Margaret's Kitchen

Margaret's Kitchen

Brenda Stacy Mastromanaco

Dedicated to my mother Elizabeth Hilliard Stacy
1919-2006

Margaret's Kitchen

© Brenda Stacy Mastromonaco 2011

Published by
Lighthouse Christian Publishing
SAN 257-4330
5531 Dufferin Drive
Savage, Minnesota, 55378
United States of America

www.lighthousechristianpublishing.com

Brenda Stacy Mastromonaco

Chapter 1

It was the tantalizing odor of fresh baked bread that caused Ash to lose his concentration. The smell came drifting in under the study door to tickle his nose, and the words and figures on the papers in front of him faded into nothingness. Ash leaped up from the desk, overturning his chair in the process.

"No!" he yelled into the empty room as he lurched over to the window. "Not again, Margaret. I can't take any more!"

For a moment Ash watched the rain drip from the eaves onto the woodpile beside the barn. By concentrating on the sights outside, he managed to drive the scent of bread out of his mind. Puddles were everywhere, with new drops forming ever widening circles in the standing water. The area in front of the barn door was more a pond than a puddle, and the stone path from the shed to the house shimmered with wetness.

That path had been Margaret's touch. She had hunted all over the farm for just the right stones. They had to be a perfect shape and color. Ash had laid the path for her in his free time, carefully measuring and digging and setting each one. Margaret had been the first one to step on it.

"Like the yellow brick road," she had cried, her eyes glistening as she danced lightly on the newly laid stones.

Now Margaret was gone and Ash felt like tearing up the path to rid himself of her memory.

He had already done so in the house. The clothes had been cleared from her closet, and he had gotten rid of all her shoes and jewelry and other personal possessions. He had no longer been able to bear the yellow flowers which smiled at him from the walls in the room they had shared, so he had redecorated the room. When that wasn't enough, he had moved all of his belongings to the spare room, and starting keeping the other door closed all the time.

And the kitchen. Chase had been close to tears when he came home from school one day to find Ash tearing apart the kitchen. Margaret's kitchen. How carefully she had planned it. The perfect number of cupboards at just the right height for her. Extra wide counters to give her plenty of work space. The aromas that filled the kitchen when she set to work had always enticed him and Chase. When they came from the barn together, the boy would bounce five feet ahead of him in his eagerness to fill himself with those smells. There were always fresh cookies, soft and moist, just waiting for his small hands to dig into. Ash had looked forward to the hot rolls at dinnertime, fresh from the big black old-fashioned oven.

Margaret had especially wanted that oven. She said food tasted better from it. To her the newer, shiny white stoves made the food taste funny. Ash couldn't tell the difference. He had laughed at her at the time, but he had indulged her.

Ash sighed and turned away from the window. He set his chair upright and surveyed the tangled heap of papers on his desk. It had been raining for two days now and, except for the regular daily chores, he hadn't been able to get anything done outside. The ground was the texture of soft cow dung and five minutes outside left Ash feeling like he'd been walking in the cow pasture for two days. The smell of the oozing black mess which coated his boots wasn't much better. Chase would wrinkle his nose as he carefully shed his own boots in the mudroom before sidling into the new kitchen. Ash didn't think Chase had gotten used to that kitchen even now after six months. It was like getting used to Margaret being gone all over again. The boy seemed to be mourning the loss.

Ash shook his head to clear it. Memories. Too many memories clinging to the cobwebs in his mind. He was supposed to be using these rainy days to catch up on his bookkeeping. Just as he did when Margaret was here. But she kept intruding now, just as she did before. He would be sitting at his desk, his bent head pondering his work, when suddenly the door would open and Margaret would be there with a plate of sandwiches and lemonade in a pitcher. Enough for two.

But now it was his imagination. When he would look up the door would be closed and the room empty.

Yesterday he had tried leaving the door open, but then he could hear Margaret in the kitchen. Singing, and clattering pans around. He had tried to ignore the sounds, but when he began smelling chocolate chip cookies he had succumbed and wandered out to the kitchen to find her.

She wasn't there, of course. Margaret had been gone

from her kitchen for over a year. It was no longer Margaret's kitchen. She no longer laughed with Chase amid the crockery and wooden spoons. Ash had trudged back to his study, and the wonderful aroma no longer filled his senses.

"This can't go on," he muttered now as he pushed the papers aside and went back to the window.

Rivulets of water made pathways down the glass. Soon Chase would be home, dripping, frowning. He didn't seem to smell the smells Ash did. Or hear Margaret as Ash did. Chase just frowned. At the kitchen, at his father in the spare room, at the loss he must have felt. The changes seemed to confuse and irritate him.

What had happened to them that they treated each other to such a cold distance? The smiles and happy moments had gone away the same time Margaret did, and Ash couldn't seem to bring them back.

"Dad?"

Ash swung around, startled to hear Chase speak so clearly behind him. The boy stood in the doorway with one hand on the doorknob. Ash frowned with sudden irritation.

"I didn't hear you come in," he said as he moved to the desk again. "Must you be so quiet?"

"I brought the mail in. I left it on the kitchen table."

"Did you wipe your feet?"

Chase nodded.

"I'm going to my room," he said, as he turned to leave.

"Hang up your jacket," Ash called after him, even though he knew Chase always did.

"I don't have any homework," was the reply as Chase disappeared.

"Don't forget to set the table for dinner...."

Chase was gone. Ash rubbed his forehead in frustration.

They had done it again. Always talking at each other instead of to each other. He couldn't even remember what Chase had said to him. All he could remember was the fact that he had been nagging the boy again. Trying to be his mother as well as father, and failing pitifully at both.

Ash stood where he was for some time, wishing that Chase would come in the way he used to, loud and laughing. The boy was too quiet now.

When he finally turned his eyes away from the door, he found the room was bathed in a murky gloom. It had grown even darker outside with the coming evening, and the dreariness of the weather had invaded the house. Shadows reached out from the corners of the room to touch him. Ash turned on the desk light, and they raced away.

Then he thought of supper, groaning inwardly. He'd never been strong on cooking. That was Margaret's place, what she enjoyed. Their meals had always been the best part of the day. Ash had liked listening to her singing in the kitchen as she prepared those meals. Sometimes she sang quietly, but his favorite time was when she was kneading bread, singing boisterously as she pounded away at the soft dough.

He sighed. Supper was up to him. He and the boy would have to eat something.

He glanced at the untouched paperwork still to be taken care of. Papers had been shuffled here and there in his unsuccessful attempts to restore order. As cluttered as his mind.

Ash turned the light off and left the room. As he

passed through the living room he flicked on a light there, chasing away the darkness. When he did the same thing in the kitchen, the harsh light in the center of the ceiling made him squint for a moment. It bathed the gleaming white appliances in light, showing the starkness of the room more than daylight did. He thought perhaps that was why Chase couldn't get used to it. This was not the homey room that Margaret's kitchen had been. Gone were the wood workbench and hanging utensils that had graced the center of the room. Gone were the warm curtains and cozy bench around the table. The cold tile floor had replaced the natural wood floor Margaret had treasured. The whole room, robbed of the warmth it had known beneath Margaret's feet, seemed to stare at him as accusingly as Chase did.

A frown rippled Ash's forehead, his mouth tightened. This was not going to get him anywhere. His imagination had been doing too much damage to him lately. He had to figure out a way to keep it under control.

Yet he stood there, the stillness creeping over him like a soft blanket, wrapping him up in his thoughts.

"Dad?"

Ash swung toward him, ready to yell at the boy for sneaking up on him. Chase pulled back in surprise. They stared at each other as the seconds ticked by on the clock over the sink. Finally Ash sighed.

"I didn't get supper, Chase."

The boy stared at him a minute longer. Then he spoke tentatively.

"There was some left from last night, Dad. Maybe we could open a can of something to go with it."

Ash stood there silently for another moment. Suddenly he wanted to reach out and touch the boy somehow. He smiled slightly.

"I guess we could at that. Want to help?"

Chase's face lit up.

"Could I?"

Ash's smile grew. He tousled Chase's dark hair, then moved to crouch down in front of the cabinet where the cans of vegetables were.

"You get out the leftovers," he said as he surveyed the contents of the cabinet. "I'll see what we have here."

Chase headed for the refrigerator. Ash ran down the list of choices out loud, but was met with silence. He turned to find the boy looking at him, his head tilted to one side and his face questioning.

"Dad," Chase said hesitantly, "did you make...bread today?"

Ash stared at him, his heart skipping a beat or two. Before he could make any reply, other than a vague shake of his head, Chase shrugged and said, "I guess the peas sound ok."

Ash watched the boy open the refrigerator door and reach inside, his heart catching up to itself inside him. He longed to ask Chase if he'd smelled other things cooking over the months since Margaret's death, or heard his mother singing. But it all sounded weird to him. It was one thing to see it as his own imagination playing tricks on him. Quite another to think it was happening to both of them.

He finally pulled a can of peas from the cabinet and dug out a pan for them. Chase had put the container of leftovers on the counter beside the stove, and Ash shoved it into the microwave, mentally cringing at what Margaret would have thought of that device. It had been a lifesaver to him over the months however, since he found it so difficult to remember to get something out of the freezer to cook.

Chase had retreated back into his silence and Ash wondered what he might be thinking about. He was regretting the distance that had developed between them, but couldn't come up with a way to end it, other than actually talking about Margaret's death. That he couldn't do. He had closed off that part of himself and had no wish to revive it.

Before long they were sitting across from each other at the table by the window, silently digging into their meager meal. Ash was grateful that the boy still ate reasonably well, in spite of their loss and the subsequent problems it had caused. He wasn't sure what he would do if Chase quit eating. His troubles at school were difficult enough. And Ash had no idea how to cope with those.

Greta looked at her son, who was standing in front of her, his upturned face both serious and anxious. She noted how tall he was getting, and that he was in need of another haircut.

"I know you'd like to play field hockey this year, Galen," she said, "but I just can't let you. I don't have time to get you to all the practices."

"That's what you said last year, Mom," he groused, turning away. "You say that every year, in fact. It doesn't matter which sport I'm interested in." He ran his hand along the sink shelf, then looked at her again. "Some of the other kids get rides from other parents. Why can't I do that?"

Greta sighed. She sat down at the kitchen table, weariness creeping into her mind as she found herself facing another difficult decision. Galen came over to sit on her lap, a pleading look coming into his eyes, and Greta smiled at him.

"Doesn't do you a bit of good to do the loving son act," she jested. "You should know that by now, Galen."

He laughed, giving her a kiss before jumping up again, his voice cheerful as he said, "I know, but it never hurts to try." He poured himself a glass of juice, standing in front of the refrigerator door to keep it from closing. "Ok, Mom," he went on, "I know you're very cautious about who I ride with. But what if you got to know Jimmy's Mom better?"

Greta watched as he drank the juice down in one breath and rinsed the glass out. Ever since Galen had turned twelve it had gotten harder and harder to say no to all the things he wanted to do. Before she could just say he was too young, but now he was no longer so young. In just a few months he would turn thirteen. And his body was changing. He had always been small for his age, but now he was beginning to stretch upward. He had nearly reached her chin when he was standing in front of her.

"You really want to play that bad?" she asked when he continued to stand there waiting for her reply.

"All my friends are trying out for the team, Mom."

"But not everybody can get on the team."

"Jimmy thinks I have a good chance," he told her eagerly, "even if I am smaller than some of the others. I'm the best player in gym class. Even Coach Gray has been encouraging me to try out."

Greta was well aware of his athletic abilities. Coach Gray had often spoken to her about the fact that Galen would be an asset to the school sports programs when he reached high school. She'd thought that she could wait until then to figure things out, but it was obvious that

Galen wanted it now, not later.

"How about I get dinner while I think it over?" she said, getting to her feet.

"Want some help?" Galen asked quickly, grinning from ear to ear.

Greta raised her eyebrows in mock horror, bringing her hands to her cheeks.

"Are you all right?" she asked, feigning concern. "Do you feel sick?"

Galen laughed, shaking his head.

As he headed for the doorway to the living room, he swung his arms as if swinging a hockey stick, and Greta had the feeling that he was already anticipating an affirmative answer to his request. She sank back down into a chair at the table, her mind flitting at once to her absent husband.

"Oh, Bob!" she murmured quietly. "Why did you have to leave us alone like this? I'm not sure how to handle the next few years. Galen really needs a father."

She looked at the picture of the three of them that sat on the windowsill over the sink. Her dark hair was longer, her face younger. And Galen, at seven, came barely to her elbow. Bob, in his army uniform, looked tall and distinguished beside her as they stood behind Galen.

The phone rang. Greta jumped up to answer it, flinching as Tom Anderson's voice boomed out at her.

"So what's the verdict? Do we get together for dinner Saturday night?"

Greta smiled slightly.

"We do not," she replied.

"When are going to give up and join me?"

"When the sky turns purple and geese fly backward."

She pulled the phone away from her ear as he roared

with laughter. As it died away, she brought the receiver closer again.

"At least you're consistent, Greta," he said. "I have to applaud the fact that you don't let me wine and dine you, and then slam the door in my face."

"Doesn't make sense to me, Tom. If I don't intend to let anything happen between us, why would I put myself in that position?"

Tom chuckled.

"I'll keep my hopes up anyway," he told her.

"I need to get dinner for Galen and I," Greta said, hoping he would take the hint.

He didn't.

"How is Galen these days?" he asked instead. "He's getting pretty big now. I see him around school. Is he a teenager yet?"

"He's nearly thirteen, Tom. And he's fine." Before he could ask another question, Greta threw out one of her own. "Did you call just to ask me to dinner, or was there something else?"

"Same old Greta," he said, chuckling again. "All business." She heard him sigh, then he became very businesslike and said, "I have a boy who doesn't read too good. Needs some tutoring. He's ten years old."

"I haven't tutored in quite a long time, Tom."

"I know that. But I thought of you, and wondered if maybe you could be enticed into this one. His name is Charles Lancaster, but everyone calls him Chase. He and his dad have a farm outside town. Lost his mother about a year ago."

"She was killed in a car accident," Greta said quietly, her mind instantly remembering the newspaper article about the accident.

There was a moment of silence, then Tom said, "I didn't realize you knew them."

Greta chewed on her lower lip, regretting her impulsive words. Then she said, "I don't. But the accident left a small boy without one of his parents."

"Like Galen?" he asked.

"Yes, like Galen."

There was another moment of silence, then Tom's voice came across the wires again.

"So you'll take on this tutoring job?"

"I never said..."

"He needs someone who understands him, Greta," Tom said, cutting in across her words. "Someone who can pull him out of himself."

"That doesn't sound like tutoring, Tom."

She could hear the smile in his voice as he replied, "Maybe not, but it sounds like you."

Greta wanted to protest but Tom went on before she could say anything.

"I'll let you think about it overnight, and call for your answer tomorrow morning," he said quickly, then the line went dead. Greta looked at the receiver in disgust, but she cradled it gently in spite of her feelings, then she turned to the stove.

"I already have so little time for everything," she murmured as she began preparing their meal. "My job, Galen, this house. I don't know how I would fit this in as well. Leave it to Tom to know exactly what would entice me though."

The thought of tutoring someone did entice her, for sure. She had really enjoyed the time she'd spent at the school right after Bob's death. It had taken her mind off her grief, and had made her feel worthwhile. Tom

Anderson, who had been one of Bob's closest friends, had gotten her the job. Of course, he was also the reason she was not still there. His constant invitations to dinner, to the movies, to plays or concerts, had driven her away from both him and the tutoring job she liked so much. She had considered Tom a Godsend in the beginning, as he had helped her deal with the tangle of insurance forms and Bob's burial, and all the other difficulties that had accompanied his death. But when she had realized that his invitations were not out of friendship or a wish to see her socialize more, Greta had begun trying to avoid him. Fortunately, the job at the school had been part time, which gave her the opportunity to use the school's inability to hire her for more hours as her excuse to leave there. Her new job wasn't as interesting, but it did bring in the money that she needed.

Galen wandered back into the kitchen as Greta put their plates on the table. He got the silverware and glasses out while she dished up the food, then slid into his chair. After she said the blessing, he began eating, talking around the food in his mouth.

"Jimmy wants me to practice with him tomorrow."

"It isn't polite to talk with your mouth full, and you may if it stops raining."

Galen swallowed, then he grinned.

"Does that mean you'll let me try out for field hockey?" he asked.

"I'll pick you up at his house after work," Greta replied. "It's about time I got to know to his parents anyway. But that doesn't mean I'm saying yes. It means I'm thinking about it."

"His dad probably won't be home when you get there," Galen said as he nodded in agreement. "Jimmy says he's a workaholic and never gets home till about seven."

Greta smiled as she watched him take another bite of his food.

"What does his father do?" she asked.

Galen shrugged slightly. He waited till he swallowed before he answered her question.

"Jimmy's never said. His mom works part time at the public library. Just till school lets out. That's why she'll be able to take us to practice. If I can play, I mean."

Greta smiled as she took another bite of her food.

"Mr. Anderson called to see if I could tutor someone," she told him after she'd swallowed the bite.

Galen looked up, a grin plastered onto his face.

"Did he ask you out to dinner again?"

Greta laughed, nodding her head.

"Why don't you just go out with him?" Galen asked, shaking his own head. "The man sure is persistent."

"It wouldn't be right, Galen," Greta replied, giving him a very serious look. "I have no intention of having any sort of a relationship with Mr. Anderson. It wouldn't be fair to accept a dinner invitation just to have a night out." She hesitated, then added, "You remember that for when you're a bit older too."

"Why?" he asked curiously.

Greta wondered if it was too early for this sort of talk, but, since he'd brought the subject up, she went on with it.

"Because there's going to come a day when you want to ask a girl out," she told him. "I want you to be sure of your motives when you do so."

Galen poked at his food with his fork for a moment, then he said, "Some of the guys at school have girlfriends already. Mark Johnson is always going on about how he takes Alyssa Green to the movies. He brags about how he holds hands with her. That's dumb."

"Bragging? Or holding hands?"

Galen laughed, and Greta realized that he seemed very open to discussing this with her. She'd been very worried about his future emotional needs. Now that worry seemed to fade as he replied to her question.

"Both," he stated firmly. "Who wants to hold hands with a girl anyway? I have more important things to do." He scooped up the last of the food on his plate and held his fork in the air as he continued talking. "Mrs. Thomas says my report on the African elephants was my best so far. She wants me to send it to one of those science magazines for kids. She's even going to get the address for me."

He shoved the bite into his mouth as Greta exclaimed, "That's super, Galen! I really liked that one too."

Galen drank the last of his milk quickly.

"Can I take my cookies to my room? I want to work on that story I'm writing for my writing class. And I have some math I need to finish up."

Greta nodded and he jumped up and started to clear the table. As he put their dishes on the counter, he looked back at her.

"I guess I'm glad you don't want to go out with Mr. Anderson, Mom," he said quietly. "I like him ok, but I wouldn't want you to marry him or anything."

"No?" she said, raising her eyebrows slightly.

Galen shook his head.

"I guess someday you'll probably get married again," he remarked seriously, "but you should do it for the right reasons and not just settle for someone so I could have a father figure around."

"You sound as if you've really thought this one out," she commented.

Galen nodded.

"Mark Johnson's mom remarried a few months ago," he explained. "His parents got divorced, remember?" Greta nodded and he went on. "I think that's why he's so... You know. About girls and all. His mom has dated all sorts of men since the divorce. Sort of like she was trying on different ones? Even Mr. Anderson took her out a few times." He took two cookies from the jar and came over to give her a kiss on her cheek. "I guess if I'm going to have a new dad I wouldn't want one who's been out with everyone else."

He disappeared out the kitchen door, leaving Greta to stare after him. Sometimes his maturity scared her. What other twelve year old would come out with something like that? She had to wonder what he was reading to develop those views.

As she got up to wash the dishes, Greta thought about what Galen had told her. She had known that Andrea Johnson had been devastated when her husband had walked out, leaving her with three young children to raise. After ten years of marriage, Ted had simply left town with another woman and begun a new life elsewhere. At first Andrea had been asking for prayer at church, but it wasn't long before she began dating herself. Greta had been appalled at the way the woman seemed to flaunt herself in front of the men at church, almost as if she were trying to prove that she was desirable still. She'd felt sorry for her too though. And, unlike Galen, Greta was aware that the new marriage was not working out as well as Andrea had hoped.

Greta plunged her hands into the soapy dish water,

amazed at the different ways people acted under the strain of death or divorce. She had not had any desire for a man since Bob's death. He'd been her soul mate, in spite of the tough times they'd had in the beginning. With him in the service, they had had to move repeatedly. She'd made friends just to lose them, over and over. It had been she who had insisted on buying a house as soon as his tour of duty was over. Bob had chosen the place, but Greta had chosen the house, and they'd joined a church almost immediately. By the time Bob was killed in a car accident, he'd been a deacon at that church and a well-respected member of the community.

A tear spilled out onto her cheek as she thought about Bob, and Greta brushed it away with her shoulder. As she let the water out of the sink and wiped it down, she glanced at the picture of the three of them again. It had been taken shortly before Bob's term in the service had ended. It wasn't the last picture taken of him by any means, but it had always been her favorite. After she dried her hands, she reached out to touch his strong face, wishing that she could touch it for real.

Chapter 2

Over their breakfast of scrambled eggs and toast the next morning, Greta spoke again of the tutoring job.

"Mr. Anderson said the boy's name is Chase Lancaster. Do you know him?"

"Chase? Sort of. He's a quiet kid. Fifth grader, I think."

"He's ten, so that would be about right," Greta replied. "I don't know when I'd find the time to do it."

"You could do it on Saturdays. I don't mind giving up some of our time."

Greta stared at him.

"Is that because you're hoping to play hockey?"

"Hockey does have practice on Saturday," he said with a grin, "but no, that's not why."

He ate a bite of his toast, his face thoughtful. Greta watched him as she sipped her coffee, her eggs sitting untouched in front of her.

"I guess it seemed like you were happier when you

were tutoring at the school," Galen finally said after the toast had been swallowed. "Like it's what you'd rather be doing. And your job isn't the greatest job in the world." Greta laughed. Galen had never been enthused about her job at Gordon's Drug Store. When the position had been offered to her, it had seemed like the perfect thing, but now, after nearly two years, it had lost its appeal, even to her. Bill Gordon, the owner, had begun unloading a number of management chores onto her almost before she'd received her first paycheck, which was for salesclerk only. She no longer worked behind the counter, unless needed, but her paycheck hadn't gone up by very much. Now she spent her time ordering merchandise and keeping track of the day-to-day bookkeeping. The number of hours she worked each week had risen since she began, but not her hourly pay.

"I guess I could at least look into the situation further," she mused as she began poking at her eggs. "Mr. Anderson will be calling this morning to find out my answer."

"Chase never gets into trouble at school, so you don't have to worry about him being a discipline problem," Galen told her.

Greta looked at him curiously.

"How do you know he doesn't get into trouble?" she asked.

"Aw, Mom, everyone knows who gets into trouble at our school," he replied. "It's so small that all the troublemakers stand out like a sore thumb."

She smiled as she pushed her eggs around her plate some more.

The size of the school here had been one of the things that drew Bob to the town in the first place. He hadn't wanted Galen in a large city school where he might get lost amid all the other students. And here the kids didn't move to the high school until ninth grade. Greta had liked that idea. She'd also liked the fact that the high school was just two blocks from the grade school. When Galen was ready to move up to ninth grade, he'd still be close to his friends in the lower grades.

Galen finished his breakfast and gathered his books together, shoving them into his backpack. Then he took his empty plate and put it on the sink shelf.

"I'll stop in to see you after school, Mom," he said as he strapped his backpack on and bent to give her a quick kiss on the cheek. "I need some new pens and more paper."

"I'll have them ready for you."

"Thanks. See you."

With a wave, he was out the door. Greta remained where she was, smiling at his youthful exuberance. Although she hadn't yet said so, she knew that she'd probably let him try out for the field hockey team. He'd shown himself to be a very responsible kid, always checking in with her after school. It had been an ordeal for her to turn him into a latchkey kid at the age of ten, but she'd had no other choice. Her paycheck had barely covered all their needs without adding the cost of child care to it. If it hadn't been for the fact that Bill Gordon said Galen could do his homework behind the counter in the beginning, she probably wouldn't have accepted the job so easily. Galen hadn't been too keen on the idea until he discovered that he could sit on the floor behind the counter and write to his heart's content without anyone even knowing he was there.

He didn't do that anymore, of course. Last year he had

begun hanging out with Jimmy Edwards after school most days. Before Jimmy's family had moved to town, Galen hadn't had any close friends. He was well-liked at school, but none of the other boys his age lived close enough for them to form friendships. When he and Jimmy had hit it off so well, and the other family lived close by, Greta had been delighted.

"Don't know why I've never taken the time to actually get to know the Edwards," she murmured to herself as she finally scraped the cold eggs off her plate into the trash. "I know they go to our church, and Jimmy is around our house on Saturdays a lot."

She glanced at the picture on the windowsill and sighed. Since Bob's death she had shied away from any real involvement with church activities. They attended Sunday morning services and Galen was involved with the kids' group there. But Greta had stopped attending the adult Bible studies, and she avoided all the activities with the women's group, for much the same reason as she'd begun avoiding Tom Anderson. It hadn't taken her very long to realize that a number of the people at church thought she should begin dating right away, maybe even remarry. Whenever she spoke of waiting to see what God had in store for her, the other women would roll their eyes and give each other funny looks.

The phone rang, breaking into her thoughts. When she picked up the receiver, Tom's voice came across the wires.

"I hope you've been thinking seriously about the tutoring."

"I have. I'd like to know more about it. I'm not sure how much time I could give this boy."

"Even just a couple hours a week would help him, I

think," Tom replied, a smug note creeping into his voice. "His father could drop him off at your house maybe, if it has to be evenings or weekends. You've boxed yourself in at that job something terrible."

Greta was not about to tell Tom that she was wishing for a different job with fewer hours, so she replied, "My job is important, Tom."

"You could get a job here at the school anytime now," he retorted. "There are openings. I'd be glad to put in a good word for you."

Though her heart jumped at his words, Greta resisted the urge to ask him about them. Instead she said, "I'm happy where I am. How would I set something up with Chase?"

"I'll call Ash and give him your phone number," Tom replied. "That's Chase's father. I already spoke to him about the possibility of tutoring. He's not entirely sure he's for it, but we're insisting."

"Who is Chase's teacher?"

"Ruth Moore. I'm sure you remember her."

Greta did. She was an older woman who was great with the young kids. Greta had always enjoyed working with her when she had been at the school. And she'd been Galen's fifth grade teacher.

"I do remember her," she said. "Perhaps I'll give her a call."

"Fine. I'll leave her a note that you'll be in touch."

Greta thought that would be the end of the call, but then Tom chuckled.

"Now, about Saturday night..." he began.

"My answer is still no, Tom," Greta inserted quickly.

"You didn't even wait for the question."

"I don't have to. Talk to you later, Tom. I need to get

to work."

She hung up the phone with his laughter ringing in her ears.

As she stood there for a minute, her hand still on the receiver, Greta couldn't help thinking about the changes that had come over Tom since Bob's death. She couldn't remember the last time she had seen him at church, yet the reason the two men had become such close friends was because of church. Even though Tom had never married, he and Bob had really connected. They had shared the same beliefs, and had served as deacons together. Now Tom seemed to be walking further and further away from those beliefs.

Greta sighed and turned away from the phone. She quickly washed up the breakfast dishes, collected her things for work, and headed out the door.

Ash finished feeding the chickens and headed for the barn, thankful that the rain had finally stopped. The October sun overhead felt warm, and he pulled off his jacket as he went into the barn. He had just picked up the pitchfork when he heard the big bell near the door begin to ring.

"Whoever is calling can wait, I guess," he murmured. "I've got work to do."

He headed for the horse's stall. The bell stopped after four rings, to his relief, but as he shoved the pitchfork into the straw on the floor, it began ringing again. Muttering under his breath, Ash went to answer the phone in the tack room.

"Lancaster here."

"Ash, it's Tom Anderson."

"What can I do for you?" he asked, wishing that the

man would just leave him alone. All this talk about Chase needing a tutor seemed ridiculous to him. So the boy was a bit slow at reading. He'd catch up.

"I have a tutor for Chase," Tom said. "Her name is Greta Jorgenson. I told her you'd be giving her a call to set things up. She works at Gordon's Drug Store during the week, so the tutoring may have to be done evenings or weekends."

Ash grunted in disgust.

"How come no one at school can tutor him?" he asked gruffly. "Isn't that what they're there for?"

"Greta used to work at the school part time," the man said. "She's probably one of the best tutors we have."

"So how much is it going to cost me?"

"Nothing. The school pays for it since it's being done at our request. You just have to work it out with her as to the when."

Tom gave him the phone number. Ash jotted it down, along with the name, and hung up the phone. As he went back to the horse's stall he wondered just who this Greta Jorgenson was, trying hard to picture the various women he'd seen in Gordon's.

"Probably some old witch with white hair and a pointed nose that he's foisting on me," he muttered as he picked up the pitchfork once more. "Tom's sense of humor is a bit warped these days."

He thought about the meeting that had taken place at the school just the week before, with Tom and Ruth Moore, Chase's teacher. He'd told them that Chase didn't need any tutoring, but that teacher of his, she'd insisted that he did. She claimed that Chase was falling further and further behind because of his inability to read well.

"Margaret would have been able to help him," Ash

said out loud as he scooped the wet straw into the wheelbarrow. "She would have told them to go fly a kite with all this talk of tutoring."

He finished cleaning out the stall, ignoring the little voice in his head which asked him why he didn't just help the boy himself.

When Galen came into the store with Jimmy that afternoon, Greta was checking stock in one of the aisles. She'd seen them through the big front window, so she had a smile ready for both boys when they appeared in her area.

"How was school today?" she asked them.

"Fine," Galen replied as he dropped his backpack on the floor. "If I toss this into the car, I won't have to carry it to Jimmy's."

"Sounds good to me." She pulled the car keys from her pocket and handed them to him. "Be sure to lock it back up. Your bag of pens and paper are in my office if you want to grab them too."

Galen shook his head.

"You can bring them with you. Jimmy and I want to get going. The sun has dried everything up real nice outside, so we can get some practice in."

They headed back outside. Greta watched them through the window as Galen unlocked the car and threw his bag onto the back seat.

"Excuse me?"

She turned to find a tall man with dark curly hair behind her.

"Yes? Can I help you?"

"They told me at the counter that you're Greta Jorgensen?"

Galen came back in to hand her the car keys. She gave him a quick kiss as he turned to go, then she turned back to the man.

"I am," she said. "What can I do for you?"

"Ash Lancaster," he said, holding out his hand towards her. "I understand you're going to tutor my son, Chase."

Greta took his hand, shook it briefly, then held her clipboard in front of her. She wasn't sure she liked the fact that he had come looking for her so quickly.

"I said I'd consider it," she said very guardedly.

He frowned.

"Tom Anderson said it was all set."

"Tom Anderson would like it to be all set," Greta replied, sighing heavily and shaking her head. She forced herself to keep looking at the man, though her insides were quivering with a mixture of anger at Tom and some unknown nervousness. "I don't know how much time Chase needs," she continued, "or where he's at in his reading. I was going to speak to his teacher before I made a decision."

The man grunted, turning away slightly.

"Was that your boy?" he asked, looking out the window.

"Galen? Yes."

"Galen. Nice name." He looked at her again, frowning slightly, then he said, "I'll be in touch then."

Greta was speechless as he abruptly turned and walked away. She felt as if a cold wind had just blown through the store. If this was what the father was like, what sort of son had he produced?

When she left work at five, Greta almost regretted agreeing to pick Galen up at the Edwards'. She was tired from being on her feet most of the day, and she wanted to call Ruth Moore to talk about Chase's tutoring. This detour was going to take up time she wasn't entirely willing to give up. And the process of meeting Jimmy's parents would not be just a quick hi, how are you idea.

She sighed as she imagined the two of them finally sitting down to supper after seven, with no time or energy left for anything else. Galen would hardly even have time to do his homework before bed.

As she drove toward Jimmy's, Greta pushed a cassette into the car tape player and Christian music filled the air around her. By the time she arrived at her destination, she felt her spirits lift in response to the music.

Galen and Jimmy were in the front yard waiting for her. Galen gave her a big smile as she got out of the car.

"Jimmy's mom wants us to stay for dinner," he informed her. "It's nothing special. Just pizza."

"Pizza? No wonder you're smiling so much."

The two boys almost dragged her up the walk. Greta was glad that Galen hadn't wanted an immediate answer. She hadn't even met Jimmy's mom yet. How could she say whether she wanted to eat with her or not?

As they reached the front door, it opened, and a slim woman with blond hair appeared.

"I don't know why we haven't already done this," she said with a laugh. "Our boys have been best friends for over a year now, and we do attend the same church."

Greta smiled in return and allowed herself to be ushered into the house. The woman spoke over her shoulder as she led Greta into the living room, with the boys following them.

"I'm Peggy, and I know you're Greta. My husband is Dan, but you won't get to meet him tonight. He never gets home until seven, at least. I never knew so many cars could break down."

"Your car isn't working?" Greta asked, a bit puzzled by the woman's words.

Peggy laughed.

"No, no," she said. "Dan is a mechanic. One of the best, I might add."

"I'll have to remember that if my car ever needs help," Greta said, smiling now that she understood.

She looked around the living room as Peggy went on about Dan's job. It was small, but neat, with matching furniture and curtains that blended well with the wall-to-wall carpeting. A fake fireplace lined part of one wall, with a shelf above it that held what looked like family photos, and the room was lit by two lamps which stood on the end tables beside the couch.

"...so Dan's a pretty popular guy," Peggy finished as the two boys came over to stand in front of Greta.

"So you'll stay for pizza?" asked Jimmy eagerly.

She smiled at him, then she looked at Peggy.

"If it's not too much trouble...?" she asked, leaving the question hanging.

Peggy laughed.

"Not at all," she replied. "And the pizzas should arrive any minute. I ordered two, just in case. And don't worry. If you had said no, I would have frozen the second one for a later time."

The doorbell rang and both boys headed that way. Peggy motioned her to have a seat and Greta did so, listening to the exchange in the hallway between the two boys and the pizza delivery man.

"We'll set the table, Mom," Jimmy said as he and Galen went through the room again.

"Galen is a good influence on Jimmy," Peggy said quietly. "We thank you for loaning him to us like this." Greta blushed with pleasure. There were times she worried about how she was doing as both mother and father, so Peggy's words warmed her heart. They chatted for several minutes, then the boys reappeared to say that everything was ready in the kitchen. Greta followed Peggy through the swinging door and found herself in a fairly large room with lots of windows, more windows than her own kitchen had. In fact, the room was larger than her kitchen too.

As the four of them sat at the kitchen table eating the pizza, Peggy told her that some of the women from their church were doing a Bible study in her home on Tuesday nights and invited her to join them.

"Galen could come over with you," Peggy added. "The boys can do homework together while we're meeting."

"I haven't been to a Bible study in quite a while," Greta admitted, not quite willing to go to one now.

"Someone told me you used to lead one."

"Several years ago, yes," Greta replied, nodding her head. "I've been too busy for much in that direction lately."

"Are you going to tutor Chase?" Galen asked.

"I told Mr. Anderson I would look into the idea," she said, then she looked at Peggy again. "Tom Anderson called me last night about the idea. He apparently told Chase's father that it was all set though, because the man showed up at the store today."

"Ash Lancaster?" Peggy said. "Dan has been trying to get him to come to church. He and Chase."

"I haven't met Chase yet," Greta told her.

The boys finished their pizza and asked to be excused, saying they wanted to get in a few more minutes of practice before Galen had to leave. Peggy shooed them out. Then she turned back to Greta.

"Ash is a good man," she said, "but he hasn't dealt too well with his wife's death. We've hardly seen him this past year. Dan keeps trying to get together with him, but Ash...well, he's become something of a hermit. I'm not trying to gossip here, but if you're going to tutor Chase, seems like you should know a bit about the two of them."

"You seem to know him pretty well," Greta mused.

"Ash is the reason we moved here," Peggy confessed. "We lived next door to them in Boston."

They began cleaning up the kitchen as Peggy told her a bit about her life in Boston and the way Ash Lancaster had urged Dan to leave a dead end job there to open his own car repair shop. She described Margaret Lancaster as a woman who loved the city, but loved her husband more.

"I know Margaret didn't want to move here," Peggy said as an end to the conversation, "but she adjusted. Ash was pretty devoted to her, so her death really hit him hard."

"And Chase?" Greta asked, not wanting to pry into the Lancaster marriage too deeply. "How has he taken the loss of his mother?"

"I think he might have done better if Ash had handled things differently," Peggy replied with a sad shake of her head. "His way of dealing with grief was to try to wipe her out of their lives. Tore apart the kitchen that she had designed, redecorated their bedroom, got rid of every picture of her. Chase retreated into himself. Jimmy sees him at school. He says that Chase walks around with his head down most of the time. No friends to speak of. I wish we could see them more, but Ash…well, like I said, he's become something of a hermit."

Greta turned the conversation to the field hockey tryouts at that point. After a bit of discussion about that, she agreed to let Peggy transport Galen to practice if he made the team. In her mind, she knew that she was going to tutor Chase Lancaster. She didn't even need to call Ruth Moore, though she still planned to. She wanted the older woman's opinion of the situation as well.

By the time she and Galen left the Edwards' house, Greta knew that she had herself a new friend in Peggy. One that would become very close, if she could carve enough time out of her busy life to let the friendship develop.

Ash sat on the couch in the darkness, listening to the night sounds in the house. The floor creaked, the refrigerator in the kitchen hummed, the living room clock ticked. He heard one of the cows give a long, drawn out moo outside.

Supper had been eaten in silence. Ash had wished he knew what to say to the boy. Chase had seemed to respond to him while they made supper that other night. But he had been distant tonight.

The darkness wrapped itself around him. He had no desire to turn on a light. He had no desire for anything at all.

Chapter 3

Greta pushed her hair out of her face and groaned as she looked at her clock on the nightstand. It seemed like these mornings were coming awfully fast these days. And as fall progressed, they got darker and darker.

She forced herself out of the bed and headed for the bathroom. She could hear Galen's radio playing as she passed his room and she hoped he was having an easier time waking up than she was. Her head felt as if it were full of mothballs or something.

Galen opened his door as she was going back to her room.

"Morning, Mom," he said cheerfully. "Today's Friday. I have that test in history class today."

"Think you're ready for it?" she asked, trying to give him something that resembled a cheerful smile.

"I studied last night before I turned off my light. Then I slept with my book under my pillow the way Dad suggested."

Greta laughed, suddenly feeling as if a weight had been removed from her..

"Do you really think that helps?" she asked him.

"Don't know, Mom, but I'm willing to try Dad's kooky ideas anytime." He headed for the stairs. "I'll start your coffee since you're dragging this morning."

"How do you know I'm dragging?" she called after him as he started down.

His laughter was the only reply, and she groaned as she headed for her room again.

"Even he can tell I don't like mornings right now," she muttered to herself.

As she pulled on some clothes, Greta thought about her talk with Ruth Moore the night before. Ruth had been very enthusiastic about the idea of Greta tutoring Chase.

"I think Tom's right," she had told Greta. "You are just the person to reach that boy. He needs to be encouraged to look inside himself and see that he's a good person."

"I thought I was supposed to tutor him," Greta had replied.

Ruth had laughed.

"When was the last time you 'just tutored' anyone," she had said knowingly. "That's why I agreed that Tom should get in touch with you. I'd already thought of you, but I wasn't sure you'd be willing."

Greta shook her head as she slipped into her shoes and headed downstairs. All these people pointing her in Chase's direction. She wasn't sure she could work the miracle they thought she could, but it seemed like she was already committed to trying.

Galen had breakfast on the table when she reached the

kitchen. His bowl of cereal was fast on it's way to being empty, and his toast was just crumbs dappling the otherwise empty plate. She noticed that his Bible was sitting next to her cereal bowl.

"Last night I was reading in Proverbs before I went to sleep," he said. "Remember how you and Dad used to read them to me and talk about them? Maybe you could use my Bible to tutor Chase."

Greta laughed, giving him a brief hug before she sat down at the table.

"Seems like everyone thinks I should tutor this kid."

"Maybe you'll like it so much you'll quit your job at the drug store."

"And go back to part time teaching?" Greta asked, raising an eyebrow as she moved to the coffee pot. "We won't have enough money to live on."

"But God says he'll take care of us and provide everything we need," Galen reminded her quickly.

Greta looked at him.

"Yes, he does," she agreed with a nod.

"So what if we have to do without a few things?" he went on with a shrug. "It's not like we need much anyway." He grinned as he added, "I'd even give up hockey if it helped you get out of bed easier."

Greta took her cup of coffee over to the table and sat down. Galen was munching on the last bite of his cereal as she poured some into her bowl. She added milk to it, then reached for the sugar and creamer for her coffee.

"What makes you think it's my job that makes it so hard to get up?" she asked him.

Galen swallowed the food before answering, reaching for his glass of juice as he spoke.

"You've been working there for two years, Mom.

Before that you had no trouble getting up. Even when Dad died you got up just fine. Alyssa Green's Dad has cancer, and her Mom has trouble getting up too. Alyssa says her Mom is depressed."

"I'm not depressed," Greta protested, then she bowed her head and said a silent prayer of thanks before picking up her spoon to begin eating. She hoped Galen wouldn't continue the conversation, but he pushed on as soon as her mouth was full.

"Not yet, maybe," he said. "But it seems to me like you're going in that direction."

Greta swallowed, shaking her head.

"Where do you get these thoughts, Galen? Aren't you the kid in this house?"

Galen laughed. He drank the rest of his juice, then got up to kiss her on the cheek.

"I read my Bible, Mom. And I listen to people talking around me instead of thinking that no one older than twenty knows anything." He picked up his books and stuffed them into his backpack, talking as he did so. "The minute you mentioned Chase and the tutoring stuff, I saw you were interested in it."

Greta smiled, watching as he slid his backpack on over his jacket. He then scooped up his dishes and put them on the sink shelf.

"Gonna meet Jimmy before school," he told her as he dropped a kiss on her cheek. "He asked me to read his report on Australia and give him some pointers."

"Maybe it should be you who tutors Chase," she teased.

"Nope. You're perfect for the job."

He was out the door before she could reply.

Greta finished her cereal, then she sat there enjoying

her coffee in the silence that always followed his departure. Galen had left his Bible on the table and after a moment she opened it to Proverbs to read a few verses before saying a brief prayer.

After clearing her things from the table, she reached for the phone book and looked up the Lancaster's phone number. The phone rang several times after she dialed the number, and Greta was about to hang up when a gruff, masculine voice spoke.

"Lancaster here."

Greta took a deep breath.

"Mr. Lancaster, this is Greta Jorgenson. You came to see me at the drug store yesterday."

"About Chase," he replied shortly.

"Yes." She paused, mustering her courage in the face of his attitude. "I spoke with Ruth Moore last night, and I'd like to set something up to get started with Chase."

He was silent for a moment, and she thought maybe he was going to tell her to forget it. Then he spoke again.

"How are you going to have time when you work all day?"

"I can meet with him evenings, or on Saturdays," she replied.

"What about your own son? Doesn't he require your time?"

Greta smiled.

"Galen is the one who suggested Saturdays."

The man grunted. Greta wasn't sure she cared too much for him, but it was going to be Chase she had to deal with anyway. So what if the boy's father was a morose and uncommunicative man?

"What about your husband?" was his next question.

She swallowed the lump that rose in her throat and

managed to calmly say, "I'm a widow, Mr. Lancaster. My husband was killed in a car accident three years ago."

There was silence again. Greta was sure he was going to just hang up the phone, but finally he spoke, even more gruffly, if that was possible.

"Sorry to hear that. Chase lost his mother a year ago."

"Yes, I know, Mr. Lancaster," Greta said gently. "I'm sorry about your loss also."

He grunted. Greta frowned at the sound, but she plunged on.

"Tomorrow is Saturday, Mr. Lancaster. Perhaps you could drop Chase off in the morning? Or I could pick him up. Whichever would be easier."

"I haven't even spoken to Chase about this yet."

Greta closed her eyes, feeling like she was going to wilt right there. Had anyone spoken to Chase?

"If you'd like to wait..."

"No," he said, cutting her off. She heard him take a deep breath, then he said, "I'll drop him off. What time would you like him there? And where is there?"

She gave him her address, then arranged for Chase to be dropped off at ten in the morning, with the suggestion that she would bring him home about noon. The man agreed.

After hanging up the phone, Greta pictured the man in her mind as she had seen him the day before. Tall and dark, with a definite outdoor look to him. Nothing like Bob. She and Bob had been close in height, and Bob had blond hair. His job as an insurance agent had called for a suit rather than the jeans and boots Mr. Lancaster had been wearing. And Mr. Lancaster had the faint smell of a farm about him where Bob had always smelled of soap and aftershave. Not that Mr. Lancaster hadn't looked clean and neat. He had looked surprisingly so for a farmer.

Shrugging away her thoughts, Greta gathered her things together to leave for work, her mind already forging ahead to what awaited her at Gordon's.

Ash hung up the phone and went back to the dishes he had been washing. He gave a brief moment to thoughts of how he would explain to Chase what was going on, then a picture of the woman popped into his mind.

This Greta Jorgenson was a smaller woman than Margaret had been, but she looked a lot like her with the dark hair and smile lines around her eyes. The brown blouse she had been wearing had brought out the brown in her eyes, and made them look a bit soft, like Tucson's eyes. Ash frowned, wondering if the woman would mind being compared to a horse. Then he grunted at the notion. There was no way she ever would know, so why bother wondering?

He finished up the dishes and headed out to the barn. As he mucked out the horse's stall, he thought of her again, wondering how she was faring after her husband's death.

"That boy must have been just about Chase's age when her husband died," he mumbled to the empty barn. "Guess he and Chase have something in common anyway."

He leaned on the handle of the pitchfork for a moment, trying to picture Margaret in his mind. When she didn't appear, he grunted angrily, wishing that he hadn't even tried. She was dead and gone. Best to just leave her there and get on with life.

As he went back to his chores, however, he thought of

the pictures he'd shoved away in a box after Margaret's death.

That afternoon Ash was by the barn chopping wood when he heard the school bus stop on the main road. He saw Chase get off the bus and stop by the mailbox before walking up the lane to the farm. He stood watching the boy, leaving the ax hanging idle in his hand.

When Chase saw him, the boy waved and began running.

"I did pretty good on my math test today," he called as he got closer. "The only ones I messed up on were those dumb word problems." He came to a stop in front of Ash and looked up at him, a scowl marring his features. "I don't know why we have to do those anyway."

"Maybe because they're teaching you to think about things in life," Ash replied. "If I told you to build me a chicken coop that had to fit into a certain space, you'd need to be able to think it out."

Chase smiled.

"I'd just have you do it," he replied. "I don't want to build some dumb chicken coop."

Ash laughed, reaching out to ruffle Chase's hair. Then he pointed to the mail.

"You can leave that on the table inside. After you dump your school bag, I need help stacking this wood."

"Do I have to?"

Ash looked down at the boy, catching himself before the word 'no' came out of his mouth. He changed it to, "There's work to be done around here, Chase. And you need to learn to do it. We used to have fun working together."

Chase frowned.

"I'm not a little kid anymore," he said. "It was fun doing it with you when I was a little kid. Now it's boring. It's your farm anyway, not mine."

Ash gripped the ax handle tightly, trying to control his rising temper.

"Go put your bag in the house, Chase. You will help stack this wood."

Chase tried to stare him down for a moment, then he headed for the house, grumbling under his breath. Ash breathed a sigh of relief.

"I think I've let things get out of hand around here," he muttered with a frown. "I've been..."

He brushed the thought away and turned back to his work. Working was definitely better than thinking. Thinking took him places he didn't really want to be. He was glad he'd shoved away those earlier thoughts about the pictures of Margaret. Looking at those would have just brought back all the anguish of losing her. Better to put it behind him and get moving forward.

When Chase came back out and began stacking the wood on the woodpile without a word, Ash tried to think of something to say to him, but nothing came. The boy kept his head turned away, and his shoulders seemed rigid, like he was still angry and sulking. Ash kept swinging the ax into the wood, feeling more and more angry himself.

"We both live in this house, Chase," he finally said, resting the ax on his foot. "We both need to contribute to the household. We use this wood to help give us heat every winter."

"So let's move to town," Chase muttered sullenly.

"You used to like the farm."

"It stinks!" Chase exclaimed, throwing a chunk of

wood extra hard, causing it to thump against the side of the barn, leaving a knick in the wood. "I always smell like cow poop when I go to school." He gave Ash a defiant look as he added, "The kids laugh at me. It's a stupid farm, and I hate it!"

He took off at a run towards the creek that ran behind the barn. Ash stared after him, surprised by the depth of frustration and anger he had heard in the boy's voice. The ax hung idle in his hands again as he watched Chase jump the creek and disappear into the woods.

Greta woke early the next morning, glancing at her clock and discovering that it was just five-forty. She thought of what Galen had said about her difficulty getting up being connected to her job, and she smiled as she realized that the weekend mornings were never as difficult to face as the ones during the week. She hadn't woken up this early in quite some time though. It wasn't even light out yet.

She sighed as she thought of the coming winter. Much as she liked the snow, she dreaded the thought of driving around in it. And the tires on her car were going to need to be replaced, preferably before there was snow on the ground. The heater had been making funny noises too, just a few days before. Greta wasn't sure just where the extra money would come from for those two items. Buying hockey equipment for Galen would be difficult enough if he made the team. He had some old equipment, but Greta had the feeling that it might not be acceptable anymore.

She reached up to turn on the small light over the bed, then pulled her Bible off the nightstand and sat up to read. Flipping the pages randomly she came to the book of

Ruth and stopped, deciding that she wanted to read it over again. She had always enjoyed reading about how Ruth had given up her life for Naomi, leaving her parents behind to travel to another country with her mother-in-law.

"Galen would probably ask me why Naomi and her husband went to Moab to begin with," she said with a smile. "Why didn't they just stay in Israel and trust God to fill their needs?"

Greta realized she had never thought about that question before. She had always just accepted the idea that Naomi's husband had moved his family to Moab because of a famine in Israel. Yet, if they'd been trusting God, they would have remained in Israel and toughed out the famine.

'But then, Ruth wouldn't have become part of their family,' she told herself. 'And she and Boaz would never have gotten married.'

Which would have changed the whole story of the Bible.

She smiled at her wandering thoughts, then began reading.

Ash found the house without any problem. It was on a small side street, in a quiet neighborhood. As he pulled up in front he wondered if the woman owned the house. Then Chase spoke.

"I don't know why I have to do this," he said sullenly. "Nobody asked me about it."

"Wasn't any need to, Chase," Ash replied. "The adults in your life make the major portion of your decisions until you're eighteen. Every year you get to make a few more on your own. But this isn't one of them."

Chase opened the door.

"It's a stupid decision," he said as he got out of the pickup.

Ash got out also and walked with Chase up the sidewalk to the door. A blue Chevy was sitting in the driveway and he noted that it looked to be in pretty good condition. Good enough to get Chase home safely.

The woman opened the door, inviting them in. Ash nudged Chase in ahead of him, then stepped in just far enough to let the storm door close behind him. The older boy he'd seen at the drugstore appeared on the stairway.

"Galen," the woman said to her son, "this is Mr. Lancaster and his son, Chase."

The boy came the rest of the way down the steps and held out his hand towards Ash.

"Pleased to meet you, sir," he said.

Ash was a bit surprised to be addressed as 'sir', but he took Galen's hand and shook it briefly. Then Galen held it towards Chase.

"I've seen you around school, Chase, but we've never met before, I guess."

Chase frowned, but he shook hands with him also. Ash decided that he'd have to do something about Chase's attitude later.

Galen invited Chase into the living room, an offer that Chase reluctantly accepted, and the two boys disappeared. The woman turned back to him after watching them go.

"I'll be using today as a get acquainted time," she told him. "Galen is trying out for the hockey team, so we'll be going over to the school in a bit. It will give me a chance to find out Chase's interests and determine which way I'd like to go with him."

"He needs tutoring in reading," Ash said bluntly,

44

annoyed that she wouldn't be sitting him down to read.

"I realize that, Mr. Lancaster," she replied quietly. "But the way I tutor him depends on the way he learns. Some kids learn best by doing things. Hands on stuff. Some learn best by sitting down with workbooks and so forth. There are probably as many ways to learn as there are kids."

Ash looked towards the living room door, then he reached for the door handle behind him.

"I'll leave you to it then," he bit out. "I have a few errands to do in town, but I'll be home by noon. The farm is easy to find, and Chase can give you directions."

The woman nodded.

Ash hesitated another moment, then he opened the door and stepped outside. He couldn't decide if leaving Chase here was the best thing to do or not. It certainly didn't sound to him like they were going to be doing much schooling, and he had plenty of work for the boy to do at home.

He looked back at the house as he reached the pickup. The front door was closed once more, yet his one small glimpse inside clung to him. Even though he hadn't been any further than the front hallway, he'd been able to feel the warmth there.

He shook his head, walked around the truck to the driver's door, and climbed in.

As he headed for the main street of town and the feed and grain store, Ash wondered what sort of woman Greta Jorgenson was. She seemed nice. A bit quiet and reserved, but pleasant enough. He wondered how Chase would get along with her.

Greta leaned against the door for a moment after

Chase's father left. He seemed so big and silent to her. "Taciturn. Uncommunicative." She smiled as she rattled off descriptive words to label him with.

She could hear the two boys talking in the living room and she pushed away from the door to go join them.

"...Jimmy's friend," Chase was saying as she walked in. "I see the two of you around school too."

"His mom says she knows you and has been to your home," Greta said.

The boy turned to give her a slight scowl.

"That was quite a while ago," he retorted. "Nobody comes to our house now."

She nodded, not sure quite what to say in reply to that. Galen grinned however.

"We don't get too many visitors here either, Chase," he informed the boy. "Mom's always working."

"So how come you're tutoring me?" Chase asked, turning to look at her again. "I can read ok and it seems like you'd rather spend your time with your own kid."

Greta smiled at him.

"As I understand it," she said, "you can read, but not well enough to keep up with your class. I'm to help you improve your skills."

"I don't feel like spending my Saturdays doing school work," he declared.

"Well," she said slowly, "we won't be doing anything today except getting to know each other. Galen needs to be at the school for hockey tryouts shortly, and you and I are driving him over there."

Chase looked at her for a moment, then he muttered, "That doesn't sound too bad, I guess. Do we get to hang around to watch?"

"Might as well," she replied. She looked at his thin jacket, wishing she'd thought to tell his father to have him dress warmly. "Will you be warm enough in that?" she asked him. "I think Galen might have a sweatshirt you could wear under it."

"Naw, I'm fine."

He hunched his shoulders a bit and turned away from her. Greta glanced at Galen. She was at a loss for what to say next. Chase seemed to be almost an exact copy of his father when it came to conversation.

"I'm bringing a sweatshirt," Galen said. "I might need it if we have to stand around waiting at all." He glanced at Chase as he said "You like snow? I can't wait till we get some snow. Last year Mom and I went sledding over on Pitcher's Hill."

Chase looked up at Greta again.

"You go sledding?" he asked.

"Oh, I like to go down the hill a couple times with him," she answered, smiling at him. "Mostly I stand around shivering while he has all the fun."

The boy smiled and Greta's breath caught in her throat. The change was enough to light her heart.

"If you're ready?" she said, glancing at Galen.

"Sure," Galen replied, scooping up the sweatshirt he had waiting on the arm of the couch.

Greta turned to head for the door.

"Maybe I could use a sweatshirt," Chase suddenly said. "I figured we'd be sitting around here. Didn't think it was all that cold out either."

Galen changed course and took the stairs two at a time, calling "I'll meet you in the car as soon as I get the sweatshirt" back over his shoulder.

Greta took Chase out to the car. He climbed into the

back seat and buckled himself into the seatbelt while she slid in behind the steering wheel. As she buckled herself in, Galen came out the door and jumped off the porch. He slid into the back seat with Chase and buckled up.

"Jimmy will be at the tryouts too," he said to Chase as Greta backed out of the driveway. "He was on the team last year. He'll most likely get on again cause he's a good player."

"You like hockey?" asked Chase.

"Sure. Basketball too, though I'm not very good at it. Too short really. In gym all the other guys can run circles around me."

"I bet they tease you about it."

"Yeah, they do. But I don't let it get to me. The Bible says God made me just right, so I figure I'm smaller than them for a reason. David was just a kid when he killed the giant."

"David?" Chase asked.

"In the Bible," was Galen's reply. "He was one of the kings of Israel. There's lots of stories about him in the Bible."

"You go to church?"

"Every Sunday," Galen told him. "I go to the kid's group on Sunday nights too. We play games and in winter we do stuff together, like ice skating and sliding parties."

Chase fell silent. Greta glanced at him in the rearview mirror, thankful that Galen was doing the talking. Chase didn't seem very open to talking to her yet, and she didn't really know just what to say to him. She had the feeling that it was going to take more than one visit to figure out how to help him improve his reading skills. First she was going to have to figure out a way to break through his walls.

The parking lot at the school had just a few cars in it when they arrived there. Galen commented that if no one showed up he'd be a shoe-in for the team. Greta parked the car and they headed for the field where they could see other people standing around. As they walked, Chase tugged the slightly large sweatshirt on over his jacket.

They were nearly to the group on the field when Greta saw Jimmy break away and run toward them.

"My mom had to run an errand, so she dropped me off," he said to Greta when he reached them. "She'll be back in a jiffy though. The parents sit on the bleachers." He waved a hand toward the bleachers, then he looked at Chase. "Hey, Chase," he said. "Haven't seen you in a while. Glad you came."

Galen gave Greta a quick kiss on her cheek, then he took off with Jimmy. Greta led Chase over to the bleachers.

"There's a blanket in the car, come to think of it," she said as they found a spot to watch from. "I might decide to go get it if we sit here too long."

"Am I going to have to do workbooks?" Chase asked her. "Cause I really hate to do workbooks. They seem really stupid sometimes."

"And what are you interested in?" Greta asked.

"I like airplanes," he replied. "I want to learn how to fly sometime. When I'm older. My dad doesn't see any reason to learn, unless I want to be in the air force or something."

He watched the people on the field as he spoke, and Greta was glad she had decided to bring him here. He seemed more inclined to talk now that he didn't have to look at her.

"What did your mom think of it?" she asked.

He glanced at her briefly, then looked at the field again.

"She thought it was a great as...aspir..."

"Aspiration?"

"Yeah," he replied. "That's the word she always used."

"Do you know what it means?" Greta asked.

Chase shook his head without looking at her, which didn't surprise Greta at all. If he was having trouble with reading, most likely he was also having trouble learning new words too.

"To aspire after something means to dream of it, maybe even yearn for it, or thirst after it," she explained. "Your mother meant that it was something worth pursuing."

"How come she didn't just say that?" Chase asking, looking at her again.

Greta laughed.

"We adults sometimes use big words to say what we mean because the bigger words seem more important. Galen likes to find out what words mean, so he's always using them on me."

"Why would he want to do that?"

"Galen would like to be a writer some day, Chase," Greta commented, smiling down at him. "He writes stories occasionally, but mostly he likes to write non-fiction. True things. Like school reports and stuff."

Chase wrinkled his nose in disgust and looked back out to the field. He was quiet for a moment, then he said, "I hate school reports. I never know what to say. And I can't spell worth beans."

Greta smiled to herself. Ruth Moore had said pretty

much the same thing about him.

"Do you have one you need to write any time soon?" she asked.

"Yeah. Mrs. Moore assigned us a report on our favorite sport. I don't even have a favorite sport. I'm too small to play any sports."

"Did you know that flying could be considered a sport?"

Chase swung around to stare at her.

"Are you sure?" he asked.

Greta nodded.

"They have aviator shows to show off their flying skills," she told him. "I've read about them before."

"Wow! Do you mean that I could write a report about flying?"

Greta nodded again. Chase turned back to the field and she saw his shoulders slump.

"Wouldn't be any good if I did," he muttered in a dejected voice. "I still can't spell, and everything gets all confused."

"We could make it part of your tutoring," she offered quietly. "Work on it together. I can help you get your thoughts down on paper in a clear order."

"Would Mrs. Moore accept it that way?" he asked without turning.

"How do you think Galen learned to write so well?"

He didn't answer, but just kept watching the people on the field. When he finally spoke again, it was very quietly, and almost as if he were talking to himself..

"Maybe this tutoring stuff won't be so bad after all."

Chapter 4

When Greta finally slipped into bed that night, she sighed with relief at being able to stretch out and relax. After dropping Chase off at the farm, she and Galen had run errands together, including a trip to the public library to search out a few books about flying. They were stacked on an end table in the living room, waiting for her and Chase to look at Monday night. His father had agreed to drop him off at seven, and they would work for an hour together before she brought him home.

Greta smiled as she thought about the farm. Chase had made them stay long enough to go see the horse in the corral behind the barn. Tucson was a large brown horse with a long mane hanging over his neck. He looked well groomed, and Chase said he could be ridden bareback. His father said the horse was mostly for hauling logs home from the woods for firewood.

The farm was big. Greta had been surprised when Chase told her they owned most of the woods across the creek in back of the barn. She could readily see how far the pasture for the cows extended, and the garden and wheat field areas. When they got back into the car Galen had said he didn't know there were farms that big in the area.

Greta reached for her Bible to read before going to sleep. As she sat up, she decided the farm must be pretty self-supporting.

"There was a vegetable garden there," she reflected, memories of her own childhood seeping into her mind. "But does that man actually can vegetables? I can't exactly see him doing that. He definitely doesn't look the type." She opened the Bible to the New Testament and thumbed her way to the book of James. "Cows, chickens. Those would provide milk and meat and eggs. Butter? Naw. He couldn't be churning butter out there."

She laughed at herself and began reading.

Greta wasn't too surprised when Peggy Edwards sought her out after church Sunday morning. They talked briefly about the field hockey tryouts, then Peggy said, "How'd it go with Chase yesterday?"

Greta laughed.

"He's quite a kid," she replied. "A bit sulky, but I think we can work together. I expected you to come over to say hello at the tryouts."

"I figured I'd let the two of you get to know each other. That's easier to do without other people around." She glanced around the church as she added, "And...what did you think of Ash?"

Greta frowned slightly, hoping that Peggy was not

thinking that she would be interested in the man. She
decided to answer the question cautiously.

"I didn't really talk to him much. Chase did insist that
we stop at the farm long enough to see their horse."

"Tucson," Peggy said, nodding her head. "That animal
must be getting old about now. How long do horses live
anyway?"

"I don't know for sure," Greta replied. "I guess I've
never thought about it."

Peggy's husband appeared at her side and
introductions were made, then they began moving toward
the rear of the sanctuary together. Galen had gone to
meet Jimmy in the foyer, as usual, for whatever snack
might be there.

"My invitation still stands," Peggy said as they reached
the sanctuary door. "I'd love to have you come to the
women's Bible study."

"I may take you up on it actually," Greta said. "As
long as you meant it about Galen coming."

"I did," Peggy assured her. "Dan sometimes leaves,
and sometimes he does something with Jimmy upstairs.
No reason why Galen can't join them, or the two boys can
even do homework in Jimmy's room. We start at seven.
If that's cutting it close, you can always come for dinner
after work."

Greta declined that offer, then winced as she noticed
Tom Anderson coming in their direction. He looked
exceptionally well in his suit and tie, but Greta doubted
that his presence in the church meant that he had renewed
his faith.

"Greta, Greta," he said as he reached them. "I knew
I'd find you here this morning."

"Easy guess," she replied, forcing herself to smile.

"This is where I am every Sunday morning."

Tom laughed, stepping closer as if to hug her. Greta backed away slightly, avoiding the intended intimacy.

"I saw Chase Lancaster yesterday morning," she said to smooth over the moment. "I think things will work between us. We have another meeting set for tomorrow night."

"Good, good," Tom said. "But that isn't why I'm looking for you." He turned to Peggy and Dan, stretching his hand out toward Dan. "And good morning to you also, Peggy, Dan."

Peggy smiled at him without answering, while Dan grasped his hand and shook it. Then Tom turned to Galen and Jimmy who had just joined them.

"So how's school going for you two boys?" he asked.

"Fine, Mr. Anderson," Galen said quietly.

Tom frowned.

"I thought you used to call me Tom outside of school. Back when I was around your house a lot."

"I did, sir," Galen replied. "But that was when my dad was alive and you were a friend of his."

Tom looked a bit disgruntled at Galen's answer, but Greta silently applauded her son. She owed him one for doing such a nice job of letting Tom know his place in their lives.

"I still think of you and your mother as friends of mine," Tom said. He turned back to Greta as he went on. "That's why I came to seek you out actually. There's one of those classical concerts that you're so fond of Tuesday night. I was wondering if you'd honor me with your presence there."

Greta resented his tone. She was sure that he was counting on her being embarrassed to refuse an invitation so publicly made, and she was glad she had already told Peggy she would go to the Bible study. She forced herself to smile at him once again as she turned him down.

"I'm afraid I already have plans for Tuesday night, Tom. I have to disappoint you, as usual." She paused for a second, then added, "But then, I think you knew I would."

He frowned slightly, then looked around the sanctuary. Greta had the feeling that he wasn't really used to having women say no to him, though she had done so repeatedly. On the phone he always treated it as a joke, but now he looked a bit irritated.

"Well, perhaps another time then," he finally said, then strode off without another word to any of them. Peggy gave a nervous giggle before asking, "Does he ask you out often?"

"Every chance he gets," Greta replied, smiling. Turning to Galen, she said, "I guess we're ready to go, Galen. I believe we have a date this afternoon?"

"Every Sunday, Mom," he shot back enthusiastically. "It's a standing date."

"A standing date?" Dan asked curiously. "Sounds intriguing."

Greta laughed as she turned to answer him.

"We play Scrabble every Sunday afternoon," she explained. "It's getting harder and harder for me to beat this kid. He knows too many words."

"Ah," Dan said, nodding his head. "Sounds like a great idea. How about we head home and play Scrabble, Jimmy? I think I could still beat you at it."

"How about Monopoly instead?" Jimmy replied. "I'd at least have a chance at that."

They headed out into the October sunshine and Greta pulled her coat a little tighter around her. The sun was feeling less and less warm as each day went by.

His book wasn't holding his attention, but Ash kept it open on his lap anyway. He normally enjoyed reading. It was his way to relax on Sunday afternoons, the one time he allowed himself that luxury. But today he felt restless, and he was vaguely concerned about the aromas that were emanating from Margaret's kitchen. The night before, after Chase had gone to bed, Margaret had baked brownies. Ash had been sitting right where he was now, but he hadn't remained there for long once the smell of the brownies reached him. The clatter of pans in the beginning he'd dealt with, but the aroma had driven him outside into the cold air. He'd left through the front door rather than approach that kitchen too. He hadn't wanted to go there and not find Margaret.

Ash heard Chase coming down the stairway behind him. He picked his book up, trying to look as if he'd been reading all along. The boy came into the room, stopped, then moved forward again to come around the end of the couch. Ash glanced his way, then pretended to go back to his book. Chase stood at the end of the couch, his hand running back and forth over the arm of the couch.

"What did you think of Mrs. Jorgenson?" Ash finally asked him, setting his book down onto his lap again. "You didn't have much to say after you came home yesterday."

"She's ok," Chase replied. "She goes sliding with Galen in the winter."

Ash couldn't picture that at all. The woman had been wearing loafers the day before. He had hesitated over the idea of her walking out to the corral to see Tucson, but Chase had been insistent and the other boy had shown interest in the horse, so he'd shrugged it off and led them to the fence. Mrs. Jorgenson hadn't seemed to mind the dirt that had gotten into her shoes though. When she'd gotten back to the grass near her car she'd simply slid the shoes off, shook out the dirt, then put them on again. Ash had been surprised to see her do that so calmly.

"Is Galen friendly?" he asked, trying to draw Chase out. He had the feeling that the boy had something on his mind, but was a bit nervous about approaching him. He wasn't sure that he wanted to talk about anything important, but at least it was an improvement over sitting with his own thoughts.

His question got Chase to look at him finally, his face lighting up.

"Yeah," he said enthusiastically. "He was really nice. He even loaned me a sweatshirt so I wouldn't be cold at the school."

Then his face closed down again and he looked away, running his fingers over the arm of the couch once more. Ash laid his book down on the end table.

"Is there something bothering you?" he asked.

"I was just wondering…" Chase began, then changed it to, "Well…" He hesitated, then he seemed to come to a decision. He turned to look directly at Ash. "It's the kitchen, Dad."

"The kitchen?" Ash repeated, wondering if Chase had smelled the brownies way up in his room.

"Why did you…well, you know…tear it apart?"

Ash sighed. He wasn't sure which conversation was worse, the one about the smells or this one. He'd always known that sooner or later he was going to have to explain his actions. He wanted it to be later. Way later. But Chase was standing in front of him now, and if he wanted to salvage their relationship before it got too late, he had to talk now.

He patted the couch beside him, inviting Chase to sit down. The boy looked vaguely surprised, but he did move closer and take the proffered seat, sitting sideways so he was facing Ash.

"When your mother died, I was angry," Ash told him. "I guess I tried to block her out of my mind, out of our lives. Sort of foolish, I think. And it didn't exactly work, did it? We're both smelling things. Stuff like bread and brownies."

"I sort of like it when I come in from school and smell chocolate chip cookies," Chase said, with a grin. "Except that I can't eat them."

Ash smiled, nodding in agreement. Then he sighed.

"In the beginning," he said, "I actually felt like your mother had gone out that night in the rain deliberately, like she knew she wouldn't be home again."

"But she wouldn't do that!" Chase exclaimed.

"I know that, Chase. But it didn't stop me from thinking it. Sometimes our thoughts just get all tangled up when we're miserable about something."

Chase was silent for a moment. It looked like he was deep in thought, his eyes on the couch cushion between them and his hands clenched together in his lap. Ash longed to pull him across the couch into his arms, but he wasn't at all sure that the boy would accept that. They had been at odds for so long that he doubted it would be this easy to get back to their old relationship.

"I don't suppose you could change it back," the boy suddenly said very quietly.

"Change it back?"

"The kitchen."

Ash smiled as he shook his head.

"Too expensive," he confessed. "I guess that's why we shouldn't make rash decisions while we're angry."

"What do you mean?"

"We tend to do, or say, things that we don't really mean."

Chase looked over at him for a moment, then returned to his study of the couch cushion.

"I don't really want to move to town, Dad," he said hesitantly. "I like the farm. I like Tucson, and the cows, and the chickens. And I really want to help you do the chores. It's just... It's just that the kids at school..."

Ash reached across the cushion and patted the boy's leg.

"I know, Chase. I know exactly what you mean. When I was a kid, some of the others used to hold their noses when I walked by them. I tried to be clean, but a farm doesn't really foster that. However, no matter where you live, or who you are, there will always be kids who make fun of you. Ask any kid who wears glasses, or one who is either very short or very tall."

"Why do they do that?" Chase asked, looking at him again. "It's so mean."

"Human nature, Chase. Human nature. They may not have the best home life, or maybe they hate themselves, or maybe they just want to be popular and think that they have to put others down in order to be top dog. We're all born selfish, Chase. It's something we have to learn to overcome."

"I guess I was being selfish when I told you I hated the farm?"

Ash nodded as he said, "And I was being selfish when I remodeled the kitchen."

Chase smiled. Then he closed the gap between them and slid his thin arms around Ash's neck, laying his head on his shoulder. Ash was startled by the gesture, but he felt his own arms move to surround the boy.

"Can we keep doing this, Dad?" Chase asked, his voice slightly muffled. "Talking? And hugging like this?"

Ash managed to give him an affirmative answer in spite of the lump in his throat. His mind went to the box of photos in the attic. He knew that sooner or later he needed to pull them out. Maybe even let Chase go through them and pick out some that he especially liked.

Greta looked around the kitchen and sighed. Was she crazy to have taken on this tutoring job on top of everything else? Chase was supposed to be arriving in ten minutes, and the dishes were still sitting on the sink shelf. Galen had needed her help with a school project after dinner, so she had waited on the dishes. Now it was too late to do anything about them. It was times like this that she wished she'd let Bob install a dishwasher.

"I think a car just pulled up, Mom," Galen said as he came into the kitchen.

"Mr. Lancaster drives a pickup."

"I didn't look out the window..."

The doorbell rang, and Greta groaned. With one last look at the sink shelf, she followed Galen out of the kitchen, turning off the light as she went.

Galen stopped by the couch, letting her be the one to open the front door. She found both Chase and his father on the porch, the man holding the storm door open.

"Come on in, Chase," she said, wishing that Ash Lancaster had simply dropped his son off and driven away. Not that she would have done that with Galen, but the less she had to deal with the man, the better she liked it.

"Is Galen here?" Chase asked, stepping inside.

"He's in the living room. You can go ahead in."

His father stepped inside also, much to Greta's consternation.

"I have to stay in town for a bit, so I can pick him up later," the man said. "No need for you to come all the way out to the farm."

"It's really no trouble, Mr. Lancaster. I don't mind the drive."

The man nodded. He shifted his position slightly as if he were going to leave, but then he stopped and looked at her again.

"I don't know when I was last called Mr. Lancaster by an adult," he said gruffly. "My first name is Ash. I guess if you're going to tutor Chase you may as well use it."

Greta forced herself to smile, nodding as she said, "I guess that means you should call me Greta then."

He looked at her silently for a moment, then nodded and opened the storm door again. Greta watched him cross the porch to the steps, then disappear down into the darkness where the porch light didn't reach. She couldn't begin to understand the man, and didn't really want to try. But she did feel a bit sorry for Chase having to live with such a person. She'd lost her spouse also, but she wasn't cold and silent as he was.

"This is a Cessna, Galen," Chase was saying when she walked into the living room a minute later. "That's what I want to learn to fly. Mom took me to see one once. I got to look inside the cockpit and everything."

Galen had apparently pointed out the stack of books from the library because Chase had one of them in his hands. Greta sat down near him on the couch and looked at the picture he'd been pointing to.

"What does it say about the picture, Chase?" she asked.

Chase put his finger under the first word in the caption and began trying to pronounce it.

"Jer... Jer...ome... Jerome?" he said.

"That's probably the man's name," she told him, ignoring the effort it took him to figure out the pronunciation. "The one standing in front of the plane."

Chase nodded, then went on with the caption.

"Jerome Wild...er be...gan flying at the age of seven...seventeen." He stopped again, looking up at her to exclaim, "Wow! Do you think I could start flying that soon? I thought I'd have to wait till I was an adult."

Greta smiled.

"I think some people have learned to fly even younger than that," she told him. "A lot depends on the circumstances. I know that in the outback stations in Australia an airplane is the only way to get to town for supplies. I would think a youngster there would have to know the basics pretty early in case of an emergency."

Chase's eyes were wide as he listened to her.

"How do you know that?" he asked.

"Books, Chase," she replied. "Books tell us all sorts of things."

He looked down at the book in his lap again as he said, "My dad likes to read. He has all sorts of books in his study."

Galen stood up.

"I still have a bit of homework to finish up," he announced. "Guess I'll head upstairs."

Greta nodded, then she turned back to Chase. He ran his finger under the words below the picture.

"Do you think I could get so I could read all these words without stumbling?" he asked.

"I'm sure you can, Chase. The first step is to read what interests you as often as possible. Like these books about flying. The more you read, the more words you'll learn to recognize."

"I have a few books at home that I've read, but none on flying. Dad doesn't want me to get too interested in it."

Chase kept his head bent over the book as he spoke, but Greta could tell that his father's wishes bothered him a bit. She felt a touch of resentment towards his father.

"My dad and I had a fight the other day," Chase said quietly.

"About flying?" Greta asked, not sure she wanted to hear anything about their personal troubles.

"No. He wanted me to do some chores with him and I didn't want to. The kids at school tease me cause I smell like a farm. I yelled at Dad that I hate the farm."

"Did you mean it?"

Chase shook his head.

"I told him yesterday that I didn't really mean it," he said. "Dad said the kids would pick on me no matter where I live." He looked up at her, his expression very serious. "Do you think that's true, Mrs. Jorgensen?"

Greta nodded.

"I think some kids tease everyone out of their own bad feelings," she told him gently. "Galen used to get teased a lot because he's smaller than most of the kids in his class."

"So…how did he get them to stop?"

"Well, it wasn't that he got them to stop, Chase. But he didn't let the teasing get to him. Not in front of them anyway. I encouraged him to be polite and friendly to those other kids in spite of the teasing. Over time, the kids came to respect Galen, and most of them stopped teasing him. He still gets teased, but a lot of it is friendly teasing rather than mean stuff."

"I think teasing is dumb," he said, looking down at the book again.

"I expect you're right, Chase," Greta said. "It would be nice if everyone could just accept everyone else's differences, but it's not human nature to do so. The Bible tells us that we're born sinners. One of our sins is our bent toward selfishness. The Bible also teaches us how we should treat others, but most people don't think it's worth reading anymore."

"My dad used to read the Bible to me. But he quit when Mom died."

"Did you used to go to church?" she asked.

"No. Mom said some churches were full of hi…hi…"

"Hypocrites?" Greta said, taking a wild guess at the word he was trying to say.

"Yeah. That's the word."

"Do you know what it means?" she asked.

Chase shook his head, then he smiled at her.

"Bet you're going to tell me though," he said.

Greta laughed as she got up off the couch. She went to the bookcase nearby and came back with a large book.

"This is sort of like a dictionary, Chase," she said as she sat down beside him again. "It gives words that are similar in meaning to the word you look up. Also words that are opposite, if there are any. It's called a thesaurus."

She flipped through the pages till she found 'hypocrite', then slid the book onto his lap. Chase frowned when she pointed to the word.

"H-Y?" he said. "Why is it spelled that way?"

Greta slid her finger under the words in the book, reading them out loud.

"Hypocrite comes from the Greek, hupokrites, which means stage actor."

"It's a Greek word?"

Greta nodded as she said, "It means to be insincere, or two-faced. Your mother meant that there were people in the church who say they believe in God, but don't act like it."

"Do you think she was right?"

"Yes," she replied, nodding, "but it shouldn't stop anyone from going to church. The Bible says that believers should gather with other believers. I understand why your mother said it though. Sometimes I get very frustrated with the people there too."

The doorbell rang and Greta looked at the clock.

"That must be your father. It's eight."

She set the books aside and got up to head for the front door. When she opened it, Chase's father stepped inside and closed the storm door carefully.

"I can wait if you're not finished," he said, glancing toward the living room.

"We're able to stop anywhere we need to, Mr....um...Ash, I mean."

The man smiled at her. Greta felt the same leap in her pulses that she had when Chase first smiled. The transformation in his face was incredible to her.

"Habits die hard, I guess," he said.

Chase appeared in the doorway and the man asked if he was ready to go. Chase looked back toward the living room with an expression of longing on his face, but he nodded and moved toward the door.

"When can I come again?" he asked, looking up at his father. "She has books on flying that I haven't looked at yet."

"Flying?" the man said gruffly, causing Greta to look at him. He was looking at her as he asked, "You're interested in flying?"

"No," she replied, lifting her chin slightly. "Chase is interested in flying. One of the easiest ways for kids to learn to read better is by reading what interests them."

His eyes bored through her and Greta wanted to shrink back from his look, but she stood her ground, challenging him to deny her the right to tutor Chase in her own way.

"When should I bring him again?" he finally said.

Greta blinked in surprise as he backed off, then she said, "Perhaps Thursday evening? And Saturday morning? I realize he probably has chores to do, but he needs to do a report for school and I'm helping him with it."

"His chores can be done by ten," the man said. "Maybe seven on Thursday?"

Greta agreed to that plan and the two went out the door. The man turned to make sure the storm door closed properly, then they disappeared off the porch and Greta closed the inside door.

"He's too touchy," she said to herself as she leaned her head on the door.

"Mr. Lancaster?" said Galen's voice behind her.

"Yes," Greta replied, turning to look at him. "But you were not supposed to hear that."

"I won't tell him you said it," Galen quipped as he came the rest of the way down the stairs. "How'd it go with Chase?"

"I'm afraid I'm still just getting to know him," Greta admitted. "He's a smart kid, really. Just a bit confused by things."

Galen kissed her lightly on the cheek and headed for the living room.

"I'm going to have a snack," he called over his shoulder. "If you're going to do the dishes tonight, I'll help."

"You sure you aren't sick?" she asked as she followed him.

"Nope," he replied. "It's just that I want you to quit your job and be home when I come in from school. If I can show you that I'll be helpful around here, maybe you'll decide to tutor kids all the time."

Greta smiled slightly, thinking about how much she had enjoyed the time with Chase. Tutoring him was a whole lot more fun than checking inventory or looking at figures all day long.

Ash was silent as he drove through the darkness toward home. Chase wasn't talking either. He'd curled up on the seat by the window after strapping his seatbelt.

A picture of the woman kept tumbling around in Ash's mind. Feisty little creature, he thought, and found that he was smiling at the way she had lifted her chin to defy him over the books about flying.

He glanced over at Chase, wondering how much the boy had told the woman about their life. He was sure Chase had said something, just by the way she'd reacted to his question.

No matter, he told himself firmly. She was just tutoring Chase. As soon as he could read better, there wouldn't be any need for the boy to go there.

Chapter 5

Greta arrived at Peggy's a little early for the Bible
study Tuesday night. Galen took off upstairs with Jimmy
as soon as Peggy let them in. Peggy led Greta to the
kitchen.

"As long as you're here early, you get to put out the
cookies," Peggy told her. She pointed to three packages
of cookies and a plate. "Doesn't matter how you put them.
I usually just throw a bunch on."

"I haven't entertained in ages," Greta said with a small
laugh. "You sure you trust me with this?"

"I do," Peggy replied as she laid napkins on the tray
she was fixing. "So, you've had your second meeting
with Chase?"

"Last night," Greta said. "It went quite well really,
though I don't know how much he's going to learn at the
rate we're going. He gets easily sidetracked."

"Don't all kids?"

"I suppose. He has a report to do for school. We decided that I would help him get his thoughts on paper clearly for that. He says his spelling is bad."

Peggy nodded.

"That would definitely go with a reading problem."

"Yes." Greta hesitated, then she decided to voice the question that was in her mind. "Has his father always been so withdrawn and uncommunicative?"

"Ash?" Peggy glanced at her, then shook her head. "No way," she said. "When Margaret was alive he was a pretty happy man. He and Dan used to have these really long talks about the Bible together. Ash always refused to go to church, but he's very knowledgeable about the Bible." She shook her head again, this time with a sad note to it. "Now Dan can't even mention it," she said. "Not that we see much of the man anymore."

"Chase said his father quit reading the Bible to him after his mother died."

The doorbell rang at that moment, ending the conversation. Greta followed Peggy as far as the living room, each carrying a tray with them. After setting hers on the coffee table, Peggy went to answer the front door. Greta slipped out of her jacket and laid it on the arm of the couch where she had dropped her Bible when she'd arrived.

Five other women joined them within the next few minutes. Three of them had been to Bible studies at Greta's home in the past. Jane Wesley told Greta that she missed her presence at their meetings and was glad to see her getting out again. Greta hoped that her presence wouldn't spark a flood of matchmaking again.

Once everyone had gotten tea for themselves, they settled in the living room and opened their Bibles and study books. Peggy sat next to Greta on the couch and shared her study book as she led the group through the second chapter of James. Greta simply listened to begin with, but Jane wasn't about to leave her out and declared that her input was very valuable to them all. Greta laughed.

"I don't know this stuff any better than all of you," she said. "And I haven't had a chance to look at the study book to see how the author has chosen to deal with it. I do know that our faith should lead to good works though. Sort of automatically. If I feel grateful to Jesus for saving me, then I should want to do things for others."

"But doing good works isn't needed to reach our goal," Vetta Brown said. "Some people act like I'm not a good Christian if I don't do stuff."

"Depends on the stuff," Alexi Barstone said. "I mean, my idea of good works may not be the same as Peggy's, or as yours, Vetta. My problem is not in the doing. It's the having time for the doing. I have to schedule good works on my calendar if I want to do them."

There was laughter and nods of agreement, and Greta decided that this was a good group. Very open and honest. Just the sort of group she had enjoyed in the past.

Later, as the study wound down and disintegrated into general conversation, Ann Taylor, who was sitting in the chair near Greta's end of the couch, turned to her and said, "So, Greta. I guess you're ready to come out of the mothballs?"

"I've never been in them," Greta replied, sniffing at her sleeve. "Do I smell like them or something?"

Ann laughed, shaking her head.

"You know what I mean," she said. "Men. There are several eligible ones in the church right now. Are you eyeing anyone in particular?"

Greta took a deep breath, shook her head, and said, "If God wants me to marry again, He will have to do the choosing. It really bothers me when you all try to set me up with somebody. That's really why I've been avoiding things lately."

There was a moment of silence, then Peggy said, "I guess that spoils your fun, huh, Ann? I bet you wanted to line her up with Al Richards, didn't you?"

"Well…" Ann drawled, smiling devilishly. "Actually I was thinking more along the lines of Nate Baxter."

Even Greta had to laugh at the idea of her dating the elderly man who insisted on sitting at the back of the sanctuary in spite of his inability to hear well.

The meeting broke up on that happy note and the women began gathering their belongings together. Ann gave Greta a hug, telling her that she was glad she'd decided to join them. Karen Maxwell and Alexi also gave her hugs, and Jane Wesley threw her a kiss as she headed for the door.

When they others were gone, Peggy called the boys downstairs. Greta pulled her jacket on and gathered up her Bible.

"I really enjoyed that," she told Peggy, joining her in the front hallway. "I'd love to come again next week if it's really ok about Galen being here."

"I wouldn't have it any other way," Peggy replied, giving her a quick hug. "I wouldn't mind getting together with you at other times either, if there's some way to work that out. Lunch or something maybe?"

"Ha!" Greta said, shaking her head. "My lunch time is so iffy that plans would be sure to fail. And now I've given my Saturday mornings to Chase. Not that I regret it. But my calendar is swimming."

Peggy laughed.

The boys came down the stairway at that moment, and Dan entered through the front door, so their conversation ended. Greta headed outside with Galen, pulling her jacket a bit closer around her as the cold night air hit her.

The next morning, Greta found herself distracted from her work by thoughts of Chase and possible ways to foster the love of reading in him. She quickly bypassed the idea of playing Scrabble with him because she knew that a child who found spelling difficult would not find any pleasure in such a game. His report would be a good place to begin, but that wasn't going to take up very much time, and doing it would not encourage him the read more.

During lunch Greta's mind suddenly convicted her of the time she was taking away from her job to dwell on Chase. When she returned to the drug store, she put her full concentration on her work and pushed all thoughts of Chase into storage for later. The day went much slower after that, but Greta felt better about the way she was using her time. The following day, however, she found herself wishing that tutoring Chase was the only job she had to do. Bill Gordon presented her with an ordering problem during the morning and she set aside everything else to take care of it. By the time she had repaired his mistake, her lunch hour had disappeared and she was left hungry and irritable for the afternoon. Despite her attempts in the past to explain her need of a definite lunch break, Bill, who always ate lunch at his desk, couldn't seem to make sure she had one.

Later that afternoon, as Greta tried to concentrate on

some paperwork in her office, there was a gentle tap on her open door. She looked up to find Chase's father standing in the doorway.

"Sorry to disturb you," he said, his voice not quite as brusque as usual.

"I needed disturbing," Greta confessed, getting to her feet. "These figures don't always come out the way I want them to."

He glanced around the office, but remained where he was. Greta waited a moment, then said, "Are Chase and I still on for tonight?"

"As long as we can make it seven-thirty," he replied, looking at her again. "I have to be in town for a meeting. I'd have to drop him at your house about twenty after, if that's possible."

"Not a problem," Greta told him. "Will I still be bringing him home?"

The man shook his head as he said, "My meeting will be done by eight-thirty. I'll pick him up shortly after that."

He turned to leave, but Greta said, "Do you have meetings often?" before she could stop herself. Chase's father turned back to her.

"Farmers in the area get together once a month," he said.

"What does Chase normally do when you go?"

"He comes with me," Ash replied shortly. "Does his homework, or sits and looks at books."

Greta nodded, deciding that she probably wasn't going to get any more information from him. The man's face had closed up again and his voice held its usual brusqueness.

"Have Chase bring paper and pencil, please," she said

as he once more turned to go. "He has a report we're going to work on."

"He says you're going to write it on flying," he said, looking at her again.

Greta smiled, even though she didn't really feel like it. His features were knit into a frown and his voice had gotten even rougher.

"Well, he's going to do the writing," she told him in an attempt to lighten up his mood. "I'm just going to help him organize his thoughts."

He nodded, but he didn't smile back. Instead he said, "I guess it won't hurt for him to write a report on it, but I'd rather he didn't get too involved with thoughts of flying."

"May I ask why not?"

He stared at her for a moment, then, very curtly, he said, "He has work to do."

"He knows he has to wait until he's older for anything like that," Greta explained, wondering just why it was that this man didn't want his son to reach for his dreams. Did he expect Chase to be a farmer, like him?

The man grunted, then he turned to leave again. Over his shoulder he said, "Just remember what I said, please."

He strode away without another word, leaving Greta to shake her head sadly. It was always hard for her to understand people like that, so full of pain themselves that they nearly crushed the joy out of those around them.

As Ash climbed into the cab of his pickup outside the drug store, he was scowling.

"That woman keeps challenging me," he muttered to himself. "Why can't she just hear what I say and leave it at that?"

Her face popped into his head as he started the truck. In spite of his frustration with her, he had to smile.

"Feisty little creature," he murmured, remembering what she'd looked like when he'd first looked into the office, with her head bent over those books and the pencil tapping against her cheek. The sight had softened him a bit, wiping out his original words. He'd gone there to tell her straight out that flying was off limits to Chase. They could do that report on something different. He'd sooner see the boy get an F for failing to do it than to encourage him in his thoughts about airplanes. Now he was still stuck with that report, and Greta Jorgenson had challenged his authority.

Shaking his head to clear away his thoughts, Ash started the pickup and headed for the school. He found a spot in the parking lot where he had a good view of the front door, and turned off the engine to wait for Chase. Just as his thoughts drifted once more to Greta Jorgenson and the boy's report, he heard the dismissal bell ring. Within a minute kids began pouring out into the sunshine and Ash scanned them for Chase. When he saw him, he stepped out of the pickup to intercept the boy's momentum toward the buses lined up nearby. Fortunately Chase saw him as well. The boy waved as he changed direction, urging the person with him to come too. As they got closer, Ash realized it was Greta Jorgenson's son.

"Hi, Mr. Lancaster," Galen said when they got to the pickup.

"Galen," Ash said, nodding in his direction, then he looked at Chase. "I was in town, so I figured I might as well give you a ride home."

"Great," Chase replied. "I don't care for riding the bus

anyway."

As Chase ran around to the other side and got into the cab, Ash looked at Galen again.

"Can I give you a lift home?"

"No, thanks, Mr. Lancaster," the boy said. "I'm headed for the drugstore to see my mother." He looked into the pickup and waved as he added, "See you tonight, Chase."

"Yeah," Chase called back.

Ash watched Galen walk away, then he climbed into the pickup.

"How was school today?" he asked as he headed out of the parking lot.

"Pretty good. A kid started teasing me, but I took Mrs. Jorgensen's advice."

His words gave Ash a start, but he kept his voice even as he said, "And what was her advice?"

"She said that Galen just ignored the teasing and tried to be friendly anyway. So I just smiled at the kid and walked away. I couldn't really think of anything friendly to say to him."

Ash smiled, wondering how the woman had come to give out advice like that in just two short visits. Apparently Chase had opened up to her more than the boy had done with him in the past year. But then, except for Sunday, he hadn't been of much use to anyone. At least he now knew something that Greta Jorgenson and Chase had talked about. And that she gave pretty good advice.

Greta was ready for Chase that evening long before he was due to arrive. The dishes were all done up and Galen had disappeared upstairs to do homework, giving her a bit of time to relax with some Christian music. When the doorbell rang, she turned off the music and went to answer it, giving Chase a quick smile while noting that his father was still insisting on coming to the door.

"Come on in," she said to Chase. "Galen is busy with homework, but those same library books are on the coffee table."

Chase headed for the living room as his father said, "I'll be here as close to eight-thirty as I can."

"Chase and I can keep working until you get here," she assured him. "I don't mind if you're a bit late."

He nodded, turning to leave. Greta closed the door and returned to the living room, where she found Chase looking through another of the books.

"This plane is flying upside down," he said as she took a seat beside him. "That must be cool."

"Not sure I'd go for that," Greta admitted. "I don't even like to hang upside down on the monkey bars."

Chase giggled, saying, "You don't go on the monkey bars, Mrs. Jorgenson. Big people don't do stuff like that."

"No?" Greta asked, raising her eyebrows. "I'll admit it's been a while since I've done it, but I'm sure Galen would tell you that I used to."

Chase considered that idea for a moment, then he turned back to the book. Greta ran her finger under the words below one of the photographs in the book, reading aloud as she did so. Then she pointed to another photo and asked Chase to read that caption. He struggled through it, with a little help from her. After that, Greta suggested that he write down some of the information about the stunts being pictured, and later, when they came to a page about a particular air show, she had him write down where it was and try to describe some of the events that took place. Both his handwriting and his spelling needed to be worked on, but she decided to wait until his reading improved before tackling anything else. The important thing was to give him some confidence in his own abilities.

Galen came downstairs about eight-fifteen. Chase immediately showed him some of the photographs in the book and Galen gave flying upside down and wing walking a negative review. Both boys agreed that it would be fun to actually go to one of those air shows though.

Greta left the boys to continue perusing the book while she made them a snack, and they passed the rest of their time chatting together. When the doorbell rang a little before nine, Chase made no move toward leaving. Greta went to the door to invite his father in, telling him that she thought Chase wanted to show him the book they'd been working with. The man frowned, but he followed her into the living room.

"You should see what these planes are doing, Dad," Chase said when he saw his father. "They're stunt planes, and they fly upside down and stuff."

Greta was surprised to see the man's whole countenance tighten up as he moved to give the book a glance. Chase didn't seem to notice as he went on talking.

"Galen and I would like to see an air show sometime," he said. "Are there any around here? Have you ever seen one?"

The man shook his head, moving toward the doorway as he said, "We need to get home, Chase."

Greta stared at him, shocked by the abruptness of his words. Chase gave him a quick look, then laid the book aside and gathered up his paper and pencil, looking a bit bewildered. Greta touched his shoulder as he passed her. "Try getting some of your ideas down onto paper by Saturday morning," she told him. "Don't worry about the spelling. We'll work on that together."

Chase nodded as he followed his father out the front door.

"He's sort of weird," Galen observed after the door closed behind them. "How come he wouldn't even look at that book?"

"I'm not sure," Greta said, sliding an arm around his shoulders and turning him back toward the living room. "He actually looked...well...I don't know. Hurt. In pain somehow, though I can't imagine why."

She sank onto the couch and picked up the book they'd been using, flipping through it in the hopes of finding an explanation for the man's actions. Galen gathered their snack dishes and headed for the kitchen.

"Such a puzzle," Greta said softly, trading the book for the next one in the stack. She began looking through it, sorry that she and Chase hadn't gotten to it first. The pictures on the first few pages were excellent, and the book seemed to be about the flyers rather than the air shows and planes. She stopped to study one picture more closely, examining the faces of the two men standing in front of an airplane. Suddenly she gasped, lifting the book to look more closely. She quickly read the caption below the picture, then the blurb beside it, biting her lip as her fears were realized.

"If that's another book on stunt flying," Galen said behind her, "Chase will be happy."

"Chase isn't to see this book!" Greta exclaimed, slamming it shut. "Don't even mention it to him, Galen, please."

"Mom?" Galen said, a vaguely worried look crossing his face.

Greta realized that it would have been better to just not say anything, but now that she had, she opened the book again and handed it to him. Galen looked at it curiously.

"The man on the right," Greta said. "And read the stuff below and beside."

"Wow!" Galen said, stepping around the end of the couch to sink down onto it. "That's Mr. Lancaster. It says the other man is his brother. They actually began flying stunt planes in their early twenties and this picture was taken right before Grant Lancaster died in an accident at an air show in Wichita, Kansas. No wonder Mr. Lancaster didn't want to look at that book, Mom. What are you going to do?"

"I don't know what to do, Galen," Greta admitted. "I can't possibly let Chase see this. I'm not even sure that I should let him do his report on this stuff. I don't want him to hurt his father any more than we already have."

"You want me to take this book back to the library tomorrow?" Galen asked. "That way Chase won't know it was here."

Greta shook her head, realizing that she owed it to Ash Lancaster to let him know that the book was in the library. How she would do that, she had no idea.

"I...I have to think," she told Galen. "To pray about the situation even."

Galen nodded, handing the book back to her. He gave her a kiss and announced his intention to go to bed, then stood up and started to leave.

"You know, Mom," he said, turning back to her, "maybe this is why you were supposed to tutor Chase.

Dad used to say that everything happens for a purpose, so why not this?"

Greta gave him a weak smile, slowly finishing Bob's old saying.

"And God works everything for good." She sighed, running her hand across the cover of the book. "Right now it's hard for me to see any good in this situation, but I'm willing to let God do his thing with it."

Galen nodded, turning once more to leave the room. Greta watched him go, grateful for his wisdom. He kept surprising her, but she liked the way he was maturing both mentally and spiritually.

She sighed again, opening the book to give the photo of Ash Lancaster and his brother another look. They looked so young, so innocent and full of life. It was hard to realize that one was dead and the other was much older and very burdened in his soul. Greta closed her eyes and began praying for him again, something that she'd found herself doing quite often since reading of his wife's accident in the newspaper the year before.

After Chase had gone up to bed, Ash sat on the couch with his head in his hands. Old memories began surfacing and he started shivering uncontrollably, so he jumped up and began pacing the floor. When that didn't help, he clutched himself tightly with his hands on his arms, trying to control his racing thoughts. Pictures flashed in his mind as if someone were clicking through a series of slides, shining them inside his head. He saw an airplane spiraling down, down, down, and he wanted to scream as he'd screamed so long ago.

"No!" he hissed, waving his arms in the air to push away the pictures. He tried to pull up a picture of

Margaret to replace the others, only to realize that he'd somehow pulled up one of Greta Jorgenson instead. "No!" he cried out again, horrified by what his mind was doing to him. He grabbed his head in his hands and squeezed it as hard as he could. "I will not think about these things!" he exclaimed, determined to block it all out. "I will not! I left it all behind and I will not let it come back!"

But come back it did, with pictures of an airplane falling out of the sky mingled with his mother's stricken face and those of both Margaret and Greta Jorgenson. Horrified, Ash staggered through the kitchen and out the back door. Out into the darkness to lose himself once again.

Chapter 6

The next morning, Greta called the drug store right after Galen left for school. She left a message on the answering machine to say that she would be in late because of a personal emergency, then she collected her things and drove out to the Lancaster farm. She knew that Chase would have taken the bus to school, and she was hoping to catch Ash before he went anywhere.

She played Christian music for the drive, but her stomach didn't really unknot itself. Greta worried that Ash would just kick her off the property and pull Chase out of the tutoring sessions. She had no idea how she would explain things to anyone, and she really didn't want to lose the connection with Chase. In just a few sessions he had made strides toward self-confidence. At least in front of her. She had no idea how he was at school.

As she drove up the farm lane, she saw Ash near the barn, chopping wood. The idea of confronting him in his house had not appealed to her at all, so the fact that he was outside cheered her up a bit. She parked the car near his truck and watched as he set aside the ax and grabbed the jacket that was draped over the fence. Then she got out of the car.

"Morning," he said, shrugging into the jacket as he approached her.

"Good morning," Greta replied, her mind going completely blank for a moment. She uttered a silent prayer as she glanced around the farm, then looked at him again. "I…I'm here about last night. About the books. Chase's report."

Her words stumbled over each other as she tried to gather her thoughts and Greta felt like she was making a fool of herself. The man was frowning at her and she was quickly losing her nerve. Instead of trying to say anything more, she reached into the car and grabbed the book, mutely holding it out toward him. At first he just stared at it, his face going pale. Finally, with shaking hands, he reached out to take it. Greta was pretty sure that he knew what he was going to find in the spot she had put a bookmark.

"I found it after you and Chase left," she said. "I…I…I'm sorry."

The man opened the book, glanced at the picture, then handed it back to her. Then he turned and strode back toward the woodpile he'd been working on.

"If you had just explained," she said, going after him, "I wouldn't have…"

He turned on her, his face fierce.

"Explain?" he bit out. "How does one explain that he got his kid brother killed by helping him learn to fly?"

"But…"

"How does one explain the sight of his brother's plane

falling out of the sky and there isn't a thing anyone can do to help him? How does one explain the horror of knowing that his mother is watching the whole thing? How does one explain the guilt and condemnation that lives with one forever?"

He continued on toward the woodpile, yanking off his jacket and throwing it violently toward the fence. It missed, but the man didn't seem notice that as he scooped up the ax again. He stood a piece of wood on the tree stump and lifted the ax over his head. Greta put out a hand, knowing quite well that the anguish driving his swing was far to powerful, but realizing that she couldn't stop him. The ax came down on the piece of wood, throwing splinters of it all over the place before burying itself deep in the tree stump.

Ash swore, making Greta flinch. He began trying to free the ax, but even she could see that it was a waste of time.

"I doubt your brother feels that you got him killed," she said quietly, moving a bit closer.

"My brother doesn't feel anything," he retorted, jerking at the ax with both hands.

She watched him fight the tool for another moment, then she closed her eyes and uttered another silent prayer. When she opened them again, he was leaning on the ax handle, his head bowed and his shoulders shaking. Greta sat down on the ground where she was and waited.

It was several minutes before he got himself under control again. She waited for him to lift his head, but he didn't.

"Grant loved flying," he finally said. "He learned before I did actually. But it was me that introduced him to stunt flying. We used to travel around to all the shows and fly. Grant was good at it. I did all right, but he was the one who always stole the show." He wiped his face with the sleeve of his shirt, then stood with his back to her, looking toward his fields. "The day he was killed he was doing a new stunt," he went on. "One that I had thought up. He'd done it in practice without any problem. No one knows for sure what happened up there. One minute he was doing the stunt, the next, the plane was falling from the sky in silence. The engine had shut down."

"I'm sorry," she whispered, not even sure he would hear her.

"I haven't flown since that day," he continued. "Sold my plane and all my gear. Went where no one knew me and started a new life."

"Did your wife know about this?"

Ash shook his head.

"Margaret and I met later," he said. "I was working on a ranch in Texas. We came east during our second year of marriage, before Chase was born. Lived in Boston for a while, but I hated it. I've always lived in open spaces. We finally found this place and bought it. The previous owners were too old to work the land anymore, and none of their children wanted it. I grew up on a farm and liked the open spaces."

"Your parents?" she asked.

He shook his head, turning his attention back to the ax.

"Sorry for swearing," he said. "I just got done telling Chase last weekend that we shouldn't say or do things in anger. Eating my own words now with this ax buried this way."

Greta laughed. He glanced over at her as he said, "I suppose you're one of those women who never loses their temper?"

"I haven't in a long time," she admitted. "But I haven't had any reason to either. Since Bob died I've avoided people who rub me the wrong way. That way I never have to stand up to them and tell them how I feel."

She was surprised to hear herself telling him this. She hadn't really admitted it to herself until that very moment.

Ash grunted and turned back to the ax.

"I may have to dig this thing out."

Greta laid the book in the grass, stood up and walked over to the stump.

"Maybe it's like that magical sword in King Arthur's time," she told him. "It takes a gentle hand or something."

He smiled.

"I think it was a king's hand maybe," he replied. "It's been a while said I read that particular book." He stepped back, motioning toward the ax. "Want to try your hand at it?"

Greta moved to stand behind the ax and wrapped her hands around it to tug. It didn't budge. She moved away again.

"I guess no one could ever say you aren't a strong man," she said with a smile.

Ash's laughter made her breath catch in her throat. Greta pushed her feelings aside and asked him if she could continue tutoring Chase. The man shrugged.

"Don't see why not," he said, scooping up his jacket and shrugging into it again.

When he headed for her car, Greta realized that he wanted her to leave. She picked up the book and followed him.

"I can try to encourage him to do his report on

something different," she said.

He stopped, turning to face her.

"He'd wonder why," he said. "It's probably time I faced this anyway. Almost anyone could have come across that book. Even one of his own classmates. I knew there had been stories done on us. Didn't know one went into a book though."

"Will you tell Chase?"

"Guess I have to, seeing that you ignored me when I said I didn't want him to be interested in flying."

Greta blushed, turning her face away from him. She couldn't come up with any defense for her actions, other than to repeat that kids needed to read what they found interesting. She doubted that he would accept that.

"You should get to work," he said, breaking into her thoughts.

Greta nodded, moving toward her car again. Once inside, she rolled down the window to say, "You'll drop Chase off tomorrow as planned?"

"Ten o'clock," he replied, nodding. "May I keep the book until then?"

Greta handed it to him through the window. Then she started the car and he stepped back, giving her room to maneuver.

Several times during that day, Greta turned to God to pray for the Lancaster home. She was glad she'd gone first thing in the morning. That gave Ash time to sort out his thoughts before Chase would come home. The tortured look on his face as he'd swung that ax had been enough to send her scurrying into God's presence immediately. The concern for Chase was enough to keep her going back.

Now that she understood his past, Greta realized that she also understood his gruff attitude and his hermit nature. He was running away. Not that she'd tell anyone that. In a way, Peggy already knew. But Peggy had no idea that there was more than Margaret's death that was causing him pain.

Shortly after school ended for the day, Galen rushed into the drug store to tell her that he'd made the field hockey team. A quick kiss had been planted on her cheek, then he had disappeared out the door, off to Jimmy's to practice. Greta smiled at his exuberance, pleased that she had allowed him to go for it.

When the doorbell rang just before ten the next morning, Greta opened the front door to find Chase standing on the porch with his father. He had the library book in his hand, along with his paper and pencil, and Greta glanced at Ash uncertainly.

"I helped Chase with his report," the man said. "It's only a rough draft though, and his spelling needs to be corrected."

Greta nodded, taking her lead from him and calmly inviting Chase into the house.

"I need to pick Galen up at the school at noon," she told Ash. "I'll drop Chase off after that, if that ok."

"I take it your son made the hockey team then?"

"He did," Greta said, smiling. "He's very excited about it."

Ash nodded, then closed the storm door and stepped off the porch. Greta watched him go down her sidewalk before she closed the inside door and joined Chase in the living room.

"So what does your report look like?" she asked as

Chase sank down onto the couch.

"My dad had tears in his eyes when he was telling me about his stunt flying days," Chase said quietly, glancing up at her. "I've never seen my dad cry. Not even when Mom died."

"Was it ok that he cried?" Greta asked gently, taking her seat beside him.

"Mom always said he was strong and tough. A real man. I thought real men didn't cry."

"God gave all of us tear ducts, Chase," she observed. "Don't you think he meant for us to use them?"

"Boys who cry at school get teased," was his reply.

Greta smiled, then turned her attention to his report, taking the pad of paper from him and beginning to read it out loud.

"When my dad was younger, he and his brother were stunt fliers. They flew airplanes and did things like flying upside down and walking on the wings. They flew in air shows all around the country and he said it was very exciting. But then his brother got killed during an air show in Wichita, Kansas, and my dad quit flying. They got written about though, and the library here in town has a book with their picture in it, and a story about them."

"Dad said maybe the library would let me hang onto this book so I can show my class the photographs in it. They're better than the ones in that other book. And the book would help me explain the stunts better."

"I can renew the book," Greta told him. "I'm sure it will be fine if you hang onto it until after your report is turned in to Mrs. Moore."

"Do you think I should still do this report?" he asked. "I mean, Dad says no one here knows he used to fly. Maybe I shouldn't tell them."

"If your dad helped you to write this, I think that means he's ready to let people know. He's even willing to let you show the kids at school that picture."

"He said he ran away from his brother's death," Chase murmured, "just like he tried to run away from Mom's death by remodeling the kitchen."

Greta stirred uneasily, feeling as if she was invading Ash Lancaster's space unbidden. She wiggled the pad of paper and suggested that they take a look at the stunts in the book and decide which ones he wanted to describe in his report. Chase accepted the change of topic, giving her the book and taking the paper from her hands.

They worked until almost eleven-thirty, then got ready to head for the school. Greta offered to let him take the book home again, an offer that Chase eagerly accepted.

As they drove to the school, Chase talked about the farm, telling her what his chores were, and what things he liked best about his home. However, once Galen was in the car, Chase fell silent. Instead, Galen talked about how practice went as they headed out of town toward the farm.

When Greta parked the car near the farmhouse, Chase gathered up his small pile of belongings and slid out of the back seat. Greta didn't see Ash anywhere outside, so she got out also and followed Chase to the back door to be sure he found his father. Chase led her through a mudroom filled with boots and jackets and other outdoor wear, and on into the kitchen. Greta looked around that room curiously as they went through it. After hearing about it's renovation, she expected it to look brand new, but to her it looked like it had been there all the time. She smiled as she realized how neat it was though. Not like her kitchen at all.

Chase continued on through another door, so she

followed him again and found herself in the living room, which was a huge room at the front of the house. Greta was sure she could fit two of her own living room into it. That too was an extremely neat room. It had an almost unused look to it, except for one corner where magazines were stacked on the floor. A wood stove took up a fair amount of space along one wall, with wood stacked neatly nearby. Another wall had a couple of book shelves along it. A matching couch and chair broke the room in half, forming a sitting area at one end and leaving the other end open.

Chase knocked on a door along the same wall as the kitchen, then he opened it. Greta heard Ash's voice say, "You're home. I didn't hear the car."

"Mrs. Jorgenson came in with me to make sure you were here," Chase's voice replied.

She heard movement, then Chase and his father came out.

"Sorry," Ash said as Chase set his belongings on a table by the couch. "I had some work to get done inside, or I would have been where I could see or hear you come."

"Quite all right," Greta replied. "Now that I know you're here, I'll get back to the car though. Galen is waiting for me."

She turned to retrace her steps through the kitchen, very conscious of his presence behind her. Chase didn't follow them, which made Greta wish she hadn't come all the way into the house with him.

"Monday night?" Ash said as she reached the door to the mudroom.

"That would be good," she replied, turning to look at him. "Chase got quite a bit accomplished today. He's going to use the weekend to think about what more he'd like to put into his report."

Ash nodded and she stepped out into the mudroom. She was thankful that he didn't follow her out, but that didn't stop her from feeling as though he watched her all the way to the car. An impossibility, considering that she had to walk around the side of the house to get there. It just felt that way. He'd most likely retreated back to the living room to deal with Chase and had forgotten all about her as soon as he'd closed the mudroom door.

Ash stood at the kitchen window watching Greta get into her car. After she had driven out of the yard, he still continued to stand there. Her face seemed to be stamped into his mind, and he couldn't get rid of it. Her perfume had wrapped itself around him as well, a light, delicate scent that drew him.

"Dad?"

He turned to find Chase in the doorway. Glad of something to divert his attention from the woman, he asked Chase if he wanted some lunch. The boy accepted and Ash began getting sandwich makings out of the refrigerator. Chase got out plates, knives, and glasses, then he stood there waiting for Ash to finish making their sandwiches. Ash had the feeling he had something on his mind, but Chase made no move to begin a conversation with him.

"How did your time with Mrs. Jorgenson go?" he finally asked.

"Good," was Chase's only reply.

Ash poured juice into their glasses and they sat down to eat. Chase took a bite right away, then laid his sandwich back down on his plate.

"Do you ever think about going to church?" he asked, totally surprising Ash.

"No," he replied, trying to give himself time to make up a good excuse if Chase said he wanted to go.

"Mrs. Jorgenson talks about God real easy," Chase told him. "It makes me feel like he's a friend of hers or something. Can God be a person's friend?"

Once again, Ash was caught off guard. He'd expected Chase to tell him that the woman had invited him to church. That he could have said no to. Now he found himself faced with a question he didn't really want to answer. He laid his own sandwich down and picked up his glass of juice.

"I suppose," he murmured, then lifted the glass to his lips in the hopes that Chase would see that as an end to the conversation.

Chase, however, just sat there looking at him hopefully, like he wanted more of an answer.

"The Bible talks about him being 'closer than a brother'," he said, silently cursing Tom Anderson for saddling him with a Christian tutor. "I guess that could make him a friend."

"You used to read the Bible to me," Chase said wistfully. "I liked it when you did that."

Ash got up, taking his glass with him. He went to the refrigerator to get himself more juice, waving the glass in Chase's direction to see if he wanted some too. Chase shook his head.

"Could I go to church by myself?" Chase asked as Ash sat down again. "You could drop me off and maybe Mrs. Jorgenson would bring me home."

"Why would you want to go there?" Ash asked.

"I think God is somebody I should get to know,"

Chase stated. "Mrs. Jorgenson told me what hypocrites are, so I know now that they aren't something that could hurt me."

Ash stared at him.

"Hypocrites?" he repeated, wondering how such a subject would have even come up during the writing of a report on airplanes.

"Mom used to say the church was full of hypocrites," Chase replied, his face serious. "I thought it was some sort of creature that might bite or something."

Ash swallowed hard, trying not to laugh. A smile snuck out though.

"Maybe they do at that," he quipped. "Bite, I mean. I've never cared for the things anyway."

Chase giggled.

With that, Ash couldn't hold the laughter back any longer.

Chapter 7

"What did you do to Ash Lancaster?"

Greta's eyes hadn't even adjusted from the brilliant sunshine outside the church to the semi-darkness inside when Peggy's voice assailed her. The other woman looped her arm into Greta's and dragged her off to one side of the foyer as Greta said, "What do you mean?"

"I mean...What did you do to Ash Lancaster? He hasn't been inside a church in all the time I've known him, yet this morning he called our house to find out when the service would start."

"What does that have to do with me?" Greta asked, glancing back toward the door she had just entered. Galen was no longer beside her and she spotted him talking to Jimmy on the other side of the foyer. "I'm Chase's tutor," she told Peggy, turning back to her new friend. "I hardly speak to his father."

"You didn't invite him then?"

Greta shook her head, giving Peggy an apologetic smile.

"I haven't even considered doing that," she admitted. "Probably should have, but I seldom see him."

It was more or less the truth, and she wasn't about to tell Peggy about her trip to the farm Friday morning. Even Galen didn't know all that had transpired there. He did know that she'd gone however, since he'd asked about the stunt flying book that evening.

"Can we sit with Jimmy's family today, Mom?" Galen asked, appearing beside her. "I promise we won't talk during the service."

Greta was relieved that she and Peggy's conversation had been interrupted. While she was giving Galen an affirmative answer, Dan joined them as well, indicating that they should all head for the sanctuary. That ended the conversation for good as they went inside to find seats.

Once they were seated, with the two boys between herself and Peggy, Greta glanced around the sanctuary. There was no sign of Ash Lancaster or Chase and she wondered if they really would show up. When the service started without any sign of them, she assumed that their plans were somehow changed. Then, during the praise and worship time, a deep voice joined in behind her and Greta knew without turning that it was Ash Lancaster. Galen turned around, then glanced at her before putting his attention back on the front wall where the words were shown.

At the end of the service, Chase touched her arm and said hello.

"Mrs. Edwards said you might come this morning," Greta said, smiling cheerfully at him.

"Is it ok that we were late?" he whispered, stretching upwards to be closer to her ear. "Dad forgot that he doesn't own a suit. He wasn't sure if he should come without one."

Greta glanced at Ash, who had begun talking to Dan and Peggy. He was wearing his normal jeans, but he had on a white sweater over a blue dress shirt in place of his usual flannel shirt. He was wearing a different pair of boots too, and his curly hair had been somewhat tamed.

"He looks very acceptable," she told Chase. "And I doubt you were the only ones to come late."

Chase grinned at her, obviously pleased with her answer.

Galen invited Chase to go out to the foyer with him and Jimmy, and Greta encouraged him to go, promising to inform his father of his whereabouts. After the boys left, she moved closer to Peggy in time to hear Ash say, "Chase wanted to come and check things out. Seems Greta talks about God while she's tutoring him, and he became intrigued."

Peggy turned to give her an 'I told you so' look, causing Greta to blush.

"So what do you think of the church?" Dan asked, earning a shrug from Ash.

"It's a church," he said.

He looked around them and Greta, figuring that he was looking for Chase, said, "The boys all went out to the foyer. Chase didn't want to interrupt your conversation so I said I'd let you know where he is."

Ash nodded, turning back to Dan.

"It sounded like your pastor knows his Bible pretty well," he commented. "Good message."

"And you'll come again?" Dan asked.

"Maybe. Maybe not."

Greta left them to their conversation, making her way out the other end of the row of chairs. It wasn't until Peggy spoke behind her that she realized the other woman had followed her.

"He's very good looking, don't you think?"

"Don't tell me you're going to try your hand at matchmaking too," Greta asked, turning to give her a stern look. "I'm not interested."

"Won't say another word," Peggy declared, pretending to zip her mouth shut and throw away the key.

Greta couldn't stop herself from smiling at her friend's antics, and Peggy smiled also.

They found the three boys munching on donuts in the foyer. Galen promised that he and Chase had only one, while Jimmy admitted to having two. Greta brushed donut crumbs off Chase's shirt.

"The music was the best part," he said, smiling up at her. "I didn't understand some of the other stuff."

"The sermon was mostly for adults, I think," Greta said. "There is a kids class during that time. You could have joined that if you'd wanted to."

"Then I wouldn't have found out what church was all about," he replied.

Dan and Ash appeared, and Ash put his hands on Chase's shoulders as he asked, "So what's your verdict about church?"

"Verdict?" Chase repeated, tilting his head to look up at his father.

"It means, what did you think about church?"

"I'd like to come again," Chase replied very seriously. "Would that be ok?"

"We'll see, Chase," Ash replied, turning his attention

to Greta. "That report seems to be coming along fine. Chase had me read it over last night."

"Your input on it was very helpful," she replied, then winced as Peggy said, "Your input, Ash? What did you add?"

Greta was afraid she had really messed up, but Ash smiled at Peggy and informed both her and Dan that since Chase's report was on stunt flying, he had shared some of his memories of his own days as a stunt pilot. Peggy looked stunned, and Dan stared at him in amazement.

"Stunt pilot?" Dan said haltingly. "You've never said anything about your being a stunt pilot."

"Wasn't anything I wanted to talk about," Ash replied, then he gave Chase's shoulder a quick squeeze. "Time to go, Chase," he said. "We need to get home."

They headed for the door, leaving Peggy sputtering with unanswered questions.

"When...How...Did Margaret know?" she was saying even as Ash and Chase disappeared out of the building. "Blast that man! How can he just walk away after dropping such a bombshell?" She turned to Greta, still speaking. "And just when did you find out? Did Ash tell you?"

Greta smiled, edging toward the door.

"Standing date, Peggy," she said, motioning toward Galen. "Got to go."

Peggy stamped her foot in frustration as Greta made her escape.

As Ash drove home from church he decided that it hadn't been very fair of him to leave Greta Jorgenson holding the ball like that. He hadn't really planned on saying anything, but when she had made that remark about his input, he'd had no choice. Not that she really meant to do it. The look on her face after she'd said it told him that she was already regretting her words. It had helped him over a rough spot though. He had wondered just how he was going to explain his silence to Dan, and what he would tell him about the past. Now the can of worms had been opened and they could go back to the conversation later. Maybe without Peggy around. She would have too many questions, and he really wasn't ready for a lot of them.

Chapter 8

Greta stood at the kitchen sink looking at the picture
on the windowsill as she waited for the dishwater to drain
out. She reached over to pick it up and run her fingers
across the image of Bob's face.

"Mom?"

She turned to find Galen standing in the doorway,
watching her.

"Yes?" she asked, raising an eyebrow.

Galen came over and looked at the picture she was still
holding.

"You thinking about Dad?" he asked.

Greta nodded, and Galen reached out to touch his
father's face also.

"I miss him," he said.

"I miss him too," Greta said. "I used to enjoy this time
of the evening when he was alive. Sometimes he'd help
me with the dishes, then we'd play a game with you and
listen to music. It was cozy. Family time."

Galen nodded, then moved away from her as he said, "Have you ever thought about getting married again?"

"Never," she replied, replacing the picture on the windowsill. "I loved your father too much."

"But if the right man came along?" Galen said curiously.

"If God wants me to marry again, he's going to have to send down lightening bolts or something to get my attention," Greta told him. "I really don't have any inclination in that direction."

"What about Mr. Lancaster?" Galen asked, making her turn to stare at him.

"Mr. Lancaster?" she repeated, dumbfounded. "Why would you mention him and marriage in the same conversation? He's got so many demons from the past hanging around him that I doubt any woman could get within a mile of him. You saw how he reacted over those books on flying."

"Yeah, but he seems to be over that now, Mom. He actually told Mr. and Mrs. Edwards about it yesterday after church."

She studied his face for a moment, then grinned.

"Mrs. Edwards put you up to this, right?"

Galen shook his head.

"I've just been thinking that you'll probably get married again someday, Mom. Not like Mark Johnson's mom did maybe, but to some man who made you happy."

"And you wouldn't mind?" she asked.

Galen shrugged.

"I suppose I would a little," he admitted, "but I want you to be happy, Mom. And Mr. Lancaster isn't so bad once you get to know him a bit."

Greta grabbed the dish towel and held it out to him,

eager to be done with the conversation.

"Chase should be here any second," she announced. "I'll let you wipe the dishes tonight since you're hanging around the kitchen."

He grinned, taking the towel from her as he said, "Chase is a good kid too, Mom. He'd make a nice little brother."

She frowned fiercely, then marched out of the room, her heart beating a weird tattoo against her ribs. She remembered thinking, just the night before, how handsome Ash Lancaster had looked at church. At the time she had reprimanded herself for such thoughts. Now she felt as if Galen had been in her mind and heard them.

The doorbell rang as she stood in the living room, struggling to compose her frayed mind. Greta went to open it and Chase bounced in eagerly, asking where Galen was.

"He's in the kitchen wiping the dishes for me," she told him. "You can go find him."

He took off and Greta turned to Ash, who remained on the porch, his hand holding the storm door open.

"I can bring him home," she said. "No need for you to come all the way back."

"I won't be," he replied with a smile. "I'm actually headed over to Dan and Peggy's. I'll pick him up in an hour. I have this thing about women driving at night, especially in the rain."

"Your wife…" she said hesitantly. "It was raining the night she died. I remember reading about it in the paper."

"That was over a year ago," he observed. "How can you possibly remember it?"

"It left a young child without one of their parents, like Galen. I actually prayed for you and Chase for several days after the accident, and I've lifted you in prayer again at times when you would come to mind."

He stared at her for a moment, then shook his head.

"You didn't even know us," he said gruffly, although she had the feeling that this time the gruffness came from emotion more than his general attitude.

"No, but I was familiar with your pain." Greta looked outside as she changed the subject. "Is it really raining?"

Ash smiled as he stepped aside. She saw the wet sidewalk below the steps, and the drips coming from the porch roof.

"I guess it is," she commented. She rubbed her arms as she felt the nip in the outside air. "And it's getting colder. I suppose winter is going to come whether I want it to or not."

"You don't care for winter?"

"Oh, I love the snow," she told him. "Bob and I used to go skiing before Galen was born, at least when he was stationed somewhere in the north. The year he was stationed in South Carolina we desperately missed the snow. I just don't care to drive in it."

"And you have to drive to work."

Greta smiled as she nodded her head. Then she shivered slightly and wrapped her sweater more firmly around herself. He instantly started to close the storm door.

"I won't make you stand in the cold any longer," he told her. "I'll come back shortly after eight?"

"That will be fine."

She watched him as he went down the steps and headed for the pickup at the curb. Then she closed the front door and went into the living room, arriving just as Galen and Chase came from the kitchen.

Ash turned on the ignition, but he didn't put the pickup in gear. He looked back at the house for a moment, seeing her in his mind as she had been, there in the doorway. Her admission about praying for him and Chase had rocked him. And she had referred to it so easily. He could tell she hadn't said it out of pride. To her it was a simple fact. There had been an urge in her to pray and she had done it.

He shook his head and looked at the street stretching in front of him.

"Why does she have to be hanging around in my mind," he mumbled into the darkness. "Margaret is the one that should be there."

He finally put the truck in gear and headed for Dan's. As he drove along he thought about what she had said about her husband, and he realized he must have been in the service during the early years of their marriage.

"Wonder what her husband was like," he said out loud, then he gave his head a little shake to clear it, reminding himself that he was supposed to be thinking about Margaret, not Greta Jorgenson.

He turned on the Edwards' street and slowed to a stop in front of Dan's. But he had to force himself to get out of the pickup. What he really wanted to do was to go back over to Greta's house and talk to her some more.

Peggy opened the door when he finally knocked on it ten minutes later.

"Hi, Ash," she exclaimed, stepping aside as she added, "Come on in. Dan is on the phone with somebody who has a problem with their car. He's nearly done, I should think."

"I don't mind talking to you for a bit," he said as he

followed her into the living room. "I'm grateful that you don't mind my inviting myself like this."

"Oh, we're delighted to have you come by. No reason for you to go home and then come all the way back in to pick up Chase."

Ash sat down on the couch as Peggy slid onto one of the chairs nearby.

"Greta always offers to bring him home," he said, "but I'm reluctant to let her. At night anyway. She does bring him on Saturdays."

"So…how are you and Greta getting along?" Peggy asked.

Ash wondered if she was hoping that something would develop between him and Greta Jorgenson. He decided that he'd better choose his words carefully or she'd pounce on them the way she had Greta's the day before. The last thing he wanted was someone trying to do any matchmaking on his behalf.

"I think she's a very good teacher," he replied. "Chase seems to be responding to her methods."

Peggy laughed.

"Not going to commit yourself to anything, huh?" she said, shaking her head. "Don't worry. I've already been warned to keep my hands off. Greta sat here last week and told a whole roomful of women that God can be the only matchmaker in her life, and that we were not to drag every eligible male to her doorstep for her approval."

Ash grinned in spite of himself.

"I would have liked to have seen that, I think," he replied.

"And I shouldn't have told you about it," Peggy said hastily. "Greta will probably hang me by my thumbs if she ever finds out."

"I'll try not to be the one to tell her," he replied as he leaned back and relaxed a little.

Dan came into the room and sat down at the other end of the couch. The talk turned to other things, and Ash was surprised by how quickly the hour passed. Neither of them brought up the subject of stunt flying fortunately, though he had the feeling that Peggy was biting her tongue. He was sure that both of them were full of curiosity about his announcement the day before, but he still didn't feel ready to share much with them. And tonight he was in their house simply to remain in town while Chase had his session with Greta.

As he climbed back into the pickup, Ash thought of what Peggy had said about Greta Jorgenson. 'God can be the only matchmaker in her life.' He smiled slightly as he started the motor and headed for her house.

Greta looked at the clock and saw that it was time for Chase's father to come. She closed the book she was holding, but Chase kept writing for another moment before looking up.

"Is it time already?" he asked.

She smiled as she nodded her head.

"But I have more I want to say," he complained.

Greta's smile grew as she reached out to tousle his hair.

"I thought you hated writing reports," she teased.

"Not this one! And I like doing it with you. It makes it easier."

"Why, thank you, Chase," Greta responded. "I've been enjoying helping you also. I've certainly learned a thing or two about stunt flying."

Chase grinned.

"Including that my dad did it?" he asked.

"Yes, including that your dad did it."

Chase looked back down at his paper.

"I have to hand this in Friday," he groused. "Do you think it will be finished by then?"

"Well, I think you're nearly done," Greta told him, glancing at his paper. "You could write down those last thoughts at home, then I could help you with the spelling mistakes the next time we get together. You do need to make your final copy though."

Chase's face fell.

"Mrs. Moore says we should do it in our best handwriting," he said. "Some of the kids wanted to do it on their computers, but she told us she wouldn't accept any typewritten reports."

"Mrs. Moore believes that kids should learn to write legibly," Greta informed him. "I remember that about her."

"What does 'le...le...'"

"Legibly?"

"Yeah. What does it mean?"

"Readable. Clear. Distinct. I usually think of the word neat when I hear legible. And I include, without a lot of eraser marks."

Chase groaned.

"That will take forever! I only have till Friday."

Greta laughed again.

The doorbell rang, and she got up from the couch. Chase began gathering his things together. As she went to the front hall, Greta considered the time constraints he was facing and decided to take an afternoon off from work if Chase's father would allow him to come an extra time.

When approached about adding an afternoon session that week, Ash said, "You work," in a very abrupt manner.

"I'm allowed time off for good behavior," she retorted.

A smile spread across his face, much to her relief.

Galen, who had come downstairs in time to hear about the plan, said that Chase could walk home with him after school. Ash looked at Chase, then said, "You have chores."

"I could have him home shortly after four," Greta countered. "Wouldn't that still give him enough time for chores? And it's just for one day. Just to get this report done."

"You don't take no for an answer, do you?" he asked, the corner of his mouth twitching slightly, as if he wanted to smile and was trying not to.

Greta blushed, but she lifted her chin and looked him in the eye.

"You didn't say no," she informed him. "You merely mentioned the roadblocks."

Ash laughed. Greta felt the flutter of butterfly wings in her stomach at the sound, but she pushed it aside and waited for him to give his answer. Ash reached out to tousle his son's hair.

"Guess I'm outnumbered here," he said. "Wednesday would be best for us."

The plan was solidified and the two of them left. Galen disappeared toward the kitchen for a snack, and Greta was left alone with some rather disturbing thoughts. The effect of his laughter on her was becoming bothersome. Attraction to Ash Lancaster was simply out of the question. He was a morose and uncommunicative man who wasn't even over his wife's death, let alone all the things from his past. And then there were her own memories of Bob. She still loved him and had no desire to remarry. Surely God would give her the desire before bringing a man into her life. Wasn't it something that she would be praying about long before it happened?

As Ash drove home through the darkness, he dwelled on her ability to make him laugh. She was as different from Margaret as black was from white, except that dark hair and her eyes. Though, if he really wanted to be truthful, even her eyes were different. Softer. He smiled as he thought of the way he had once compared them to Tucson's eyes.

"Dad?"

"What?" he said, glancing over at Chase.

"Do you think you'll ever get married again?"

"Married?" he repeated, his mind going straight to Greta Jorgenson.

"Yeah. Some of the kids at school said that you'll probably do that."

Ash frowned. Why did kids always have to be saying stuff like that anyway? Why tell Chase something just because they think it *might* happen?

"It won't be anytime soon, if I do it at all," he replied tersely.

"What about Mom?"

"What do you mean?" he asked, his frown deepening.

"Didn't you love her?"

Ash glanced at the boy again.

"Of course I loved her," he replied. "Why would you think otherwise?"

"How can you marry someone else if you love her?" Chase asked, persisting in keeping the conversation going. "And Mom always said that marriage was for life. How come some of the kids at school don't have their real father living with them, and they talk about some new man their mother has married."

Ash sighed, wishing he could somehow avoid this subject entirely. But he knew it wouldn't go away. Especially not when Chase would begin to see more and more oddities like this as he reached puberty.

"Sometimes people decide they can't possibly live together," he replied, "so they get divorced. Your mother and I didn't believe in that. We believe that if two people decide to get married, they should learn to work things out together."

"Mrs. Jorgenson's husband died, like Mom. She hasn't gotten a new husband."

Ash thought of Peggy's words about that subject and he smiled to himself. He couldn't very well repeat those things to Chase however.

"Not everyone gets married again, Chase," he finally said, very quietly. "Some people think they need a mate, especially if they're divorced. When you're alone because of death, you tend to feel differently."

"Why?"

Ash groaned inwardly. If these were the kind of questions that the tutoring business was going to bring up, was it worth it? He had thought he had a few more years before Chase would begin asking about this sort of stuff.

"Divorce is difficult," he said slowly. "The one left behind often feels like they must have done something terribly wrong, or that they aren't....uh...likable. When a husband or a wife dies, the person left behind has a lot of other feelings."

"How did you feel?"

"When your Mom died, all I felt, besides anger, was emptiness," he said a bit gruffly. "Like a part of me had been wrenched out and buried with her."

Chase was silent the rest of the way home.

Only half of Greta's mind was on the women's Bible study the following night. The other half was stewing over her reaction to Ash Lancaster's laughter. She thought that she was enjoying him just a little too much. At the oddest moments, his face would come into her mind, or she'd remember something he had said or done. Not that they had seen each other all that often. The day that she had driven out to the farm about the book had been the most time they had been together.

The women were discussing the first twelve verses of the third chapter in James. Greta attempted to stay with the conversation that flowed around her, but she wasn't taking anything in very well. Fortunately no one asked for her opinion. Even Peggy, who was seated right beside her, was allowing Greta to maintain her silence.

"Were you even here tonight?" Peggy asked once all the others had left. "What's going on that you're so quiet?"

"Tired, I guess," Greta murmured, now feeling completely worn out. "I probably should have cancelled. Stayed home."

Peggy examined her, then shook her head.

"It must be awfully hard to be a single parent," she observed. "Working all day, then racing home to put supper on the table. Me? I work at the library because I want to, not cause I have to. And I designed my own hours there. No fulltime work for me. I want to be here when Jimmy comes home from school."

Greta sighed.

"I would love to be home for Galen," she confessed, "but it's impossible. Part time work just doesn't pay the bills."

"What about some other job?" Peggy asked. "Gordon's isn't the only place in town."

"Galen wants me to quit my job at Gordon's and go back to tutoring at the school, which is what I was doing right after Bob died. I suppose that's something I can do at home, but I don't know about the money. I know I'm supposed to trust God for our finances, but isn't Gordon's the job he provided?"

Peggy smiled, shaking her head.

"Confusing, huh?" she said.

"Very. And I'd better get Galen out of here before I fall asleep on your couch."

Peggy called the boys and Greta slipped her jacket on.

As she drove home, Greta considered the possibilities of other jobs around town. None were really to her liking though. Tutoring young kids in reading and writing was something she enjoyed doing, and it didn't take as much preparation as actual teaching, though she would probably be allowed to substitute teach. That wouldn't guarantee her enough hours though.

Galen was quiet during the short drive, but when they arrived home he got himself a snack and joined her in the living room. They talked about school and field hockey for a few minutes, then he headed for bed. Greta put on some music and turned off all the lights in the living room so she could relax for a bit before bed.

Wednesday dawned clear and somewhat warm. Greta drank in the smell of fresh mowed grass when she arrived home at two for Chase's session. She could see it was her next door neighbor who had mowed, probably for the last time until spring. The leaves were beginning to fall too.

She went inside to wait for the boys to arrive, thankful that Galen was willing to make sure Chase got there alright. She felt that Chase's time around the other boys was almost as important as the tutoring, so the walk home would provide the two of them to get better acquainted.

When the boys walked in, Greta took one look at Chase and knew something had happened. He had dirt on his face and he looked as if he'd been crying. There was a tear in the sleeve of his jacket and mud on his pants. Her eyes flew to Galen.

"A couple of the boys in Chase's class decided to have a bit of fun with him," Galen explained. "They took the book about stunt flying away from him."

"Galen got it back," Chase said.

"I got outside just in time, I think," Galen added. "Though Chase had already gotten hurt."

Greta knelt down in front of Chase and looked at his face. His cheek looked like a bruise was forming on it. She touched it gently.

"Did you tell someone in the office?" she asked.

Chase shook his head.

"Chase didn't want to, Mom," Galen said. "He thought it would just make the other boys pick on him even more."

"You could be right," Greta admitted, looking Chase in the eye. "Let's get you cleaned up. I'll sew your jacket while you're working on your report."

Galen followed them to the kitchen. Greta asked him to get a snack for himself and Chase while she took a cloth and cleaned up Chase's face.

"How come you're not married," Chase asked.

Greta stared at him. She heard Galen laugh softly.

"Because God hasn't brought a man into my life that he wishes me to marry," she told him.

"What does God have to do with it?"

She grabbed a paper towel and began wiping some of the mud off his jeans.

"Well, Chase," she said as she worked, "the Bible says that Jesus needs to be the Lord of my life. I'm supposed to look to him for everything I need here on earth. I figure that means he should make my decisions for me."

"All of them?"

"The major ones especially," she replied. "Like where to live, and what job to have, and whether I should get married or not. I don't want just any husband. I want who God wants for me. And if God doesn't want me to have one, then that's ok too."

She finished cleaning off his pants and stood up. Chase slid off his jacket and hung it on one of the chairs at the table while she threw away the paper towel. As she rinsed out the cloth she'd used on his face, Chase said, "Could we use the Bible to help me read better?"

Greta turned to look at him, then at Galen. Galen was almost laughing, and she knew he was remembering how he had offered her that idea when he was trying to convince her to tutor Chase. She smiled slightly.

"I guess we could do that. After we finish your report we'll get started on it."

The three of them went into the living room. While the boys ate their snack, Greta read the new things that Chase had added to his report.

Ash had spent the morning hauling a tree home from

the woods with Tucson. After lunch he had used the power saw to cut the trunk into usable pieces, and now he was splitting wood again. He had his back to the farm lane, but every inch of him was waiting for the sound of Greta Jorgenson's car. All day he had been looking forward to seeing her again, though he had tried to wipe that fact out of his mind through the heavy exertion of hauling the tree. He told himself that she was just a woman who was tutoring Chase. He told himself that he had no wish to be involved with another woman. He even told himself that it would never work out, trying to blend two families such as theirs. Plus, they had hardly spoken to each other. She was nice enough, but she had never expressed any interest in him. In fact, he had the feeling that she didn't really like him very much.

He stopped chopping long enough to wipe away the sweat from his forehead and glance at his watch. Three-thirty. He shifted his position so he could see the farm lane, then hefted the ax and swung it down on another stick of wood, his mind going swiftly back to the previous week when he'd buried the ax in the stump. It had taken him a while to get it out, and he couldn't help smiling at the memory. She'd been very easy to talk to that day. A good listener, yet very feisty when she needed to be.

Setting aside the ax again, Ash wiped away more sweat and surveyed the pile of wood he'd managed to make. He picked up several pieces and carried them over to the woodpile by the barn, carefully beginning a new stack where the old one ended.

"She probably wouldn't look twice at a farmer anyway," he mumbled. "Town girl. That's what she is. Loafers, probably heels. Not quite the same sort as Margaret, but close enough. Takes a special kind of woman to live on a farm."

Ash knew he was trying to make excuses for not being involved with her. He moved back and forth between the scattered wood and the woodpile, wiping away the sweat each time his hands were empty. After awhile, the newly split wood was gone and the stack by the barn was much larger. Ash stuck the ax into the stump and headed for the barn, glancing at his watch as he went. Four-ten. He had a bit of time to throw hay down from the hayloft to Tucson's stall in readiness for his supper.

When the car finally drove into the yard, Ash left the barn, a quiver of excitement racing swiftly through him. He stood still for a moment, watching as Greta stepped out of the car, sending a wave in his direction. His heart swelled at the sight of her, then plummeted to the souls of his feet as he realized exactly what he was feeling.

"No!" he silently screamed, struggling to stand right where he was. "Not love. Not love," his mind panted, even as his heart told him otherwise.

Chapter 9

"How come Mr. Lancaster barely spoke to you, Mom?" Galen asked as they drove back down the farm lane. "He acted like he didn't even want you around."

"I imagine he had to do extra work today since I took Chase away from him," Greta replied, though she was also wondering just why the man had acted so strangely. Not only had he barely spoken to her, but he'd seemed very stiff and almost angry.

"You didn't even get to tell him about Chase's problem at school," Galen said.

"Wasn't planning to," Greta said. "I had cleaned Chase up. It's probably better to just let it go. Hopefully it isn't something that will happen again."

"I'll keep an eye on him. So will Jimmy."

"I'd appreciate that, Galen. Chase has enough to deal with in his life without getting beat up at school."

Galen fell silent and Greta turned on the radio, hoping that he wouldn't go back to the conversation about Ash Lancaster. The man was very confusing, very friendly one minute and the next, very unfriendly. A Dr. Jekyll and Mr. Hyde personality for sure.

They arrived home and Galen took off up to his room. Greta made dinner, her glance repeatedly going to the photo on the windowsill.

After tossing and turning most of the night, Ash had to fight his way out of a troubled sleep when the alarm went off at four-thirty. He pulled on his clothes and went out to the barn, his mood in tune with the drizzly day that met him. He was angry at himself for being attracted to Greta Jorgenson, and equally angry with Tom Anderson for getting her to tutor Chase. His life had been difficult enough without her entrance into it.

Once he'd taken care of Tucson and the cows, and had turned them out into the pasture, Ash headed back to the house to get Chase out of bed and fix breakfast. He tried to be civil to the boy, but with Chase being the reason Greta Jorgenson had gained entrance to his home, it wasn't very easy. Chase apparently sensed his black mood. He remained silent through breakfast and got himself ready for school with no prodding at all.

After the school bus took the boy away, Ash went back to the barn to begin mucking out the stalls. He hadn't gotten any further than collecting the pitchfork and wheelbarrow when the phone bell pealed, calling him away from his chores. It was Tom Anderson, which didn't sooth his mind at all. He barked at the man, telling him that he was too busy to talk, and slammed the phone down again.

"Should never have let this tutoring stuff start," he muttered as he grabbed the pitchfork again. "Chase can read just fine. I had trouble when I was his age too. He would have grown out of it, just as I did."

He ignored the fact that it had been his grandfather who had tutored him past the rough spot, using the Bible and teaching him about God at the same time.

The telephone bell pealed again.

"Now what?" he asked the empty barn angrily. "How many times do I have to be disturbed this morning? I'll never get out to the field at this rate." He dropped the pitchfork beside Tuscon's stall and headed for the phone, still muttering to himself. "I swear I'm going to get one of those answering machines and let it do the talking for me." And, when he picked up the phone, he nearly snarled "Lancaster here" into it.

There was a moment of silence, then Greta's voice said, "I'm sorry to disturb you, Ash, but we didn't decide when Chase should come again. "That report is due tomorrow, and he needs to make his final copy. He was going to work on that tonight if he came."

Ash felt his anger drain away, quickly replaced by an intense longing to see her face. The hand holding the receiver shook and he had to switch hands, fighting to maintain control over his emotions.

"Ash?" she said, and he could hear concern in her voice.

"I'm here," he bit out through clenched teeth.

"If I've caught you at a bad time, you could give me a call later. Either here at the house or at Gordon's."

"I'll do that," he replied quickly, nearly slamming the phone down.

When he got back to where the pitchfork was, Ash scooped it up and began furiously forking away the old wet hay. He closed his mind to everything but the job at hand, frustrated with himself for reacting to her the way he did.

When he finished in the barn, he headed for the field. But, no matter what he did or how hard he worked, Greta Jorgenson stayed with him, lingering in his mind. At lunch he stomped into the house without even removing his barn boots, climbed the stairs all the way to the attic, and yanked out the box of pictures he had stuffed there after Margaret's death. He carried it back down to the bedroom they had shared and dumped the pictures onto the bed. Then he sat down and looked at every single one, tears rolling down his face as he allowed all of his grief to flow free.

Greta found the message on her answering machine when she arrived home from work that evening. Galen had called down from upstairs when she walked in, so she was alone in the kitchen when she listened to it.

"This is Ash Lancaster," the voice said. "I'm not sure I want the tutoring to continue. I need some time to sort things out and make a decision about it. I'll get back to you."

She listened to the message three times before erasing it. His voice had the same abrupt quality in it that had been there the first few times she had seen him. In fact, it had been there when she'd called that morning. She couldn't think of anything that might have caused it, any more than she could understand what had occurred the day before. And had he already told Chase there would be no more tutoring?

Greta remained standing in front of the counter where the answering machine was for several minutes after the message was gone, feeling somewhat alone. Then Galen walked into the kitchen and she moved to the stove to start dinner.

"So when is Chase coming again?" he asked.

"Tonight or Saturday morning?"

"Mr. Lancaster isn't sure he wants to have the tutoring continue," Greta said. "He left a message on the answering machine."

"How come adults act so weird?" Galen asked. "I mean, it was obvious that the tutoring was helping Chase. Why end it?"

"I don't really know," Greta said, keeping her face turned away from him so he wouldn't see that she was troubled by this turn of events. "We'll just have to wait and see what he decides after thinking things over."

Galen was silent for a moment, then she heard him leave the kitchen. She forced herself to get their dinner, to not think about Ash Lancaster's behavior.

Friday and Saturday went by without a sound from the Lancaster household. Greta wished that she could at least find out if Chase had finished his report and turned it in, but she didn't dare call. No matter how many times she went over things, she couldn't come up with an explanation for what had happened. Ash Lancaster's actions were a complete mystery to her.

When they arrived at church Sunday morning, Galen headed straight for the place where the Edwards family was already seated. Greta followed him into the row, noting that the row behind them was already full. She greeted the people before taking her seat beside Galen, then leaned forward to say good morning to Peggy and Dan. The service started, leaving no opportunity for small talk. Something that she was very thankful for. She was sure that Peggy would have asked about the tutoring.

The pastor spoke on compassion. Greta found herself very interested in his message, looking up the passages he mentioned, and taking notes. Galen sat quietly beside her, sometimes looking at her Bible with her. At no time did she glance around the church, determined to not care if Ash and Chase were there or not. However, at the end of the service, as Galen and Jimmy went by her to go to the foyer, Greta saw Ash and Chase leaving the sanctuary.

"Now that is very strange." Peggy said.

Greta glanced at her and saw that Peggy had apparently spotted them also.

"Why would Ash leave without at least coming over here to speak to all of us?" she asked. The she made a noise of disgust. "Just when I think we're getting somewhere with the man, he closes up again!"

"At least he still came to church," Greta said quietly.

"Do you know what's going on?" Peggy asked, giving her a rather intent look.

Greta shook her head.

"All I know is that he left a message on my machine Thursday afternoon," she confessed. "He's not sure he wants the tutoring to continue."

Peggy looked toward the back of the sanctuary again.

"I'll have Dan give him a call this week," she stated firmly. "Maybe even tomorrow." She turned to Greta again, saying, "So you'll come Tuesday night?"

"Sure," Greta replied, relieved that Peggy wasn't going to ask her any more questions about Ash Lancaster. "I'm enjoying the study, even if I am tired. I've always liked the book of James."

"So have I. This is the first time I've tackled the whole book at once though. Usually I just study one passage or another."

Greta picked up her Bible.

"I need to go collect Galen and get home," she told Peggy. "He wants to do some project after our Scrabble game, so we need to get moving."

Peggy walked out to the foyer with her. They found Galen and Jimmy outside with Dan, and Greta waved goodbye as she and Galen headed for the car.

"Chase and his dad were here," Galen commented. "Jimmy and I saw them for a second in the foyer, but Mr. Lancaster said they couldn't stop to talk."

"I imagine they have plenty of work to do, even on Sunday."

Galen shook his head.

"The other day Chase told me his dad never does more on Sunday than what's absolutely necessary," he informed her. "His dad spends Sunday afternoons reading most of the time."

Greta tucked that piece of information away in her head as they headed home.

Ash sat in the living room with an unopened book on his lap. He could hear Chase upstairs in his room, thumping around, but it was the other noise that held his attention. From the kitchen came the sound of pans being moved around, and quiet singing. The smell of coffee filled the air.

He squeezed his eyes shut, determined to block out the sounds by picturing something else. But when Greta Jorgenson's face popped up, he opened them again.

"I'm being driven crazy by two women," he muttered softly. "One isn't even alive, and the other is...."

He didn't finish his thought. The smell of meatloaf

drifted out from the kitchen, and he realized that he no longer smelled coffee.

"This is my imagination," he told himself. "That's all. I'm over tired."

He groaned silently as he remembered the previous night and the sleeplessness that had invaded him. After tossing and turning for over an hour, he had come downstairs and done paperwork in the study till after two.

"At least I managed to catch up on that," he said now.

He thought about the church service that morning. The pastor had given a good message on compassion, but his mind had wandered a bit. He had hoped that sitting in the back would make being there easier, but he'd found himself looking over toward where Greta and her son were sitting with Dan's family. She'd been very engrossed in the sermon and had not even looked around.

'I doubt she even wondered if we were there,' he thought. 'And I refuse to allow these feelings to grow at all. If Chase wants to continue going to church there, we will sit where we can't possibly see her.'

Somewhere in his brain he knew that not seeing her wasn't going to matter, but Ash ignored the reality of it.

"I don't suppose you'd care to explain what's going on?" Tom Anderson said as soon as Greta answered her phone at work Monday morning. "I just got a call from Ash Lancaster. He's requesting a different tutor, or no tutor, depending on whether Ruth Moore says Chase could do without now."

Greta's heart sank.

"I…I'm not really sure what happened, Tom," she said. "Things were going quite well, I thought. I helped Chase write a report, and we made plans about what to do next."

"So Ash hasn't spoken to you?"

"No," she replied, not telling him about the phone message she'd received.

"Well, I have no choice but to do what he's requested."

"I understand, Tom," Greta said. "Thanks for calling to let me know."

After hanging up the phone, Greta stared at the wall for several minutes, her anger growing. She felt like she'd been tossed aside like an old dishrag and she didn't much care for the feeling. What right did the man have to just cancel the tutoring without an explanation? If there was a problem, he should have talked to her about it. She doubted that it had anything to do with the plan to use the Bible. He hadn't even known about that on Wednesday afternoon when he'd acted so strangely.

Sure that she would not get any work done feeling as she did, and with her anger fueling her, Greta grabbed her jacket and went to tell Bill Gordon that she had a personal emergency to attend to. She felt as if she had been using that excuse a lot lately but she couldn't help it. She was determined to find out why Ash had ended the tutoring in such a fashion.

On the drive to the farm, she tried to clear her tangled thoughts and come up with a plan of what to say. But her mind refused to calm down. Not even music seemed to help. Twice she wondered if going to the farm was the right thing to do, but her anger took over and she continued on her way. Then, as she went up the farm lane, she finally began praying. By the time she parked the car she was regretting her rash decision to come, but it was too late. If he'd seen her driving in, he would wonder why she turned around and left if she chose to do that.

She parked her car beside the pickup and stepped out. The whine of a saw reached her and Greta followed the sound around to the back of the house. Ash looked very busy, running a power saw through a board lying across a makeshift worktable in the back yard. She stopped, now hesitant to approach him. He had obviously not seen her drive in, so if she left right away, he'd never know she had come. But that wouldn't answer any of her questions, and she really did want some answers.

The noise of the saw suddenly stopped and Greta saw that the cut had been completed. Part of the board fell to the ground while Ash ran a hand over the part still on the worktable. She took a deep breath, exhaled slowly, then moved closer.

"I'd like to know what happened," she said quietly, not even waiting for him to notice her there. "Tom Anderson tells me you asked for another tutor."

Ash was clearly startled to see her there. Every muscle in his face tightened and his body went rigid.

"You could have called to ask me that," he said.

"You may not have bothered to answer the phone," she said, shaking her head. "Besides, I prefer to confront people face to face if I'm going to do it at all."

Ash set the saw on the ground and unplugged the cord from the extension wire coming out the window nearby. When he straightened up, he didn't look at her.

"Chase will do fine with another tutor," he said.

"That's not an explanation," she stated, wishing that he would look at her. "I would like to know why you made this decision."

"Because I did," he replied, stepping away from the worktable.

Greta had the impression that he was going to head into the house and she reached out to touch his arm as she said, "I'm not leaving until I hear an explanation, Ash. I think I have a right to ask that of you."

Ash turned to face her finally and Greta took a step backwards when she saw the fierce look in his eyes.

"An explanation," he repeated, taking a step toward her. "Ok, I'll give you one."

He grabbed her by the shoulders, hauling her forward into his arms. Greta instinctively raised her hands in defense, but he ignored them, crushing them between their bodies. As his head came down, she turned hers aside. Ash let go of one shoulder to force her to turn it back and she had no choice but to accept his kiss. The scent of his aftershave and sweat mingled together in her nose, and she could feel every inch of him against her. Surprise rooted her to the spot.

The kiss ended as abruptly as it had begun. Greta nearly fell as he let go of her, but Ash caught her, holding her steady for a moment. Then he said, "I hope that is sufficient explanation, Mrs. Jorgenson," in a gruff tone before striding away toward the back door of the house.

Greta stared at the door, her hand at her lips. Tears filled her eyes. She shook her head, then wiped the tears away before heading for her car.

Chapter 10

Greta went home instead of going back to work. She felt even worse than before--confused, angry, embarrassed--and she didn't think she could face anyone until she could pull herself together.

The message light on her answering machine was blinking. She stood in front of the kitchen counter watching it, reluctant to listen to the message, yet knowing that if it was him and if she left it for Galen to hear later, it might make the whole situation even more intolerable. She finally pressed the button, and Ash's voice filled the room.

"I apologize for my actions, Greta. I never intended for that to happen. Please forgive me."

Greta played it again. Tears filled her eyes and rolled down over her cheeks as she listened to his voice. She continued to stand there, replaying his message over and over as her tears splashed onto the counter.

Ash felt as if he were being tortured by a thousand demons. He had tried to shut it all out with work, but he kept picturing Greta's face in his mind. Her shock and confusion. He couldn't understand himself. Kissing her was the last thing he'd wanted to do, yet the need to do so had completely overwhelmed him.

When work hadn't washed away the memory, Ash had taken a long hot shower and reexamined the old pictures of Margaret. But it was the light, gentle scent of Greta's perfume that seemed to hang in the air all around him. He had abandoned the pictures and retreated to the living room, and now he was just waiting for Chase to arrive home from school. Ash hoped that doing chores with the boy would clear his mind.

He heard the back door bang, then Chase's voice called him.

"In the living room, Chase," he called back, and the boy appeared in the doorway. He hesitated there a moment, then came slowly into the room.

"You ok?" Chase asked, looking at his clothes.

Ash realized that his clean work clothes were probably confusing Chase and he gave him a weak smile.

"Had sawdust all over me," he confessed, hoping that Chase wouldn't question his explanation. "Took a shower cause I felt rather grubby."

"What are you working on?" was the boy's next question.

"Just a crazy idea probably," Ash replied. "How was school?"

Chase's shoulders slumped in dejection and Ash feared that something had gone terribly wrong.

"I got an A on my report but I have no way to tell Mrs.

Jorgenson," Chase said. "I don't understand why she can't tutor me anymore. And I avoided Galen today at school cause I didn't know what to say to him. I thought he would be my friend, but now I don't know if he can be."

Ash closed his eyes, regretting his impulsiveness even more. If he'd just left things alone, Chase would not be feeling as he was and he would never have kissed Greta the way he had.

"So Mrs. Moore thought your report was that good, huh?" he said.

"She even had me share it with the class," Chase replied. "I even got to show them your picture. They thought it was really cool, you being a stunt pilot and getting written about in a book."

There was very little feeling in the boy's voice, though Ash could see that he was at least a bit proud of his achievement. Chase seemed rather lost though.

"Did I do something wrong, Dad?" the boy asked. "Was it my report? I asked Mrs. Jorgenson if I should really do it still, and she said it was ok. Is that why you said she can't tutor me anymore?"

Ash sighed.

"It had nothing to do with you, Chase," he said, shaking his head. "Your report was great and I'm very proud of the way you worked so hard on it."

"Then why…?"

"It's me, Chase. I got confused and angry with myself and did something dumb, like when I changed the kitchen. It's hard to explain, and I'm sorry this all happened. I'm sure Mrs. Jorgenson would be very happy to hear your good news though. How about I let you call her later?"

"I've never called anyone before," Chase announced solemnly. "Could you maybe call her for me?"

"I'll dial the number," Ash told him. "After that you're on your own."

Chase nodded, then turned to leave.

"Guess I'll change my clothes and get my chores done," he said.

"Want some help?"

Chase looked at him in surprise. Ash smiled, moving to get up also.

"I'm not getting anything else done around here right now," he said. "Just sitting around being angry with myself isn't much fun."

Chase grinned, then disappeared up the stairs to change his clothes. Ash wandered out through the kitchen to the mudroom and changed into his outdoor boots. By the time Chase joined him, he was in the barn.

After supper, Ash pulled out Greta's number and dialed the phone. He listened to the first ring, then he handed it to Chase and walked away to lean against the counter. Chase listened for a minute. Ash knew the moment Greta picked up the phone by the smile that spread across the boy's face.

"Mrs. Jorgenson, this is Chase," he said quickly. "I got an A on my report and Mrs. Moore had me share it with the whole class."

Chase's whole demeanor was different in this telling of his news. His body moved with excitement, and his voice was eager and excited. Ash felt a stab of pain at the realization that his son had a better relationship with Greta Jorgenson than with him.

"I got to show everyone the pictures in that book too,"

Chase was saying.

There was a brief silence as Chase listened to the woman. Then he said, "Yeah, the other boys liked it. Tommy Nichols asked me if there were any other books at the library about stunt flying. He said he likes planes a lot."

There was another silence. Chase's face grew serious as he listened.

"Ok," the boy said. "I'll tell him."

He said goodbye and hung up the phone, then turned to Ash.

"She said if you change your mind, she's still willing to tutor me," he reported.

Ash nodded and Chase went on.

"I really do want Mrs. Jorgenson to tutor me, Dad. We were going to read the Bible together. That's how I was going to learn to read better."

Ash started to shake his head, then moved to crouch in front of Chase.

"Right now that's an impossibility," he said, "but how about you and I read the Bible together? Maybe we don't even need a tutor. It'll be just you and me getting to know each other again."

"That would be great," Chase exclaimed, wrapping his arms around Ash's neck.

"Yes," Ash murmured, his arms sliding around Chase also. "Yes, it would be."

Greta hung up the phone, hoping that she had done the right thing by telling Chase she was still willing to tutor him if his father changed his mind. She wasn't at all sure that she wanted to be anywhere near the man, yet she was not willing to just dump Chase by the wayside. He needed help. He needed to be around other people. She wasn't at all sure that Ash Lancaster would pay attention to his son's needs. The man had a habit of closing himself off in order to protect himself from life's troubles. Greta knew that never worked for anyone.

At work on Tuesday, Greta set aside all of her concerns and concentrated on the things she had failed to complete the day before. Although she had returned to work after lunch on Monday, her mind had refused to settle down, and Bill Gordon had not been pleased when she didn't have some reports ready for him. By getting to work a bit early Tuesday, she was able to have those reports on his desk before he walked in.

That evening, she and Galen arrived at Peggy's just after seven. Greta would have preferred to not go, but Galen had already made plans with Jimmy so she forced herself to face Peggy's possible curiosity. By arriving late she escaped it for the moment, but she wasn't so sure that she could get out of the house before the others.

As the women were taking their seats in Peggy's living room for the Bible study, Greta realized that she was the only single woman in the room. Ann Taylor was a woman in her forties with three teenaged kids. Her husband worked at the local lumber company, and Ann was a bank teller at the bank Greta dealt with. Jane Wesley and her husband, Cliff, owned a small garden shop right next to their home, which had been started as a way for Jane to stay home with their son when he was a baby. The boy was now a young man of twenty and off at college. Karen Maxwell and Vetta Brown both worked at the high school, Karen in the library and Vetta in the cafeteria. They were both younger than Greta was, in their early thirties, and they both had two children. Karen had two girls while Vetta had a boy and a girl. The last woman, Alexi Barstone, was about Greta's own age of thirty-seven. She and Hank had been married just a few years, and they had no kids. Greta wasn't sure if Alexi worked at all since she didn't really know her very well.

Their study that night was a continuation of the third chapter in James and Greta told herself that she really had to pay attention to what was going on. Peggy began by reading from the book they were using, then Ann commented on the fact that people who display worldly wisdom usually ended up leaving the church. Greta immediately thought of Tom Anderson. When Bob had been alive, Tom was in church every Sunday. Now it was surprising to see him there.

"Worldly wisdom doesn't seem to go too well with church," Vetta mused. "It's like this passage says, 'God's wisdom is peace loving and gentle, and willing to yield to others'. The world's wisdom says we should get what we want in whatever way we can."

"I think it's interesting that this comes right after the passage on controlling the tongue," Alexi commented. "Most of the stuff said by people who have worldly wisdom is said out of selfish ambition."

Greta began flipping back through her Bible as she said, "I was reading Psalm 111 this morning. Yes, here it is. 'Reverence for the Lord is the foundation of true wisdom. The rewards of wisdom come to all who obey Him.' Verse ten." She glanced around at the others. "I think probably people drift away because they aren't in obedience when they're using worldly wisdom. I don't know if they actually realize they aren't though."

"I think some do," Alexi said. "They choose to walk away because they want what the world offers."

Again, Greta thought of Tom Anderson.

Later, as the group was breaking up, Greta pleaded tiredness and asked Peggy to call Galen while she gathered up her jacket and Bible. Peggy hesitated, looking as if she really wanted to chat for a bit, but then she went to the stairway and called the boys.

On the way home, Galen told her that Jimmy's father had tried to call Ash Lancaster the night before. He'd gotten no response.

"Perhaps they were out somewhere," Greta offered. "He meets with the other farmers in the area at times."

"I kind of miss Chase," Galen said. "Yesterday at school I sort of had the feeling that he was avoiding me. Not that we ever see each other that much there. Last week he was watching out for me though."

Greta made no reply, totally unsure of what to say.

Wednesday morning after Chase left for school, Ash tore the window out of the back kitchen wall and began widening the area in readiness for the new picture window he'd picked up the day before. He knew that his actions were rather rash, but anything was better than spending time with his own thoughts.

"Too bad changing this window won't get rid of those smells," he mumbled to himself as the odor of peanut butter cookies came drifting out through the opening to assail his nose.

The problem had actually gotten worse after he'd told Greta Jorgenson that he wasn't sure he wanted to continue with the tutoring. The night before it had been a roast beef dinner with all the fixings, and Monday night, after Chase had gone to bed, Ash had heard Margaret singing in the kitchen. Over the weekend he and Chase had been plagued with a variety of smells. Each time they walked into the house there had been a different one.

Ash didn't think that Chase was hearing the things that he was, but then, he hadn't thought Chase was smelling anything before. Usually the sounds happened at night though, after Chase went to bed. Pots and pans rattling, singing, water running.

"I can't live like this much longer," he groaned, mopping the sweat off his forehead with his arm.

He glanced over to where the new window was leaning against the house, wondering just how he was going to get the thing into position once the hole was ready for it.

When he'd started this project on Monday morning he had been too tired and frustrated to really think about what he was doing, just the way he'd been when he remodeled the entire kitchen. All he could think about was the fact that Margaret was driving him crazy with her comings and goings, and Greta Jorgenson was driving him crazy just by being alive. Having her show up right when he was sawing wood for the project had been the last straw.

It was noon by the time he finished preparing the hole for the picture window, and Ash went inside feeling like he'd taken on an impossible task. Chase was obviously too small to help him, and there was no way he was going to call Dan Edwards. He could almost hear all of Peggy's questions if he did that.

As he sat at the kitchen table eating his lunch, Ash tried to think of someone he could ask to help him get the window in place, but no one came to mind. He'd pretty well isolated himself, though he did get together with some of the other farmers. He wasn't going to call any of them though.

He turned to look at the hole in the wall, smiling as he considered what Margaret would say if she saw it. "Ash Lancaster! What have you done to my kitchen? What a mess you've made!" That had been her reaction to everything he'd done in the house over the years. The upstairs bathroom, the living room, building the mudroom even, though he'd done that for her sake so she wouldn't have all the dirt tracked into her kitchen.

As he sat there staring at the hole and thinking about Margaret, the smell of coffee drifted by him. Ash turned, expecting to see Margaret standing behind him, but there was no one there.

"No!" he exclaimed, jumping up from the table.

He reached the back door in two strides, slamming it shut behind him as he went through the mudroom and on outside.

Never before had the smells begun when he was right there in the kitchen. He was always somewhere else in the house and they drifted in to him. Having it begin while he was right there startled Ash and sent him off to the barn to find something to drive Margaret out of his head.

It was over an hour before he ventured near the house again. Ash couldn't even face the idea of working on the window if Margaret was going to haunt him the whole time. He'd put the time to good use though, cleaning the barn and thinking. And now he strode into the house with determination, passing through the kitchen and living room, and heading straight to the door that led upstairs.

At the top of the stairs Ash opened the door to the master bedroom, took a look around it, then headed for the room he was now occupying next door. He pulled open a dresser drawer and scooped up an armful of clothing, then headed back to the master bedroom.

Forty-five minutes later the job was done. As he stood in the master bedroom looking at the clothes he had just hung in the closet, Ash decided that he wasn't sure he could really handle moving back in here, but somehow he had to get past all these feelings inside himself. He was tired of listening to Margaret singing in the kitchen. And he was tired of smelling things cooking that weren't really cooking.

He moved to close the dresser drawer that held his socks, then he looked at his watch. It was nearly time for Chase to come home from school. He glanced towards the small table in the corner where he had put a picture of the three of them, Margaret, Chase, and himself.

"I have to let go, Margaret," he mumbled. "I can't keep trying to shut everything out this way."

He looked around the room once more, then the sound of the bus stopping at the end of the lane reached his ears. Ash sighed heavily. This would be just one more thing to explain to Chase. It would have been a whole lot better to have dealt with Margaret's death the right way a year ago instead of putting the boy through all these changes.

The week dragged by for Greta. After having a taste of tutoring, her job at Gordon's became a huge millstone around her neck and she longed to toss it off. By Friday she was contemplating giving Tom Anderson a call to see if there were any other kids who could use her help.

Peggy had called Thursday evening to say that the library book on stunt flying had been returned.

"I nearly died of shock when I saw Ash's picture in it,"

she'd told Greta. "And he isn't answering his phone at all. Dan has tried every single day. It's the same thing he did right after Margaret died."

Greta had hung up with a hollow feeling inside her. She had prayed for both Ash and Chase again, determined to continue banging on heaven's door until God worked the situation through to its end.

With no Chase to tutor, Greta was free to take Galen back and forth to his field hockey practice on Saturday. His first game was to be the following Monday. Greta was sorry that she would miss it, but she knew Bill Gordon would not appreciate her taking the afternoon off again. Instead, she arrived at the school before practice was over to watch Galen. They went to the mall afterwards, ate lunch, then shopped for some items that Galen was growing out of.

"Can we stop at that bookstore too?" Galen asked as they wandered through the mall.

Greta agreed. She headed for the fiction area while Galen disappeared into another area. Pretty soon he came back, a book in his hands.

"Look what I found, Mom," he exclaimed, holding the book out toward her.

It was the same book that the library had. Greta took it from him, opening to the page with Ash's photograph.

"Chase would love to have his very own copy," she murmured as she closed the book again. "I'm not sure if I dare buy it though."

"I think you should," Galen replied. "I walked with Chase out to the bus yesterday. He said he wished he could have kept the library book. His dad brought it back."

Greta sighed, once more troubled by the way things

were turning out for Chase.

"Chase says the other boys don't tease him anymore," Galen said. "They're too busy asking him questions about stunt flying to bother."

She was happy with that piece of news and thanked Galen for passing the information on to her. Then she looked down at the book in her hands again.

"You know what, Galen?" she said slowly. "I think I will buy this book for Chase. I think it's time for Mr. Lancaster to see that there are people who care about his son enough to ignore his stubborn attitude."

"Way to go, Mom!" Galen exclaimed, grinning broadly.

Greta smiled, reaching to give him a gentle tap on the cheek.

She purchased the book and they left the bookstore. Greta had no idea just how she would give Chase his gift, but she was determined to do so. The only time she would see him was at church, and then only if his father still chose to go. She decided that if they weren't there the following morning, she would drive out to the farm and put the package into their mailbox.

Later that night, after Galen had gone to bed, Greta wrote a short note to Ash, slipped it into an envelope, then put it into the book. She wasn't sure she was doing the right thing, but after much prayer she had decided that she wanted to know if she had done anything to provoke him into kissing her. Plus, she knew that she had never really accepted his apology. Telling Chase to let his father know that she was still willing to do the tutoring was definitely not an acceptance of his apology.

Ash sat in the dark living room listening to the sounds

of the house. After two nights in the master bedroom he was beginning to relax, but it was still hard to go up those stairs and face it. The first night had been the worst. He'd actually stayed up till nearly two a.m. because he was so afraid to go in there. And once there, he'd found it very difficult to go to sleep. So many memories had haunted him.

The second night he'd forced himself to go up shortly after ten. It had been at least midnight before he had drifted off to sleep, but he had stayed put, listening to the night sounds around him and reliving old memories again.

Chase had not said anything about the change. But then, Chase hadn't said anything about the kitchen when he'd remodeled it, or about the master bedroom when he'd done that over. Nor was he mentioning the big hole in their kitchen wall, covered only by a tarp. Ash shook his head, still defeated by the problem of getting the new window into place.

He glanced up at the clock on the living room wall. Nearly eleven.

Before heading for bed, Chase had made sure they were still going to church in the morning. Ash wasn't at all certain he was ready to face Greta Jorgenson yet, but he did want to go to church. And he didn't really want to sit in the back of the sanctuary. He wanted to sit where he could catch every morsel the pastor had to offer him. He'd finally come to the conclusion that God was his only source of relief from Margaret's kitchen maneuvers.

When Peggy saw the package Sunday morning she held out her hands as she said, "For me? How sweet of you, Greta."

Greta laughed, shaking her head and clutching the

package to her chest.

"It's for Chase, if he comes today. Galen and I found that stunt flying book at the mall yesterday."

"What a perfect gift for him," Peggy said, clapping her hands in approval. "Dan has been trying to contact Ash all week, but no luck. I wanted him to go out there yesterday. Dan said no. He doesn't want to lose Ash's friendship by being too pushy."

"Well, I'm going to be a bit pushy," Greta confessed. "Chase is important to me, and I want him to have this book. If Ash Lancaster doesn't like it…"

"He can lump it!" Peggy shouted gleefully, then clapped a hand over her mouth as people around them looked at them in surprise.

They both giggled.

When the service began, Ash and Chase had not appeared. Greta forced herself to give all of her attention to the service and not worry about whether or not they would come. She enjoyed the praise and worship time, and took notes during the sermon, then bowed her head as the pastor began giving the altar call. He asked those who felt they needed forgiveness to go forward, and there were rustling sounds here and there in the congregation. The worship team began playing quietly, and the congregation joined in. Greta got to her feet, glancing toward the front of the sanctuary to see how many had gone forward. She was stunned to see Ash about to kneel down before the altar.

Chase found him at the altar when the service ended. Ash slid his arm around the boy as he said, "I'd like a few words with the pastor. How about you go say hello to Mrs. Jorgenson for a moment?"

"Can I really?" Chase said, looking very eager.

Ash nodded. Before Chase could take off he told him to be outside at the pickup in five minutes.

The pastor came back over to him right after Chase left, and they spoke for several minutes. Ash found him to be easy to talk to, a likeable man in his fifties with slivers of gray beginning to show in his hair. He told the pastor nothing about himself, but requested some of his time during the week to talk.

When he reached the pickup, Chase was standing beside it with a package in his arms.

"Galen and his mom bought me a present," he said. "It's sort of a reward for my A, she said. Can I open it right away? Before we go home, I mean? Mrs. Jorgenson said to wait till I got out here, so I wouldn't keep you waiting."

Ash unlocked the pickup as he said, "Open it inside." Then he walked around to the driver's door and got in. Chase was tearing the paper away, scattering it on the floor of the truck in his eagerness to see the present.

"It's my book!" he exclaimed, holding it up for Ash to see. "Brand new though. Wow! My very own copy."

Ash started the pickup, motioning toward the wrappings on the floor. Chase slid off the seat to scoop them up, then buckled himself in.

"I told her about us reading the Bible together," he said as Ash pulled out of the parking spot. "She looked happy to hear it." He was flipping through the book as he talked and suddenly held something out toward Ash. "This has your name on it, Dad," he said. "Maybe Mrs. Jorgenson wrote to you?"

Ash glanced at what he was holding, then reached over to take it. A whiff of her perfume swam by his nose and he saw that it was an envelope. He jammed it into his jacket pocket and continued driving.

Chase chattered all the way home, distracting him from the questions in his mind. Ash was glad to be distracted, but once home he was eager for Chase to go upstairs to change. When the boy had finally gone, he pulled the envelope from his pocket.

'Ash,' the note inside said, 'I hope you'll allow Chase to keep his gift. I truly feel he is more important right now than whatever has passed between us. I do accept your apology, and I will continue to pray for both of you. I'm sorry if my actions were, in any way, the cause of your behavior. Greta.'

He read the note again, then slid the paper back into the envelope. The scent of her perfume clung to him, but Ash found that he didn't really mind it. In fact, he rather liked it.

Chapter 11

Greta woke up early on Tuesday morning, much to her surprise. She'd gotten so used to struggling out of bed when the alarm went off that waking before the alarm confused her. She decided to get up though, and do a bit of extra reading in her Bible.

She'd spent the past two days wondering if Ash Lancaster would call her, then chiding herself for hoping that he would. She had told herself repeatedly that her concern was for Chase, not his father. But a part of her had really wanted him to call.

During breakfast, Galen asked if they were going to the Edwards' home that evening.

"Jimmy said his dad was going to try to get home early and do something with us."

"As long as Bill Gordon doesn't run me ragged today, we'll go," Greta replied. She wasn't sure she wanted to spend any extra time with Peggy, but she did want to go to the study.

"Anything I should do here this afternoon?" Galen asked.

Greta shook her head, smiling at his generous gesture. He'd been offering more and more of his help lately, but she wasn't quite sure why. It may have started because of her decision to allow him to play field hockey, but she didn't think that was the reason it was continuing.

Galen left for school and Greta began getting ready to leave also. As she was taking a package of chicken out of the freezer for their supper, the doorbell rang. She hurried through the living room, wondering who would come to her house so early.

Ash Lancaster was standing on the front porch.

"I waited till I knew Galen must have left for school," he said as he opened the storm door. "Would you have a few minutes to take a walk with me? I'd like to talk."

Greta nodded, her heart tumbling over itself as she reached for her jacket.

"I want to thank you for buying Chase that book," Ash said as they began walking down the block. "I think it's already his most treasured possession."

"Galen was the one who found it."

"Chase told me," he replied, nodding his head.

Greta was glad that it was a bit difficult to actually look at each other while walking. She wondered if that was why Ash had suggested it, but she wasn't about to ask him. Her heart was still hammering just from the sight of him standing on her porch and she had no wish to say something that might cause him to stop walking and look at her.

It was a minute before he spoke again, and when he did, Greta was even more glad that they weren't facing each other.

" I also want to reassure you that there was nothing in your actions to…" he said, his words drifting off into silence. Then he tried again. "You acted very…"

He fell silent at that point. Greta wasn't sure if she should say anything, but she was grateful that he was letting her know that she hadn't done anything wrong.

They walked in silence for a ways, then Ash began speaking again.

"I admire you, Greta," he said quietly, "for the way you seemed to have handled your husband's death. You're a very strong woman, in spite of your size."

Greta smiled without looking at him. She kept her eyes on the sidewalk ahead of them as they approached the end of the block. They turned the corner before he spoke again.

"Chase and I have been reading the Bible together."

"He told me," Greta replied.

"I can already see some improvement in his reading, though maybe it's my imagination."

"I doubt it," Greta said, glancing into the yard they were passing. "I think all Chase needed was some support. Someone to show him that he's worthwhile."

"Guess I haven't shown him that this past year."

Greta glanced at him.

"You were going through a difficult time, Ash," she said. "You lost your wife."

He continued looking up the street, and she looked away. After a moment he spoke again.

"Somehow I doubt you pushed Galen away when your husband died."

Greta stopped herself from looking at him again by watching a car as it came toward them on the street. It turned at the corner and she went back to watching the sidewalk ahead of them. They reached the end of another block and turned the corner before she responded to his words.

"You're right," she told him. "Galen and I drew closer to each other when Bob died. We read the Bible together a lot, for comfort and to show him that God is always faithful. Our church family helped us quite a bit, at least at first."

"And then?" Ash prompted.

Greta frowned slightly as she thought of what had happened to make her pull away from everyone.

"I'm afraid it didn't take long for the women from church to decide I should get back into action," she told him. "And Tom Anderson, who had been Bob's closest friend, was happy to oblige them by asking me out places. I found myself beginning to resent their intrusions."

"Tom said you used to work part time at the school."

"Yes," she said, nodding. "He was the one who actually got me the job, which I needed desperately at the time, but he was also part of the reason I ended up leaving, though I never told him so."

They walked in silence for a moment, then Ash spoke again.

"Were you ever angry at God for Bob's death?"

Greta took a moment to consider how to answer that question.

"No," she finally said. "I always knew that death would come, though I didn't really expect it quite so soon, or so violently. Bob and I had both talked to Galen about heaven quite often, and had tried very hard to let him know that death comes to us all. We wanted him to realize that he needed to decide where to spend eternity."

They reached the last corner, the one that completed

the circle and took them back to her house, and they turned it. Greta could see his pickup ahead and she realized that she didn't really want to reach it. She knew he would leave when they did.

"I've been told you feel that God is the only matchmaker you need," he commented.

"Peggy must have told you that," she said with a laugh. "I won't hold it against her, I suppose."

She wished he would walk more slowly to stretch out their time together, but he kept to the same pace. The distance between them and the pickup grew smaller and smaller as they continued walking in silence.

When they came alongside the pickup they stopped, and Greta turned to face him, looking up at him, her heart beginning to beat faster as she wondered if she would ever see him again, even socially.

"My offer to help Chase still stands," she said carefully, "though he probably doesn't really need me now that he has you."

"I'm not much good at looking up things and writing reports," Ash said, looking at her finally. "It takes time, and I have too much to do around the farm. I'd appreciate it if you could continue to make yourself available for that side of things."

Greta nodded. She had the impression that there was more he wanted to say, but he looked away. His glance swept over the neighborhood, then came back to her. He rubbed the back of his neck with his hand.

"Greta..."

He stopped. Greta waited for him to say what was on his mind. Finally he gave just a flicker of a smile.

"I'm sorry," he said. "I'm not used to feeling the way I do right now. I'm not even sure I want to feel this way.

I've spent the past week looking at pictures of Margaret and struggling to work through the past."

He gave her such a serious look that Greta found herself trembling slightly. She wondered just how he *was* feeling. Was his heart beating as fast as hers as he looked at her? Was he shy and eager all at the same time? Did he feel as if he could melt from anticipation?

Ash sighed heavily but he didn't take his eyes from hers as he continued.

"Trouble is," he admitted, "when I close my eyes and try to see Margaret, it's you I see instead."

Greta struggled to keep her composure. She felt her heart grow a pair of wings that fluttered against the wall of her chest in a desperate attempt to get out. At the same time, she also wanted to flee from the strength of his feelings. She knew that wouldn't help him at all though. He probably wouldn't even understand it if she were to run inside and slam the door in his face. Worst of all, something within her was trying to light fires where she didn't want them. Or maybe she did and it was she doing the lighting herself.

Ash put his hand on the hood of the pickup. He hadn't taken his eyes off her, and Greta forced herself to match his look.

"I've made you late for work," he said.

"I've been late before" Greta replied quickly, not really wanting him to leave in spite of her own tangled feelings. "As long as I get my work done, my hours are a bit flexible."

Ash nodded.

"I..." he began, then he stopped, taking a deep breath and letting it out slowly. Finally he looked away. "I need you to be part of our lives," he said. "Chase's and mine.

I need to work through these feelings." His eyes came back to her as he asked, "Can you manage that?"

Greta looked down at the sidewalk under her feet, sure that it was moving somehow. She felt like it was shaking her and she wanted to grab onto Ash's jacket to steady herself. At that moment she remembered her words to Galen. They'd been said in jest, but now they seemed somewhat prophetic. "If God wants me to marry again, he's going to have to send down lightening bolts or something to get my attention." Was this the 'or something'?

She realized that Ash was still waiting for her answer.

"I believe I can, Ash," she said, looking up at him once more. She saw him relax slightly, and she smiled at him as she added, "I think I have some feelings of my own to work through also."

He gave her a rather quizzical look and Greta sighed, deciding to just admit the truth and get it over with.

"In case you missed it last week," she remarked quietly, "I didn't exactly fight you off."

He stared at her for a moment, then a smile appeared on his face.

"I think I've been so busy with my own thoughts that it hadn't connected yet," he said. "I'm sure I would have gotten around to it sooner or later. That kiss sort of lingers around the edges of the fog in my brain. I've refused to dwell on it."

Greta laughed.

"Well, you certainly got your point across," she told him. "It was more than enough explanation."

Ash grinned sheepishly, then turned to walk around the truck. Greta watched him go with a mixture of relief and regret dancing their way through her heart.

Greta's admission made his heart feel lighter. As he drove away, Ash decided that when he got around to letting himself dwell on that kiss, he was going to enjoy it a lot more knowing that she hadn't been completely repulsed by his actions.

"She could actually laugh about it," he said aloud, surprised that she'd want to. But then, a lot of things about Greta Jorgenson surprised him. She was so different from Margaret.

He smiled as he passed the last of the houses that marked the town's boundaries. The road stretched ahead of him, leading him home to the farm. But this time, he didn't feel all the loneliness that he had often felt on this drive the past year.

When Chase came home that afternoon, Ash was working in the garden near the house, turning the soil and getting it ready for the winter. He leaned the hoe against the fence as Chase came up the lane.

"How was school?" he asked when the boy reached him.

Chase give him a big smile.

"Real fine!" he announced happily. "Tommy Nichols asked me if I wanted to play ball with the rest of them at recess. I managed to get a hit even."

"Great!" Ash said as he returned the smile. "Want a snack before chores?"

Chase looked up at him, a confused look on his face.

"Is everything ok?" he asked.

Ash laughed, reaching out to give the boy a quick hug.

"Better than it's been in a long time, Chase," he replied, crouching down in front of him. "I had a talk with Mrs. Jorgenson this morning. We worked out an arrangement. I'll continue reading the Bible with you here at home, and she'll be available to help you with reports that you get assigned. Does that sound ok.?"

"Yeah!" Chase said enthusiastically. "Does that mean everything is all right between you and her?"

"More or less," he said as he nodded slowly, curious as to why he asked.

"Good!" was Chase's immediate response. He grinned happily as he added, "Cause if you ever decide you want to get married, I'd rather have her than anybody else. And she's available. All you have to do is talk to God about it."

Ash threw his head back and laughed. He grabbed Chase and dragged him down onto the ground to tickle him. The boy giggled, gasping for breath and Ash let him go, sitting down beside him.

"You're a little crazy, Chase," he said as Chase caught his breath. "You know that? I can't hardly get past your mom's death, and you're trying to set me up with another woman."

"I figure you must be sorting stuff out," Chase told him as he sat up. "You've moved back into the big bedroom."

"You noticed that, did you?"

Chase nodded.

"And Sunday you were happier after you read Mrs. Jorgenson's letter."

Ash looked at him curiously.

"How do you know I read it?" he asked.

"You took a long time to come up and change," Chase replied. "I didn't come down cause I didn't want to disturb you."

Ash grinned.

"I think you're getting too smart, Chase Lancaster," he announced. "Maybe I should have asked you months ago about how to work this through."

"I'm not sure I would have known back then," Chase responded seriously. "Hanging around with Mrs. Jorgenson and Galen showed me stuff I didn't know."

Ash tousled Chase's hair, then he stood up.

"Work or snack?" he asked.

Chase got up, picking up his school bag.

"Snack, please. I'm starved!"

Ash laughed as he put his arm across Chase's shoulders. They walked to the back door together, then he let Chase go ahead of him into the house.

When Greta pulled up in front of Peggy's house for the Bible study that night, she groaned as she realized that none of the other women were there yet. Galen looked at her.

"What was that for, Mom?" he asked. "Don't you want to be here?"

Greta smiled at him.

"I want to be here, Galen," she replied. "I just don't want to be here yet." He looked at her so quizzically that she laughed. Then she told him, "Mrs. Edwards sometimes asks questions I'd rather not answer."

"About Mr. Lancaster?" Galen asked.

"Now why would you think that?" she replied, tilting her head and trying to act as if that couldn't possibly be the reason.

Galen grinned at her as he said, "Jimmy says his mom is sure that you know more than you're saying about why Chase can't come to our house to be tutored. And tonight at supper, you told me he'd be coming just when he needs help with a report. That means you and Mr. Lancaster have talked at some point between Sunday and today."

Greta made a face.

"My son, the detective," she groaned. She opened the car door. "If I have talked to him," she remarked, "which I have, I'm not going to discuss it with Mrs. Edwards."

They both got out of the car, and Greta looked at him over the hood of it.

"And I'd appreciate it if you didn't say anything," she told him. "Maybe she won't ask anyway."

Galen laughed as if he doubted that as much as she did herself.

She walked around the car and they started up the walkway together. Before they got very far however, Greta heard another car pull up, and she breathed a sigh of relief when she turned to see it was Ann Taylor.

"You can go ahead in, Galen. I'll wait for Mrs. Taylor."

He gave her a kiss on her cheek and whispered, "Coward," before heading for the door again. Greta smiled as she watched him go, then she turned to say hi to Ann as the other woman joined her.

Dan and the boys went out to do a good deed, and the women discussed the first ten verses of chapter four in James. Greta enjoyed the discussion they had about ways to stay close to God in spite of the worldly temptations they all faced on a regular basis. She especially liked Peggy's suggestion of reading the Bible for ten minutes for every five minutes spent looking through a catalog or window shopping at the mall. Peggy had said it in jest, but Greta thought that it was a worthwhile practice if one was bent toward spending too much money.

They were all reluctant to end the study for the night, but Karen finally closed her Bible, admitting that she had responsibilities at home. The others nodded in agreement, and very shortly the house had emptied out. Greta found herself alone with Peggy, and her friend immediately asked if she had heard anything at all from Ash.

"I spoke with him this morning," Greta reluctantly confessed. "He seems fine. Will Dan and the boys be back soon? Galen and I need to get home."

Peggy laughed, shaking her head.

"You weren't exactly subtle about changing the topic," she said. "I swear you're one of the most close-mouthed women I know. I guess that's best though, isn't it?"

Greta nodded and Peggy began talking about other things. Dan and the boys came in about ten minutes later, and she and Galen left almost immediately. On the way home, Galen told her that Dan had taken them grocery shopping.

"You didn't bring any back," she mused.

"They were for an elderly woman," Galen said. "I've seen her at church a couple times. Mr. Edwards said she's pretty housebound, and has limited income. They deliver stuff to her every so often, like mayonnaise and spaghetti sauce. Stuff that won't go bad. We brought her some bread too. Jimmy says she likes to put loaves of bread in the freezer so it will keep longer. It was sort of fun, Mom. Taking her that stuff and watching how happy it made her."

Greta smiled as she turned into their driveway. She knew that Dan was a pretty busy man, so to hear that he took time out to do good deeds like this one was a bit surprising, but she liked it.

Galen headed for bed as soon as they went inside, leaving Greta to unwind on her own. She put on some music and settled onto the couch, finally allowing her mind to go back over the conversation with Ash. She still wasn't sure exactly what his feelings were, but at least he had admitted that he wanted to get to know her better. Her own feelings were pretty confused. She felt that God wanted her to get to know him better, but part of her felt like she was somehow betraying Bob's memory with the attraction she felt for Ash. And how could either of them really consider remarrying? They both had young boys. Galen loved his father, and she was sure that Chase was still very much attached to his mother. In spite of Galen's question about what she thought of Ash Lancaster, could he honestly accept another man's presence in her life?

"Oh, Bob," she whispered softly, "what am I supposed to do here?"

There was no reply, and Greta decided that what she really needed was her Bible and some sleep, not music and a head full of questions.

Greta woke up early again the next morning, stretched lazily, and looked out the window into the semi-darkness.

"Lord," she whispered, "Is Ash really the man you are intending for me to marry?"

It was the question that she'd fallen to sleep with, in spite of the time she'd spent reading her Bible.

Pushing herself up into a sitting position, she turned on the light and reached for her Bible once more. She opened it to the book of James and reread the verses they had covered at the Bible study the night before.

"When you bow down before the Lord and admit your dependence on Him," she read aloud, "He will lift you up and give you honor."

Greta closed her eyes for a moment, savoring those words. Then she smiled, opening them back up as she realized that her question had just been answered.

"Ok, God," she whispered, "I do depend on you for everything. I will let you work this out in your own way. And I will continue to be a friend to both Ash and Chase."

She read the entire chapter once more before setting her Bible back on the nightstand. Then she got up to begin her day.

Ash found that each night he slept in the master bedroom it became easier to do so, especially if he took the time to study Margaret's picture and think about their years together while he was there. After a week of it he was able to go upstairs at nine-thirty to get ready for bed, as he normally did. And he felt rested in the morning instead of feeling groggy and disoriented.

It was now Margaret who filled his nights, but it was Greta who filled his days. In fact, she always seemed to be on his mind the moment he woke up. Her brief note was in the pocket of one of his shirts, safely tucked away but still accessible whenever he wanted to pull it out. Which he did every so often just to breath in the scent of her and to study her neat handwriting. He wasn't ready to see her again though. The walk they had taken together had not been all that easy,

About ten o'clock Friday morning he headed for the woods with Tucson to take down a dead tree he'd spotted from the edge of the field. Ash figured it would round out his winter wood supply quite well. However, the job took longer than he'd figured and he missed lunch, finally arriving home just after two-thirty. He was unhooking the trunk of the tree from Tucson's harness when he saw the bus drop Chase at the end of the lane.

The boy saw him almost right away and started running up the lane. Ash finished unhooking the horse and led him back through the gate into the field.

"You've earned some relaxation time, boy," he said as he took the harness off.

Tucson whinnied as if agreeing with him. Ash stepped away from him and the big horse began munching on the grass at his feet.

"Mrs. Moore gave us a new report to do, Dad," Chase said as he reached the fence. He climbed onto the bottom rail and hung over the top of the fence. "That means I can go to Mrs. Jorgenson's again."

Ash smiled at him as he rolled up the harness.

"We'll have to let her know about it, I guess," he said, walking toward the gate. "We could speak to her in church Sunday."

"Not before then?"

Ash laughed at the downcast look that appeared on Chase's face.

"I've never seen you this eager about doing a report," he kidded. "Today is Friday. Sunday is only two days away."

Chase's shoulders slumped a little, but he nodded.

"Guess I should put my stuff inside and do my chores. Am I going to smell anything in there?"

Ash grinned, shrugging as he said, "I haven't been inside since this morning."

As Chase stepped down off the fence and began walking away, Ash suddenly realized that he hadn't actually smelled anything cooking all week.

"Hey, Chase?" he called, stopping the boy. "Are you

really still smelling things?"

Chase turned around, his face thoughtful. He came back to the fence.

"I think I did on Monday," he said, "but maybe not since then."

Ash nodded.

"Is Mom trying to get our attention?" Chase asked. "Can someone who has died do that?"

"I'm more inclined to think it's God," Ash replied. "Like the handwriting on the wall that we read about the other night in Daniel. One time he used a talking donkey to get someone's attention. And there's always the burning bush in Exodus, with Moses.

"So maybe he's speaking to us through Mom's kitchen?"

Ash nodded and Chase frowned in concentration.

"Why would God want to get our attention?" he finally asked.

Ash looked down at the ground around his boots for a moment, then at Chase again.

"Maybe he thinks it's time for us to get serious with him, Chase," he replied. "Put the past away and look to the future. That doesn't mean forgetting Mom. Neither of us will ever forget her entirely. But when God shuts one door, he usually opens another. We need to be willing to accept what he sends."

"Like Mrs. Jorgenson?" Chase said, grinning broadly.

"Mrs. Jorgenson seems to pop up in your conversations an awful lot, Chase," Ash said, chuckling softly. "I admit she's a very nice person, and I guess God sent her into our lives for some reason. We'll have to wait to find out just why."

Chase looked up at him for a moment, then he headed

for the house. Ash watched him go, wondering if the boy really wanted him to bring another woman into their home.

It was Sunday before Greta saw Ash again. Galen had reported having several conversations with Chase at school, mostly at the end of the day as they were leaving the building. And he'd also passed along the news that Ash and Chase had gone to the Edwards' to visit Thursday evening. Greta had had to be content with that. She wondered how Ash was doing with his memories, but, since there was no way to find out, she simply put the whole situation back into God's hand and went about her work.

She and Galen sat with the Edwards' again at church. Greta felt like they'd somehow slipped into a ritual, but she didn't really mind the arrangement. It actually felt good to have a friend to sit with. And, when Ash and Chase slipped into the row behind them just after the service began, she was doubly thankful for Peggy's presence nearby. It kept her from feeling embarrassed by the fact that Ash was directly behind her. His choice of seating could be contributed to his friendship with Dan rather than any interest he might have in her.

During the praise and worship time, Ash's strong voice wrapped itself around Greta. She ignored the urge to turn and look at him, focusing on the words she was singing instead of the flutter of her heart. She was surprised by his knowledge of the music though, considering that he had not gone to church before.

After the praise and worship time ended, Dan and Peggy turned to tell Ash good morning. Greta twisted in her seat to touch Chase's knee.

"How's school going?" she asked.

"Great!" he responded enthusiastically. "Mrs. Moore gave us a new report to write, so I get to come to your house again."

Greta told him she was glad, then turned back around as the pastor began speaking from the pulpit. She'd been afraid to actually look at Ash, nervous of her reaction to seeing him. Her pulse had sped up just at the sight of his leg beside Chase's, and she had to force herself to pay attention to the pastor's words.

As soon as the service ended, Ash leaned forward.

"If you don't look at me soon," he whispered into the ear farthest from Galen, "I'm going to melt from anxiety. Have I done something wrong?"

Greta turned around, smiling at his words.

"Good morning, Ash. It's good to see you here this morning. I hope all is well at your house?"

He chuckled softly, then turned to say hello to Galen and Jimmy. The boys asked if Chase wanted to go to the foyer with them, but he shook his head and said, "I have to talk to your mom about my report, Galen. I need to get started on it right away, so we have to decide when I'll come to your house."

Greta laughed and told him that she'd never seen anyone so eager to do schoolwork, then she asked him what the report was on.

"We have to choose an animal," he declared. "I think I'd like to write about horses."

"Any particular breed?" she asked.

"Breed?" Chase repeated, looking rather confused.

"Horses are like people," Galen said. "Chinese, French, Americans. Horses can be Arabians, Clydesdales, Lippizzans. There are lots of different breeds."

Chase frowned, glancing at his father.

"What is Tucson?"

"Morgan," Ash replied.

"Can I do my report just on Morgan horses?" Chase asked, looking at Greta again.

"I'm sure you could," she replied. "And perhaps your dad will let you come over after school one day this week. That way we could go to the library together to look for books on horses."

"Tuesday or Wednesday would be fine," Ash said quickly, before either she or Chase could actually look at him. "Whichever is best for you."

Greta turned to look at him anyway, and saw a muscle twitching in his cheek. She smiled brightly at him as she said, "I don't suppose you were a jockey in your teens or anything like that?"

Ash stared at her for a moment, then he started laughing. Greta saw Chase look up at him with a quizzical expression on his face. She reached over to touch the boy's knee.

"I was kidding, Chase," she told him.

"Is that like the nice, friendly teasing you were telling me about?" he asked, looking at her very seriously.

"Yes. That's exactly what it was. Friendly teasing is the kind the person being teased can laugh at and enjoy too."

Chase nodded, smiling happily at her answer.

Galen again invited Chase to join him and Jimmy in the foyer and this time the younger boy agreed. The three of them left, and Greta realized that Dan and Peggy had also disappeared. She and Ash were more or less alone.

"Tuesday would be good for me," she said, smiling

nervously. "I'll let them know at work that I'll be doing a half day again."

"I'll tell Chase," Ash replied. "Perhaps he can walk to your house with Galen again?"

"And we'll have him home by four-thirty," Greta said, nodding her head. "I'm supposed to be at Peggy's for a Bible study that night. It'll be rather nice to not have to rush home from work to get supper."

"Chase and I visited over there the other night," Ash said. "I saw Dan Thursday morning at the garage and he told me they were concerned about my disappearance. Decided I'd better come out of hiding."

"So you admit that's what you've been doing?"

Ash shrugged, then he grinned.

"Habit," he said. "And thank you for not telling them about…well…"

"I tend to take my personal stuff to God rather than to other people," Greta said, saving him from saying anything more. "I wouldn't have wanted Peggy to be upset with you about anything."

"Thank you," he said, smiling at her. "I appreciate your choice. So…Just what did God say about the whole thing?"

Greta laughed.

"He said to bow down to him," she replied, "and to admit my dependence on him."

Ash's smile grew broader.

Greta stood up, feeling that they had sat there together long enough to make some tongues begin to wag. Ash got up also and they moved to the end of their rows, then he allowed her to precede him down the aisle. They found the others outside and joined them. Peggy immediately asked Ash when they could go out to the farm again.

"We haven't visited you in ages," she told him. "Jimmy was just telling Chase that he'd like to see Tucson again."

"Maybe some Saturday," Ash responded. "If Greta helps Chase with his reading on Saturday mornings, she brings him home afterwards. Maybe she would stick around too."

Peggy looked at Greta as she said, "Did he just ask you for a date?"

"Oh, we have dates all the time," Greta shot back, hoping to startle Peggy out of any teasing she was looking to do. "Ash drops Chase off, then he picks him up later."

Ash and Dan laughed, and Dan gave his wife a quick hug.

"That will teach you to poke your nose into Greta's life," he told her. "She's too quick for you."

Peggy grinned wryly.

"I guess I deserved that," she confessed, then turned back to Ash. "So how about this coming Saturday? Jimmy and I could bring our lunch and eat with you."

When Ash looked at her, Greta nodded as she said, "I could work with Chase Saturday morning, yes."

"And stay for lunch when you bring him home?" he asked.

Greta nodded, her stomach muscles acting as if they were snakes twisting around each other at the bottom of a dark pit. She was sure that what he was really asking was whether or not she could be in his home, around him, after what had happened between them. The fact that he continued to study her for a moment after she'd nodded seemed to back up that theory.

She was glad when Dan began talking about field

hockey right after that. Ash turned his attention to the new topic, and very shortly after that they all went their separate ways.

The first few rounds of their game went well, but soon Greta's mind began wandering. She thought of Ash's laughter, then of the proposed trip to the farm, then the way he had studied her face after she accepted his invitation to lunch. Galen had been excited about the trip, had spent lunchtime talking about it. Now he was silent, his head bent as he studied his letters and plotted ways to win their Scrabble game.

"It's your turn," Galen said, breaking into her thoughts.

Greta looked at her letters, then at the board. She grabbed two letters and laid them down to form the word 'owl' without hardly thinking about it. When Galen quickly laid an 'h' in front of it, covering a 'double word score' spot, she groaned, noticing that an 'f' was sitting on her rack. If she'd been paying attention, she could have gotten more points. Not only did Galen get the double word score for the word 'howl', he also got it for the word 'hurt' that he put down with it.

"That puts me twenty-three points ahead of you, Mom," Galen said.

"I see," she replied, telling herself that she really had to concentrate on the game instead of Ash Lancaster.

However, as soon as she had taken her next turn, her mind began wandering again. She thought once more of how Ash had laughed about her jockey joke. She loved the sound of his laughter, and, if she was going to admit it, the way his laughter made her feel.

"Your turn again, Mom," Galen said, this time with a

note of disgust in his voice.

She laid down three letter tiles to form the word 'fret', just to watch Galen cover up the 'triple word score' spot that she'd left open for him.

"You're not even trying, Mom," Galen complained grumpily.

Greta looked at their scores. Galen was now almost forty points ahead of her.

"I'm sorry," she said. "I guess my mind isn't really on this today."

Galen snorted.

"If he were here, I'd probably be fifty points ahead of you!" he exclaimed.

Greta tried to look as if she didn't understand what he was talking about.

"Who?" she asked innocently.

"Mr. Lancaster," Galen announced, "as if you didn't know." He shook his head, giving her a look that said he thought she was a bit weird. Then he said, "You're beginning to act like some of the girls at school."

"I am not!" Greta exclaimed, but she had to turn away to hide the quick blush that spread over her face.

"You're blushing!" Galen yelled, pouncing on that fact.

Greta decided she'd better curb what was happening before it got out of hand, so she said, "You just keep your thoughts to yourself, young man," in what she hoped was a stern voice as she turned to look at him. "This situation is difficult enough without you teasing me."

Galen grinned.

"I wonder how Chase feels about it," he said.

"I doubt Chase knows anything about it," Greta replied, moving the letter tiles around on her rack as she tried to decide what word to play next.

"I think he does."

"What do you mean?"

"Chase is watching what goes on between you and his father," Chase replied. "Like this morning when you teased Mr. Lancaster after church. I think he was surprised by his father's laughter."

"He doesn't laugh all that much, I suppose," she mused, wondering if Galen was right and Chase did suspect that maybe she and his father liked each other.

She saw Galen look at the Scrabble board, then he looked at her.

"Should we throw in the towel on this one?" he asked. "Or are you going to get your head out of the clouds and concentrate?"

Greta made a face, but her sense of humor got the better of her.

"My head is not in the clouds," she retorted, smiling at Galen. "Mr. Lancaster doesn't live in the clouds."

Galen gave a shout of laughter, dumping himself over on the couch in glee. Greta had to laugh too, in spite of herself.

Ash heard Chase come down the stairs and he laid his open book across his knee. He'd been just half reading anyway. The other half of his mind had been on Greta Jorgenson and the fact that she was coming to his house again. So far her visits had been unscheduled. In fact, except for the times she had dropped Chase off, no one even knew about her visits.

"Dad?" Chase said as he entered the room. "Can I ask you a question?"

"Sure," Ash said, patting the couch beside him.

"Come have a seat."

Chase joined him on the couch, his face looking very thoughtful.

"Did you like it when Mrs. Jorgenson teased you?" he asked.

Ash smiled, remembering how surprised Chase had been when he'd laughed over Greta's question at church.

"Well, Chase," he said, "I didn't really mind it when she teased me. In fact, it felt sort of good, sort of like she was treating me the same way she'd treat Mrs. Edwards or you or her son. That's what friendly teasing is all about."

"So you like being around her?" Chase asked.

Ash grinned, suspicious of just where this conversation was headed.

"I like being around Mr. and Mrs. Edwards too," he replied, hoping to head Chase in other directions. "It's good to have friends again."

"But you'll keep Mrs. Jorgenson in mind if you ever decide…you know…that you want to get married or something?"

"I will definitely keep her in mind," Ash said, matching Chase's serious expression. "No doubt about that."

Chase gave a satisfied sigh and got up from the couch.

"Guess I can go back to my book now," he said. "I feel better knowing that you like her. I think she's really nice, and I like Galen a lot."

He headed for the stairway, leaving Ash with just one thought.

'Keep her in mind? I can't seem to get her out of it!'

Chapter 12

On Monday, Greta began giving some serious thought as to how she and Galen could survive on less money. Bill Gordon's messy paperwork had her stumped straight through her lunch time, and he didn't seemed too pleased when she told him she would be doing a half day on Tuesday. Greta found herself really looking forward to the planned trip to the library with Chase because it seemed so much more interesting than being cooped up all day in the drug store, and she ignored Bill's displeasure.

Galen turned down the chance to go to the library, saying that he wanted to get his homework out of the way before going to Jimmy's. Peggy had called to invite them to supper, so Greta gave him permission to go there as soon as he was done studying.

"I'll take Chase home when we're done at the library," she told Galen before leaving the house. "I'll meet you at Jimmy's after that."

"Sounds good," Galen said, heading upstairs to get started on his homework.

When they got to the library, Greta inquired about non-fiction books on horses and they were directed to several locations, both books for kids and books for adults. Chase had no problem finding more than enough to satisfy him. Once they were checked out, Chase stuffed them into his school bag so he could begin his research right away.

On the ride home, Chase was silent and Greta found herself thinking about the boards Ash had been working on the last time she was at the farm. She wondered what they were for and whether the project had been finished that day or not.

"Dad was reading about David and Goliath last night," Chase said suddenly.

"That's a good story," Greta replied. "It used to be Galen's favorite."

"Does he have a different favorite one now?"

Greta thought about that for a minute.

"I'm not really sure, Chase," she finally said. "I do know that he reads his Bible every night before going to sleep."

"I think Dad does too," Chase remarked. "We read it downstairs during the evening, but I always have to get it from his bedroom." He paused, then he added, "He moved back into the room he and Mom used to share."

Greta's heart skipped a beat. She tried to keep her voice calm as she asked, "Do you ever wish he could also turn the kitchen back to the way your mother had it?"

"I used to," Chase replied, "but not anymore."

"Why is that?" she asked curiously.

Chase hesitated for a moment, then he said, "Nothing

will bring her back, Mrs. Jorgenson. I used to wish it would."

"Sounds like you've pretty much come to terms with your mom's death," Greta observed.

"Dad feels better now," was Chase's reply, "so now I'm not afraid of him disappearing too. When he was so angry, I got scared that he didn't want me anymore."

Greta swallowed hard to dislodge the lump that formed in her throat at his words. She wanted to just stop the car in the middle of the road and pull the boy into her arms, but she forced herself to keep driving.

"I told my dad that it would be ok if he married you," Chase said after a moment.

Greta's heart plummeted, then soared, and she had to hold onto the steering wheel very tightly to keep from careening all over the road. Fortunately, the farm lane appeared and she turned into it, then stopped the car.

"Sometimes you and Galen startle me with your perceptions," she said, turning to Chase.

"Per...perceptions?" he repeated.

"Your thoughts," she clarified. "Your ideas."

"Why would they startle you?"

"You make everything sound so simple. We adults tend to get things rather confused sometimes." She took a deep breath, looking up the lane toward the farm. "I'm not sure you should repeat things that are said between you and your father though."

"I'm sorry," Chase replied quickly.

Greta smiled at him, reaching over to touch his leg.

"It's ok, Chase," she said. "I know you didn't mean to break a confidence. And I really do appreciate knowing that you like me enough to tell your father he could marry me."

She put the car in drive again and continued up the lane.

"Most stuff said in conversations can be repeated," she explained, "but not personal things. Can you understand the difference?"

"I think so," Chase replied. Then he asked, "Are you going to tell Dad what I said?"

"No way, Chase," Greta stated firmly. She glanced at him as she stopped the car beside Ash's pickup. "Now it's a personal thing between you and I."

Chase grinned broadly in response to her words.

As they got out of the car, Greta saw Ash coming from the barn. She felt a rush of pleasure at the sight of him, in spite of the embarrassment she had felt over Chase's revelations. She stood by the car, waiting for him to reach it.

"No Galen today?" he asked right away.

Greta shook her head.

"He's at Jimmy's," she replied. "I'm headed there for dinner and the women's Bible study."

Ash nodded.

"We got some neat books, Dad," Chase called out as he got his book bag from the back seat. "I'll take them inside before I do my chores."

He took off without waiting for a response, and Greta found herself blushing slightly at the obviousness of his actions. She was sure that Chase was leaving her alone with his father on purpose. What made it even worse was the fact that Ash hadn't taken his eyes off her since she'd arrived.

"I'll see you Saturday morning?" he asked.

Greta nodded.

"Ten o'clock," she said. "As usual."

"We'll be there."

She wanted to go, yet she wanted to stay. And Ash still didn't look away from her.

"Is everything ok, Greta?" he asked quietly.

Suddenly she knew what he was looking for. He wanted some reassurance that she didn't mind being there.

"What were you building?" she asked, smiling slightly.

"Building?" he repeated, looking confused.

Greta motioned toward the rear of the house.

"The day I came to confront you about the tutoring, you were sawing boards in back."

Ash's face broke into a smile.

"And it's taken you all this time to ask?"

"I hadn't thought about it before," Greta admitted. "I guess I had other things on my mind."

He chuckled, finally turning away to look at the house. Greta followed his gaze, wishing that Chase would come back out.

"He's probably in there giving us time alone," Ash said ruefully.

Greta turned to stare at him, and Ash's smile broadened.

"Chase thinks I should marry you," he reported, much to her embarrassment. Before she could respond he added, "No matchmakers, huh?" as he looked at the house.

Greta didn't dare tell him about Galen.

They were both silent for a moment, then Ash told her that she should get to Peggy's before they started supper without her. Greta didn't really want to leave, but Ash was opening her car door and she had no real choice but to get in. Instead of closing her door though, Ash squatted down beside her.

"I like your perfume," he told her. "The scent of it was on your letter."

"I didn't put it there," she said quickly, blushing a bit at the thought.

"I know," he replied. "But it was there."

He stood up, closed the door and moved away, giving her room to turn the car around and leave. Greta did so, but reluctantly. What she really wanted to do was to just stay there at the farm and talk to him for the rest of the evening.

By Friday morning Greta had to admit that she was just passing time until Saturday. Her mind just was not focusing on anything. And Friday evening as she did the dishes, she realized that she had hardly glanced at Bob's face all week.

"Galen's right," she murmured, reaching for the photograph. "I am acting like a schoolgirl."

Greta knew she had no wish to forget Bob, yet she also didn't want to give up a chance at happiness with another man for him.

She sat down at the table with the photo in her hand, thinking about her three years as a widow. Galen had done a lot of growing up during those years. He was soon to be a teenager, and high school was just around the corner.

She ran her finger over Bob's face, instantly remembering the day it was taken. They had gone to a carnival with two other couples from the base. There had been three other children besides Galen with them, and they'd had quite a bit of fun going on rides and playing the games along the midway, all ten of them sticking together the whole afternoon. It had been one of the other couples who had the camera. Rick, the one who owned it, had taken pictures during their time together. Then, just as they were getting ready to leave the carnival, Cassie, his wife, had insisted that he get a family picture of each family, something they could hang onto to remember the afternoon. Bob had been the one to snap the picture of Cassie and Rick, with their little four year old daughter. A passerby had agreed to take a picture of all ten of them too. Later, after the terrible accident that had happened on the way back to the base, the camera had been found undamaged and Bob had had the pictures developed.

"Those were the last pictures ever taken of Rick and Cassie and little Louisa," she said sadly, remembering how grateful Rick's parents had been to get them.

Greta ran her finger over Bob's face again.

"We've had our share of hurts too, haven't we?" she asked him, her mind going back to another car accident. One that had happened even earlier.

'Life always goes on,' she told herself silently. 'And God always leads us forward.'

She stood up and moved back over to the sink, reaching up to replace the picture on the windowsill. Then she began doing the dishes again, this time with memories of her marriage on her mind.

When Ash pulled up in front of Greta's house Saturday morning, Greta was raking leaves in her front yard. She turned around as he shut the pickup off, stopping her work to give them a quick wave. Chase jumped out and carried his bag over to the porch before going to where she was. Ash stepped out more slowly, his gaze resting on her as she talked with Chase.

"Galen isn't helping you?" he asked as he finally walked over to them.

"He was," Greta replied, "until Peggy picked him up for practice a few minutes ago. She's going to pick up both boys after practice and take them out to your house. Dan was going to try to get away, but he wasn't sure he could."

Ash nodded.

"If you give me the rake, I'll finish this up for you."

"You don't have to do that," she said very quickly. "It will wait."

Ash smiled.

"Don't you know you're not supposed to look a gift horse in the mouth?" he asked.

"A gift horse?" piped up Chase.

Greta laughed. Ash took the rake from her as he answered Chase.

"Means I'm offering her a gift and she should be polite enough to accept it," he told him. "It's a saying, like 'an apple a day keeps the doctor away'."

"Oh," Chase said. "I didn't know that raking leaves was a gift."

Ash chuckled as he began raking leaves into the pile Greta had already started. She watched him for a moment, then she sighed.

"If you're that determined, I guess I'll let you do it," she said, giving in.

Ash smiled at her.

"Where would you like the leaves when I'm done?"

"You'll find a pile of them out back. I compost them and spread it on the lawn." She started to turn away, but then she looked at him and added, "The lawn cart and rake go in the garage. And thank you."

"My pleasure."

He watched her go into the house with Chase, the rake motionless in his hands until she had disappeared. Then he began raking again.

As he worked, Ash wondered just who did all the things around Greta's house that her husband would have normally. She looked far to small and delicate to do any hammering of nails or things like that. Even the sight of her raking the leaves had wounded his heart in a way he hadn't expected.

Then he thought of his own mother and all the work she'd done around their farm while he was growing up. The memory made him smile since his mother hadn't been that much taller than Greta, yet she'd worked in the fields right alongside him and Grant and their dad whenever a need arose. Maybe the fact that Margaret never went near the barn had given him a lopsided view of women.

He finished raking the leaves into a big pile and loaded them into the lawn cart. When he reached the backyard with it, he found that that area had already been cleaned up. A large pile of leaves was sitting in one corner, alongside another large pile of composted materials.

"Obviously she takes care of this job herself," he mused as he dumped his load into the pile.

He glanced around, admiring the neatness of the yard. A few scraggly looking flowers grew along the back of the house still, a memento of what had probably been a very flourishing flower bed during the summer. He looked up at the two story house, wondering once again if she owned it.

"I'm willing to bet she owns it," he murmured to himself, his mind leaping ahead to the question of whether or not she'd even consider moving out to the farm.

That thought stopped him cold and Ash quickly strode over to the garage to put the rake and lawn cart away.

"You're getting ahead of yourself, Ash Lancaster," he muttered as he closed the garage up again and headed back out to his pickup. "Just because you're attracted to the woman doesn't mean you gotta marry her."

The thought of her owning the house brought to mind some other issues though, and Ash couldn't seem to get them out of his mind. As he drove home he couldn't help wondering what it would be like to move into a house where your spouse had lived with an earlier partner. He couldn't picture himself sleeping in the same bed that Greta and her husband had slept in. The whole idea was a bit repulsive to him. How could he possibly ask Greta to live in the farmhouse?

The more he thought about it, the more he decided that marriage between them was impossible. Unless they simply bought a new house somewhere.

"No way I'm going to sell the farm," he stated firmly as he turned into the lane leading up to his home.

He stopped the pickup and looked around his property, at the fields he'd been plowing for quite a few years now, at Tucson in the pasture by the barn, at the house where he and Margaret had lived.

No, there was no way he was going to sell this place. If he and Greta married, she was just going to have to deal with the situation as it was.

He put the truck in gear again and made his way up the rest of the lane. He parked near the house and walked to the barn, thinking about the chores he was now behind on. Chores he'd set aside in order to bring Chase into town.

'Who are you kidding?' he asked himself silently. 'You wanted to go in just as much as Chase did. In fact, if you had your choice, you'd still be there, sitting in her living room and drinking in the sight of her.'

"Great!" he exclaimed out loud. "Now I'm talking to myself."

Suddenly the absurdity of the situation made him chuckle. Shaking his head, Ash looked up at the sky.

"Ok, God," he said calmly, "I'll let you figure this all out. I'd appreciate it if you let me know just how I can have Greta and this place though. She's a fine woman and I've got a lot of feelings for her already."

Leaving it at that, he went on into the barn to do his work.

As it got closer to twelve however, Ash found that he kept looking down the lane, hoping to see Greta's car. Each time he did it, he shook his head and forced himself to go back to work, but it wasn't easy.

"She won't be here till close to twelve-thirty," he told himself. "Why do I keep looking for her?"

Finally he headed for the house to clean up a bit. There was no way that he wanted to appear in front of his guests fresh from the barn. They were supposed to be eating lunch with him.

He tossed his work boots onto the mat in the mudroom and hung up his jacket before going into the house. As he washed his hands at the kitchen sink, he looked down at his shirt and decided to change it. That meant a trip upstairs.

As he reached the top of the stairs, Ash stopped, his mind going to the room at the other end of the hall. The room he'd slept in for the past year. He walked down the hallway to it and opened the door to look around it.

"It's smaller than the master bedroom," he said to himself, "but it wouldn't take much to turn it into one."

He retraced his steps to his and Margaret's room and stood in the doorway looking around that one also. He tried to see it through Greta's eyes, but finally just shook his head and began changing his clothes.

A car came up the lane as he was tucking his clean shirt into his jeans, and Ash crossed the hall to look out a front window. It was Greta and Chase. Going back to his room, he grabbed a sweatshirt, then he headed down the stairs.

Chase came into the house, with Greta behind him, just as Ash reached the kitchen. The boy looked at him eagerly.

"Wait till you see my report," he said. "We did a lot on it."

Ash resisted the urge to look at Greta, who had stopped just inside the door. Instead he tousled Chase's hair as he said, "That's good, son. The other boys should be here soon though, with Mrs. Edwards. Why don't you put your bag on the stairway and come back to set the table."

"Ok," Chase replied, heading immediately toward the door to the living room.

When he finally did look at Greta, Ash felt a rush of pleasure course through him. He wanted to just sweep her into his arms, but he forced himself to calmly walk over to the refrigerator, sure that she would probably panic if he were to kiss her right then.

"I figured everyone could make their own sandwiches," he said as he opened the refrigerator door.

"Sounds good," Greta replied. "Is there anything I can do to help?"

He tried to think of something she could do that didn't require her to be too close to him, but he decided that no matter where she was, it was too close.

"No," he finally said with a shake of his head. "You can stay right where you are."

He hoped that Peggy and the other two boys wouldn't take too long to get there. They would at least offer some protection against all the feelings that were now storming through him.

Chase came back into the room and began getting plates from the cabinet. Ash opened the refrigerator drawer and pulled out the packages of sandwich meat he had picked up the day before, taking them over to the table and setting them in the middle of it. As he returned to the refrigerator he saw that Greta was looking around the kitchen and he wondered what she thought of the place. Then he noticed that she was biting her bottom lip and pinching at the sleeve of her blouse with her fingers.

"Anything else I need on the table?" Chase asked.

Ash pulled the juice from the refrigerator and turned to look at the table.

"Plates, knives, glasses," he said. "Looks...No. We have guests, Chase. Definitely need napkins for guests."

He set the pitcher of juice onto the table and went back over to the counter for the bread, realizing too late that it was right behind where Greta was standing. He stepped closer to her, saying "Bread," and pointing to the counter. Greta turned to pick it up, holding out both loaves toward him. Ash took them, picking up the delicate scent of her perfume at the same time.

"Chips," he mumbled. "We picked them up this morning. I left them in the pickup, I guess."

"I'll go get them, Dad."

Chase was out the door before he could stop him, and suddenly Ash was alone with Greta again. He wanted to say something to her, but his mind went blank. He pushed the silverware around the table, then readjusted the glasses.

"Ash?"

He looked over at Greta and found a slight smile dancing across her face.

"You're about as nervous as a young boy on his first date," she commented.

Ash laughed shakily as he retorted, "You're a close second, I think."

Greta's smile widened as she pushed away from the counter and stepped toward the table.

"I'll admit it," she said. "This is not the easiest thing for me to do."

"Because of what happened that day?"

"No," she replied, shaking her head. "You tend to make me feel..." She broke it off as she slipped into a chair by the table, not looking at him. Then she said, "I keep telling myself that I shouldn't feel this way, but the truth is, every time I'm near you I want to..."

She stopped again and Ash could see that she was struggling with how to explain her feelings. Suddenly his own feelings didn't seem so important. He knelt on the floor in front of her, taking her hands in his.

"Greta, I'm sorry," he said quickly, looking into her eyes. "I really don't want you to feel the way I'm feeling. I mean, I do, but I don't." He shook his head in confusion as he said, "Does that make any sense?"

"Tons," she whispered.

They stared at each other for a moment, then Greta put a hand on each side of his face and leaned forward slightly to kiss him. Ash felt like he was drowning in her scent again, just as he had the last time they'd kissed. This kiss was different though. It was soft and inviting instead of hard and punishing, as his had been.

Ash heard voices approaching the back door just as Greta pulled away from him. He stared at her for a fraction of a second, then he got to his feet, turning away to pull himself under control.

"We're here," said Peggy's voice as Chase opened the mudroom door and came back in, potato chips in hand.

Jimmy and Galen followed him, with Peggy in the rear. Ash saw her glance around, a smile on her face, then she looked rather startled as her gaze swung around to where Greta was sitting.

"Ash!" she exclaimed. "What have you done to the kitchen?"

Ash followed her glance to the new picture window, groaning silently as he wondered how he was going to explain it to Peggy.

"Cool, Mr. Lancaster!" Jimmy exclaimed before he could say anything. "A picture window!"

"I had some time on my hands," Ash said, deciding to just gloss over the whole thing and not explain it. "Just thought it would look nice."

"I like it," Peggy said, coming over to the table. "And the kitchen is so big that it doesn't really matter if the table is out further. I absolutely love the way the window sits in an alcove like that. But I'm afraid I'd load up that neat shelf with pictures and knickknacks if I lived here."

Ash didn't dare look at Greta. She would know exactly when he'd begun the work, and he knew that even now she was probably putting two and two together and figuring out why. At least, part of the why anyway. She knew nothing about the smells and sounds that had been plaguing them since Margaret's death.

Fortunately Chase announced that he was hungry at that moment, so Peggy wasn't able to question him about the window any further. Ash pointed out the sandwich makings and told everyone to dig in, which the boys immediately did.

All through lunch, Greta wondered if she had made a mistake by kissing him. Ash hadn't had any time after the kiss to say anything, and ever since he had seemed to be ignoring her. He'd relaxed after Peggy and the boys had come into the house though, especially once the picture window had been spotted and explained. She hadn't noticed it when she'd arrived, but then, she'd been in the kitchen just once before. Besides, she'd been too involved in Ash to notice much of anything.

Ash had been talking to the two older boys as everyone was making their sandwiches, asking how practice had gone and when their next game was. But while they were eating, Greta couldn't help noticing that he still wasn't speaking to either her or Peggy.

Peggy had apparently noticed it also. She kept giving Greta curious glances, which Greta kept ignoring, forcing herself to eat the sandwich she had made.

Greta decided that she didn't regret her impulsive kiss, even if Ash did. She'd been wanting to do that since the moment she'd walked into the kitchen and saw him. He'd looked so tall and strong, and she'd been filled with so much love for him right then and there. It hadn't taken long for her to get nervous though. He'd seemed a bit too relaxed, as though having her in his kitchen didn't bother him one way or the other. Then she'd seen little things that made her examine the situation a bit more closely. Like the way he hadn't wanted her to move from beside the door. When he had finally been forced to come near her for the bread, she'd realized that he was holding himself very firmly in check.

"Can we go outside now?" Chase asked, causing Greta to realize that everyone had finished their lunch. "I want to show Mrs. Jorgenson and Galen around."

"Thought you did that the first day she brought you home," Ash replied, and Greta saw Chase shake his head.

"I just showed them Tucson that day," he informed his father. "They never saw the barn or the fields or all that stuff."

"I'm not so sure Mrs. Jorgenson or Mrs. Edwards would want to examine the barn too closely," Ash told him. "I don't think they'd appreciate getting anything on their feet in there. But we can go see Tucson."

Chase jumped up from the table, ready to run out the door, but Ash stopped him.

"We need to put things away here first," he said, and Chase glanced at the table.

After the lunch items had been cleared away, they put on their jackets and headed outside. The three boys headed for the corral that held Tucson. Peggy, Greta, and Ash followed more slowly.

"How old is Tucson, anyway?" Peggy asked.

"Almost nine," Ash replied. "He's getting rather old. I keep thinking I should warn Chase that we may not have him much longer, but I keep putting it off."

"One of those books may tell him how long horses live," Greta said quietly.

Ash ran a hand through his hair.

"Guess I better say something soon then," he replied.

They ducked between the rails of the fence that separated the yard from the fields and walked around to the corner of the barn. Another fence formed three sides of a corral there, with the barn as its fourth side, and the three boys were standing by the horse inside it, petting his neck and sides. Chase had gotten some hay from somewhere and he was giving Tucson pieces of it.

"Can we ride him," Jimmy asked as the three adults stopped at the fence.

Ash looked at Peggy and Greta.

"I know Jimmy can ride," he said, "but what about Galen?"

"He's never been around a horse," Greta replied. "Not that he looks uncomfortable right now."

She had been surprised to see Galen right there with the other two, his hand stroking the horse's neck. As she watched, Chase handed him some hay and showed him how to hold his hand and let Tucson eat off it.

Ash ducked through the rails and went over to the boys.

"One at a time and just in here," he said to the three of them as Greta leaned on the fence to watch them. "Want to be first, Galen? Or would you rather watch the others before trying it?"

"I'll watch, thanks," Galen said very quickly. "He looks sort of big close up."

Greta smiled at Galen's words.

"So what did we break up when we arrived?" Peggy whispered as she too leaned on the fence.

Greta kept watching Ash as he gave Jimmy a hand up onto Tucson's back.

"What makes you think you broke up something?" she asked quietly.

"Because your face showed it," Peggy retorted. "And Ash seemed... I don't know. A bit shaken?"

Greta looked at her.

"Why would he look shaken?"

"Not exactly shaken," Peggy replied, giving her head a slight shake. "You know what I mean."

Greta shook her own head as she said, "I don't. Maybe you should explain it better."

Peggy stared at her for a moment, then she smiled.

"Ok," she quipped. "I get the message. Hands off, Peggy. Let the two of you work things out on your own." She shook her head and turned to watch Ash and the boys as she said, "You two are so much alike, yet so different. You're both very private people."

Greta laughed gently. She put an arm around Peggy and squeezed slightly.

"Have to keep people like you off guard," she jested, making Peggy giggle.

"You're succeeding," Peggy told her. "I still don't even know why Ash stopped the tutoring, nor why he stayed in seclusion for over a week. He changed the subject when Dan asked him the night he and Chase visited."

Greta looked back to where Ash was helping Chase up onto Tucson's back, pleased by that information.

It was now Chase who was sitting on the horse's broad back and Greta realized that they'd somehow missed Jimmy's ride. Chase rode around the corral once, then he slid off Tucson and Ash turned to Galen.

"Want to try it?" he asked.

Galen stepped closer to the horse.

"Could I just sit on him?"

"Sure," Ash replied, cupping his hands to give Galen a

hand up.

As Galen settled onto Tucson's back, Greta watched the emotions on his face. First there was a bit of fear, then a mixture of amazement and awe as he looked down.

"If you decide you want to make him go," Ash was saying, "you give him a gentle squeeze with your knees. Tucson is trained to turn by touch rather than with a bit in his mouth. If you tap him on the right side of his neck, he turns left. That how the reins work on him."

"He's awful big," Galen said. "I don't know how Chase can control him like he does."

"It's not so much control as it is building a relationship with him," Ash replied. "A horse knows when it's rider is unsure of themselves."

"Does that mean Tucson knows I'm a bunch of nerves up here?" Galen asked nervously.

Ash laughed.

"See how his ears are twitching back and forth? He knows."

Galen looked down at Ash, and Greta saw that he was a little afraid again.

"He won't do anything to me, will he?"

"Not Tucson," Ash assured him. "Some horses would take advantage of a green rider. But I've got Tucson trained to carry Chase. If Chase were hurt, Tucson would bring him home without ever letting him fall off."

Greta breathed a quiet sigh of relief. Having been around horses for the first eighteen years of her life, she knew just how skittish some of them were.

Galen reached out and rubbed the side of Tucson's neck, then he looked down at Ash and said, "I think I'm ready to get down."

Ash helped him off the horse, then he turned toward

the fence.

"Either of you want to try him out?" he asked, looking at her and Peggy.

Peggy shook her head.

"Not me," she stated firmly. "I am definitely not a horse person. I think I told you that before, Ash."

"Can't fault me for trying," he said, shrugging slightly. Then he looked at Greta. "How about you, Greta?"

She had planned to just shake her head and remain by the fence, but a spark of mischievousness caused her to duck between the fence rails and walk over to him.

"I guess I'll give it a go," she said, imitating the shrug he'd given a moment before.

Ash smiled down at her as he held his hands out the way he had for Galen. Greta nearly backed out of her plan when she realized that she'd have to touch him to get up onto Tucson, but then she put her hand on his shoulder and her foot into his hands, and stepped up, sliding her leg across the wide back.

"You did that like you've done it before," Ash commented as he looked up at her.

Greta smiled down at him, taking Tucson's mane loosely into her hands.

"I was born and raised on a horse ranch in Montana, Mr. Lancaster," she said as she squeezed Tucson gently with her legs.

The big horse obediently moved forward underneath her. Greta heard Peggy laugh at the same time as the three boys gave a crow of delight on her other side. She also heard Ash's soft comment as she moved away from him.

"I owe you one, Mrs. Jorgenson," he said very quietly.

She made her way around the corral, enjoying the feel

of the horse beneath her. This was something that she hadn't done in years, but it came as naturally to her as cooking and cleaning did. And even the fact that she could feel Ash's gaze on her the whole time couldn't diminish her pleasure at pulling off her joke.

Peggy and Jimmy left about three-thirty. Greta had planned to leave at the same time, but as the Edwards were getting into their car, Chase announced that he wanted to show Galen his collection of horses.

"I guess you could," Greta said reluctantly, "but just for a moment. We need to get home also."

The boys disappeared into the house and Greta said goodbye to Peggy and Jimmy. As soon as Peggy had driven down the lane, Ash turned to her and said, "Thank you."

"For what?" Greta asked curiously.

He came over and stood in front of her, reaching out to touch her cheek.

"In the house, before lunch," he commented. "You made things a lot easier. Your kiss was very reassuring."

Greta blushed slightly, her heart dancing inside her as he ran his hand down her cheek in a very light caress. Just as she was wondering if her was going to kiss her however, he said, "A horse ranch in Montana?"

She laughed softly, nodding her head.

"I was born in my parent's bed because there was a snowstorm and no one could move anywhere. My dad had to cut the cord himself."

"Your mother was ok?" he asked.

"Yes," she replied, smiling up at him. Her heart was slowing its pace a bit now that he'd taken his hand away. "My dad sort of knew what he was doing since he raised horses. But he vowed to never do it again. My brother was born in a hospital with a doctor in attendance. Dad took my mother into town a week before the baby was due and they stayed there waiting for her time to come."

"What about you?"

"Oh, I was left on the ranch in the care of the housekeeper," Greta replied. "The foreman ran the ranch while my parents were gone."

Ash gave a slight whistle.

"That big a spread, huh," he commented.

"Pretty big," Greta admitted. "Dad sold horses all over the place."

"Do they still live in Montana?"

Greta shook her head.

"Dad died when I was nineteen," she told him. "He had a heart attack while out riding. My mother sold the ranch and moved to Florida. My brother was eighteen at the time. He had just graduated from high school and was headed for college." She looked up at the house as she said, "Where do you suppose those boys are?"

She looked back at Ash in time to catch the smile that spread across his face.

"Maybe they've teamed up," he suggested, moving away from her a little.

Greta laughed, agreeing that it might be so.

They were both quiet for a moment after that, but Greta felt it was a relaxed quiet rather than a nervous one. Ash was looking out over the fields, which gave her a chance to examine him a bit. She took note of the curls that brushed the collar of his jacket and the shadow that marked the line of his jaw, then she saw a small scar near his left ear.

"You still like horses?" he finally asked, turning back

and causing her to blush slightly at being caught in her perusal of him.

"Sure," she replied, nodding her head. "Haven't been on one in years though."

"How many years?"

"Not since my father died," she admitted. "I was in college at the time. Mom did ask if I wanted to keep my own horse, but Junco was getting sort of old, like Tucson. Plus, I didn't have any place to keep him. Then Bob and I got married, and we were moving around too much for horses."

"Apparently Galen hasn't said anything about your past to Chase," he mused, and Greta shook her head.

"I guess we haven't really talked about my past much lately," she admitted. "Not that I was trying to hide it."

Ash smiled at her reference to his actions, and Greta gathered the courage to repeat a question she'd asked him once before.

"Your parents?"

He looked away and Greta thought he wasn't going to answer, but then he said, "My parents were at the air show when Grant was killed. My mother collapsed and had to be rushed to the hospital. She died the day after Grant's funeral." He turned back to her, his face grim. "My father began drinking himself to death and finally finished the job five years later. Not a pretty story."

"I'm sorry. I shouldn't have asked."

"I would have told you sooner or later," he said, smiling as he added, "preferably later."

There was another moment of silence, then Ash ran a hand through his hair, glancing toward the house.

"Maybe they'll come out when dinnertime comes," he said ruefully.

Greta laughed as Ash headed for the house to round up the two boys. She was sure now that they were staying inside on purpose, giving her and Ash some time alone together. She wasn't about to confront Galen about it though. He was already too willing for her and Ash to hit it off.

"God's timing, Galen," she murmured to herself. "Ash needs to work through his feelings concerning Margaret before he can think about anyone else."

She looked around the farm while she waited for the three of them to come back out. It was taking on a very wintry look, with scattered stalks of old corn standing forlornly in the field and leaves fluttering around the yard from the trees. Greta pulled her jacket more closely around her as she began to feel the chill in the air. When she heard Galen's voice she turned to look toward the house, almost relieved to see Ash and the boys coming across the yard toward her.

After Chase went to bed that night, Ash sat in the living room trying to read his Bible. Every so often, a thought would pop into his head, and he would find himself dwelling on something Greta had said, or the way she looked, or the way the wind blew her hair as she sat on Tucson. Finally he set the Bible aside.

"This is getting me absolutely nowhere," he said out loud.

His mind drifted back to her kiss. It had been such a gentle kiss, but there had been something more to it that he couldn't quite put his finger on. He remembered the way her hands had felt on his face, soft and warm. Then he realized what it was. That kiss had been her token of surrender, he was sure.

The thought filled him with a very quiet joy, yet it also evoked feelings of fear as he thought of all the things that could happen in the future. What if he lost her, as he'd lost so many others? Was it worth it to go into another marriage, just to have it collapse at his feet?

'With God all things are possible,' said a small voice within him, reminding Ash of his commitment to leave the whole future in God's hands. He smiled to himself, then bowed his head and began praying.

Chapter 13

Greta was singing softly to herself as she made breakfast the next morning. She'd woken early and had read her Bible, then she'd just laid there in bed reminiscing about the day before. Ash had been a very good host, in spite of the fact that he hadn't spoken to her or Peggy all through lunch. He'd made up for it later, while the boys were exploring the barn. The three of them had gone back into the house and sat at the kitchen table talking, and Ash had quizzed them about what was going on in the church. Greta wondered if perhaps he was planning to get involved in some of the things they discussed, such as the youth ministry since he'd asked quite a number of question about it.

Galen came into the kitchen as she finished making their scrambled eggs. Without a word he set the table and poured her coffee. Greta gave him a cheerful smile as she set their plates onto the table and sat down in her seat across from him.

"You never said what you thought of Tucson yesterday," she said after they had prayed. "Did you like getting up onto him?"

"He's huge," Galen replied a bit forcefully. "When I was sitting on him, I felt like I was three miles off the ground. I can't believe you used to ride those things when you were my age."

"I was raised around them, Galen. It makes a difference. To me, they were just part of my life."

"Do you think I could ever learn to ride like you?" he asked.

"I imagine you could," she said. "You'd have to get comfortable around horses first though. As Mr. Lancaster said, horses can sense when someone is nervous and unsure of themselves."

They ate in silence for several minutes after that. When Greta finished her eggs, she leaned back in her chair to enjoy her coffee, watching Galen as he continued to eat.

"You were singing when I came in," he commented out of the blue, a bit of a smile on his face as he glanced across the table at her.

"Yes, I was," Greta replied. "It's a gorgeous morning and I feel great."

Galen's smile grew and she was pretty sure she knew just what he was thinking.

"Then it has nothing to do with Mr. Lancaster?" he asked, confirming her suspicions.

"Maybe it does, maybe it doesn't," she remarked casually, then she pointed her fork at him as she added, "And you and Chase don't need to deliberately leave the two of us alone together."

"Why would you think we did that?" Galen retorted, failing at his attempt to look innocent. "Chase was showing me his collection of horses."

"A big collection?"

Galen nodded.

"His mother used to buy them for him," he said. "Don't know why she didn't tell him about the different breeds though."

"Maybe she didn't know all that much about horses. Only that Chase liked them."

"Sort of weird, isn't it?" Galen questioned with a bit of a laugh.

"What's weird?"

"Well, Chase likes airplanes and horses. Mr. Lancaster used to fly planes, and you were raised around horses."

Greta smiled.

"Coincidence, Galen," she said. "Just a coincidence. Lots of kids like both airplanes and horses."

Galen grinned at her as he scooped the last of his scrambled eggs onto his fork and Greta wasn't fooled for a minute by that grin. It wasn't the last of his teasing about Ash Lancaster.

Ash followed Chase up the side aisle of the sanctuary and into the row of chairs behind Greta. He smiled slightly as he realized that Chase purposely made sure he would sit directly behind her. The service hadn't started yet, and Galen turned around to speak to Chase. Ash leaned forward and said, "Good morning," near Greta's ear. She turned around to smile at him and Ash felt a surge of pleasure streak through him.

"Good morning to you also," she said.

He caught the scent of her perfume and tucked it away inside his mind, determined to behave in a manner that wouldn't reveal the strength of his feelings toward her.

"Chase mentioned this morning that we haven't set another date for him to come over," he said in a business-like voice. "I have a meeting Wednesday night. If that works for you, I can drop him off and pick him up after my meeting."

"That works for me. His report is due on Friday and he could probably use a bit more help with it."

"He worked on it at home last night," Ash told her. "He needed some words spelled for him."

Greta nodded, then she turned around as the pastor began speaking at the front of the sanctuary. Ash ignored the urge to touch her hair, putting his attention on the pastor's words instead.

All through the service he was very conscious of Greta's presence in front of him, but Ash kept his attention from straying by closing his eyes and focusing on whatever was happening at the time, whether it was prayer, praise, or the pastor preaching.

At the end of the service, Galen and Jimmy invited Chase to go to the foyer with them, as Ash knew they would. Greta turned in her seat again.

"So when do I get repaid?" she asked.

Ash had no idea what she was talking about, but he saw the smile that played around her mouth. He had the feeling he was going to get teased about something again.

"Ok," he said, "I'll bite. What do I owe you?"

Her smile broadened.

"I'm not sure really," she mused, tilting her head to one side. "Your words were, 'I owe you one, Mrs. Jorgenson'."

"You weren't supposed to hear that," he scolded, chuckling as he said it.

"So what do you owe me?"

"I'll have to think about that for a while," he said. "You like to tease me, don't you?"

"I like to hear you laugh," she answered. "When I first met you, you couldn't even smile."

Ash felt as if his heart was thawing out after a long winter. He reached out to touch her cheek, feeling the softness of her skin under his fingers.

"I don't mind being teased by you," he said. "It actually makes me feel...warm. However," he said, taking his hand away, "If we don't move, I'm going to kiss you, Greta Jorgenson."

Greta laughed as she stood up. She picked up her Bible and made her way out of the row of chairs, then headed for the back of the sanctuary. Ash stood up, smiling as he turned to watch her go. This teasing could go both ways, he decided. And yes, he liked to hear her laugh also.

When he got to the foyer, Greta was standing with Peggy and Dan. The three boys were nowhere to be seen. As he went over to join the conversation Greta was having with the other couple, Peggy turned to him.

"I was just telling Greta that if the two of you aren't busy tomorrow night, we'd like to have you over for dinner and an evening together. The boys can have pizza, then do something up in Jimmy's room while we adults eat."

"I'm free," Ash replied, glancing at Greta. "How about you and Galen?"

"Galen and I can come, yes," Greta said, nodding her head.

"Good," Peggy said. "Our house isn't exactly set up for dinner guests, of course. We get to eat in the kitchen."

"I think the food will taste the same no matter where we eat it," Dan said with a laugh. "And we're all close friends."

The foyer was already pretty empty, with just a few people still lingering to talk. Ash looked out the door and saw Jimmy, so he figured Chase was outside also.

"I need to collect Chase and get moving," he said. "We're working on a project this afternoon."

"Galen was eager to go home for your standing date too," Peggy said to Greta. "He says he's going to cream you today."

"He probably will," Greta replied with a quick laugh. "I think he's been reading the dictionary lately."

She smiled at Ash, then headed for the door, calling, "I'll see you tomorrow night," over her shoulder.

"Are you remodeling again because you're angry?" Chase asked once they were headed home.

Ash chuckled.

"I think this time I'm remodeling because I'm happy," he replied. "But I'd appreciate it if you'd keep our little project to yourself for the moment."

"Is it a secret?" Chase asked.

"Sort of. I'm not sure what's going to happen in the future, but I'd like it to be a surprise if…"

"If you and Mrs. Jorgenson get married?" Chase asked, rushing into the middle of Ash's words.

Ash chuckled again, reaching over to tousle Chase's hair.

"Something like that, Chase. Something like that."

He could see that his words had made Chase very happy.

Galen called her at the drug store after school the following day. He explained that he'd been invited to Jimmy's for the afternoon and assured her that they were going to do their homework together before supper. Greta willingly agreed to that plan, telling him that she would be stopping at home to change her clothes before going to the Edwards house. She was glad that it would give her a few minutes to herself. Something she didn't have a lot of as a single parent who worked all day.

After changing into a clean shirt and pulling on a pair of jeans, she looked at herself in her bedroom mirror critically, wondering if the lines on her face were beginning to show her age.

"I can remember when thirty-seven seemed ancient to me," she said, smiling at her refection. "Now it seems like a pretty good age."

She tucked her shirt into her jeans, and pulled a pink sweater on over it. After slipping her shoes back on, she went downstairs to head out to her car.

When she opened the front door, Ash was standing beside his pickup at the curb. He straightened up as she walked over to him.

"Galen said you were going to come home to change. Thought I'd come pick you up."

"Because you have a thing about women driving at night?" she asked, stopping in front of him.

"Not entirely."

The look in his eyes was enough to stop her from asking anything else. Greta felt her face become rather warm and was glad the semi-darkness would cover it up.

"So do I get to drive you to Peggy's," he asked, "or are you going to be stubborn and drive yourself?"

"Are you a safe driver?" she inquired with mock seriousness.

"Very."

"Are you safe to be around?"

"I'll be on my best behavior," he replied, a smile forming on his lips.

She put her hand up to her chin, with one finger across her mouth, and pretended to consider the situation carefully. Ash's smile grew.

"How would we get home?" she said, grilling him even more. "I don't think that cab is big enough for four."

"You could sit on my lap," he said, his smile widening.

This time her face roasted and Greta ducked her head. Ash laughed, then he said, "We could go in your car and leave the pickup here."

She looked over towards her car, then back at him.

"Do I get to drive?" she asked, pulling the keys from her pocket. When he laughed again she hastily held them out as she added, "On second thought, I think you would make me too nervous to drive."

She turned and headed for her car. Ash caught up to her easily.

"I don't mean to make you nervous," he told her, and Greta nodded, saying "I know" as she continued walking.

Ash opened the passenger door for her, then closed it after she got in. Greta watched as he walked around the front of the car to the driver's side.

"So what about me makes you nervous?" he asked as he slid behind the steering wheel.

"It's your whole presence in my life," Greta replied truthfully. "Things were going along fine before. I was happy with it just Galen and I. Now there seem to be all these emotions running around inside me. I'm not sure I like them." She paused, then admitted, "Or maybe it's that I like them too much and I'm afraid it won't last."

"Then you'll have to be satisfied being just you and Galen again?"

"Yes."

He started the car and backed out of the driveway. Greta didn't think he was going to continue the conversation, but once he was headed toward Peggy's, Ash said, "I know the feeling. It took me quite a while to accept Margaret into my life after my mother and Grant died. And Margaret never knew my father, though he was still alive when we were married. I never even told him I was getting married."

"Why not?"

"Too painful. He was a drunk, and I was still running away." He glanced toward her, smiling. "I think I've finally stopped running. When you brought that book out to the farm, I realized that I had to face my past and work through my feelings."

He stopped in front of Peggy's, turned off the car, and turned in his seat, holding the keys out to her. Greta shook her head.

"I'm not driving home" she stated firmly.

He closed his hand around the keys and reached for the door handle.

"I would like to sit here and continue talking to you," he said as he opened his door, "but I'm going to make myself get out of this car and go in for dinner. If we stay here I know I will end up kissing you."

Light flooded the car as color flooded into her face yet again and Greta hastily turned her head away. She heard him chuckle as she opened her own door and escaped the confines of her car.

"I see you found her all right, Ash," Peggy stated when she opened her front door for them.

"No problem," Ash replied. "Greta was right where Galen said she would be."

Greta laughed as she took her jacket off. Peggy hung it on a hook, then hung Ash's on top of it even though there was an empty hook next to it. Greta saw Ash's eyebrow go up slightly, and she ducked her head to hide her smile.

Peggy led them into the living room, talking as she went.

"Dan just called, and he's on his way." She glanced back at Greta. "The boys are feasting on pizza in the kitchen, if you want to go let Galen know you're here."

"I will, thanks."

Greta went into the kitchen and found the three boys sitting around the kitchen table with a pizza box in between them. Most of the pizza was gone. Galen grinned at her.

"Chase can eat almost as much pizza as Jimmy and I," he said.

"As long as you don't make yourself sick," Greta said, looking at Chase.

"I'm done," he replied with a grin. "They're a piece ahead of me."

Greta went over to give Galen a kiss on his forehead. "School go all right?"

"Yeah." He smiled up at her as he said, "Mrs. Thomas got a call from that science magazine. They were checking to make sure the work was mine. She thinks they're going to use it."

"That's great, Galen!" she exclaimed, looking over at

Chase. "Galen sent one of his pieces to a science magazine for possible publication."

"Is he really gonna get paid for it, Mrs. Jorgenson?" Jimmy asked.

"If they use it."

"Wow!" Chase said, sitting up straighter. "You mean anybody who writes stuff gets paid?"

"If someone chooses to publish what you wrote," she answered with a nod, "you get paid in some way. Some magazines pay by giving you a free subscription, but most give monetary payments."

"Monetary?"

"Means money, Chase," Galen said quickly. "Mom is always using big words to say little things."

Greta gave him a playful swat as Chase grinned.

"I like it when she does that, Galen. It makes me think more."

"Galen likes it too," Jimmy said. "Gives him more ammunition for their Sunday Scrabble games."

Greta left the three of them to their pizza and went back out to the living room. Dan had arrived and was sitting on the couch with Peggy. Ash was sitting in one of the easy chairs. He looked up as she came in, smiling mischievously.

"We're out of luck, Greta," he said. "They grabbed the couch."

Dan and Peggy both laughed. Greta felt a rush of embarrassment, but she shoved it aside as she decided to play along with his joke.

"Sharing a chair is much cozier anyway," she said as she sat down on the arm of his chair and slid her arm around his shoulders.

She nearly laughed as Peggy's mouth dropped open in

surprise. Ash chuckled, then said, "You're right. Couches let you sit too far apart. Look at them, one at each end."

Greta giggled at the expression on Peggy's face. Dan was laughing so hard he had tears on his cheeks and Peggy finally smiled slightly.

"You two are joshing, right?" she said.

Greta moved to a chair nearby as she said, "Had you going there, didn't we? Serves you right for your little maneuvers."

"Hanging our jackets on the same hook was a nice touch, Peggy," Ash added.

Peggy blushed, making Dan start laughing again. She made a face at him, then smiled ruefully.

"Ok, guilty as charged."

Ash leaned forward.

"You're going to have to let Greta and I sort things out on our own," he said seriously. "I think we can both agree that there is an attraction between us, but neither of us are sure where it's going." He smiled, settling into his chair again. "So now that we've broken the ice here, can we all enjoy the evening together?"

To Greta's relief, Peggy nodded.

The conversation turned to other things and Greta relaxed. She was glad they had brought it all out into the open and had admitted that an attraction was there. Even though she knew she'd probably get quizzed by Peggy later, at least this evening there wouldn't be any undercurrent going on.

When the boys came out of the kitchen, they announced that they were headed upstairs to Jimmy's room. After they disappeared, Peggy got up.

"Must be time to clean up after them and set the table

for us," she said as she headed for the kitchen door.

"I'll help," Greta said as she jumped up.

She followed Peggy into the kitchen, nearly bumping into her when Peggy stopped with a gasp just inside the door. Greta looked beyond her and saw that the table was all set, with candles in the center of it. She started laughing, and both men came to see what was going on.

"I don't believe it!" exclaimed Peggy. "They cleaned it all up and set the table!"

"Jimmy?" Dan said. "No way!"

Ash laughed, walking over to the table to pick up a candle.

"I think this is the work of Galen and Chase, with Jimmy as an accomplice."

"Galen and Chase?" Dan asked.

"It seems the boys are doing a bit of matchmaking on their own," Greta said. "They keep deliberately leaving us alone."

"And Chase has informed me that when I decide to get married, I'm to keep Greta in mind."

Peggy giggled.

"No wonder you two are so attuned to any matchmaking efforts," she said.

Ash put the candle back onto the table, smiling slightly.

"A nice touch anyway. Might as well leave them there."

He and Dan headed back to the living room. Greta leaned against the counter.

"So what can I do to help?" she asked.

"There's nothing to do," Peggy told her. "There's lasagna in the oven, which needs just a hot mat on the table." She opened the refrigerator and pulled out a pan of Italian bread. "I'll toss this in the oven for a minute, then we can eat." As she moved to the stove she glanced at Greta. "Ash has come a long way in a very short time."

Greta nodded, but didn't say anything. Peggy smiled, then slid the pan into the oven before going to the door to tell the men dinner was ready.

When Dan and Ash came in, they sat across from each other. Greta took the seat to the left of Ash. Peggy put the lasagna onto the table and got the bread out of the oven. After she sat down, Ash grinned.

"Not going to light them?" he asked jokingly.

Peggy giggled as Dan got up to grab matches from a drawer.

Greta was very conscious of Ash as they ate their dinner. He talked easily with Dan and Peggy about a variety of things. She liked listening to his voice, and when he would look at her, she was sure there was a slight twinkle in his eye, as if he were sending her quiet little bolts of affection.

"Greta is awfully quiet," Peggy said suddenly.

Ash turned to look at her.

"I've noticed," he said.

"I'm just enjoying the conversation," she said quickly. "And this lasagna is terrific. I never have the time to make this sort of meal anymore."

Peggy put her fork down and leaned back in her chair to pat her stomach.

"I am stuffed," she said. "And I have a question for Ash."

Ash raised his eyebrows as he said, "A question?"

"I wasn't going to ask it tonight," she said, "but you seem so relaxed. And if I'm being nosy, just tell me and I'll shut up. I'm just curious about your stunt flying days.

I saw your picture in that book. You and your brother."

Greta saw his jaw tighten, but Ash didn't tell Peggy that she was being nosy. Instead he said, "Grant actually learned to fly before I did. He got his pilot license at nineteen and began flying for a crop duster. I guess that's sort of how we ended up doing stunts. A crop duster flies down low to the ground. He takes chances really." He leaned forward, pushing his plate aside to lean his forearms on the table. "I suggested going to see an air show near where we lived, and we were very quickly sucked into that life. I got my pilot's license, and we talked some of the other pilots into teaching us stuff. After awhile we scraped together enough money for a plane. By the time Grant was killed, we had two planes. My father thought our lives were rather exciting. My mother was terrified every time we flew. They were there when Grant went down. What happened killed my mother."

"And your father?" Dan asked.

Ash shifted slightly so that his arm was touching hers, and Greta decided perhaps he needed support. She laid her hand on his arm.

"My father drank himself to death," Ash said. "He lost the farm within a year, and died within five."

"And Margaret knew nothing of this?" Peggy asked. "She once told me that you were orphaned at a young age."

Ash smiled slightly.

"I led her to believe that," he admitted, laying his free hand on Greta's. "It was easier than living with the truth."

"Well, I'm glad I can once again talk about the Bible with you," Dan said. "I've missed our discussions. For someone who never went to church, you know a lot about the Bible."

Greta felt Ash's grip on her hand tighten, and she looked at him curiously. There was a tightness about his face that hadn't been there a moment before.

"I grew up in church, Dan," he said, his voice a bit rough. "My grandfather was an Assembly of God pastor in Wichita. Before Grant and I got involved in stunt-flying, I was planning to become a pastor myself."

Greta felt as though the floor had opened and dropped her through it. She heard Dan give a low whistle, and Peggy's slight gasp. Ash turned to look at her. She forced herself to keep her eyes on him.

"So that's why you sing the songs so easily," she said softly, "as if you know them."

Ash smiled.

"That's all you can say?" he asked.

"No," she replied, giving him a small smile. "But that's all I'm going to say for the moment."

He laughed. Greta felt his grip relax again, then he took his hand away.

After Chase was in bed that night, Ash sat in the living room thinking about the evening. Greta had certainly taken his revelations calmly. He was sure Margaret never would have. Margaret had been excitable. What his mother would have called high-strung. She had been fun to be with, and he had loved her very much, but his past was never something he'd wanted to share with her.

It had been as they were sitting in Dan and Peggy's living room after dinner that Greta had finally asked a question about his past.

"You left your life behind and went somewhere that no

one knew you in order to start over," she had commented. "How is it that you didn't leave God behind also?"

Ash had smiled at her question, since it came out of the blue in the middle of a different conversation. How like Greta to catch him completely off guard with the way her mind worked.

"It's a little hard to leave God behind, Greta," he had replied, and had been delighted when she blushed.

But it hadn't stopped her. He grinned now as he thought of the way she had challenged him.

"You tried after Margaret's death."

Ash had nodded silently.

'Sometime I'll answer her question,' he thought now.

He hadn't been able to, there in front of Dan and Peggy. And Greta had seemed to understand. She hadn't pressed the issue. Instead she had gone right back to the previous conversation as if the question had never been asked.

'It's like that day she brought the book out,' he thought. 'I broke down and she just simply waited for me to pull myself together. A silent presence. Totally non-threatening. That's what made it so easy to tell her about it.'

He reached for his Bible on the end table nearby. Greta's face appeared in his mind, and he smiled. He felt pleasure seep through him at the thought of her, and rested his hand on his Bible while he enjoyed his thoughts a moment longer. Then he opened the Bible and began reading.

Chapter 14

Greta and Galen arrived at Peggy's on Tuesday night before anyone else. Galen disappeared up the stairs with Jimmy, and Peggy told her she could help lay out the refreshments. As they worked, Peggy told her about some new books that had come into the library. Some of which she wasn't very happy about.

"I wish we would stock more Christian books," she said mournfully, "but the librarian tells me that the ones we do have don't get used very often."

"Maybe we should sign them all out at once," Greta commented.

"Get all the women here tonight to sign them out also?" Peggy asked, and they both laughed.

As Peggy continued fixing the tray of cups, she very casually asked how things were between Greta and Ash.

"I'm not trying to pry," she added quickly. "It's just that I care about both of you."

Greta smiled.

"He's a very complex man, Peggy. Just when I think I know him, he throws a monkey wrench into the pot."

"Like last night?" Peggy stopped working, holding a cup in midair as she stared at Greta. "I was so shocked when he said he had planned to become a pastor. To me, Ash has always been a farmer. He loves the land. He works hard at making improvements, and building up the soil." She shook her head slightly. "Hauling all those logs home and chopping them up for firewood is not the work of a pastor."

The doorbell rang, and Peggy quickly put the cup down onto the tray, then hurried out to answer it, leaving Greta to finish up in the kitchen. When she brought the tray of crackers and cheese to the living room, Vetta was sitting on the couch, telling the others about a fight she had with her husband. Only Peggy looked uncomfortable with Vetta's talk. Greta put the tray down carefully on the coffee table.

"So, have any of you learned anything of value from this study?" she asked as she took a seat.

The others looked at her curiously.

"Of course we have, Greta," Ann said, frowning a bit. "This study has been great!"

"What did we study here last week?" Greta asked, looking around at them all. When they were silent, she said, "I wasn't here at the beginning of this study in James, but I do know that James 1:22 says that it is a message to obey, not just to listen to. If you can't remember what we studied last week, how can you possibly remember what we studied four weeks ago and obey it?"

Everyone stared at her in confusion. Peggy leaned back in her chair, smiling.

"What are you talking about, Greta?" Karen asked, eyeing her suspiciouly.

"I'm talking about the beginning of chapter three. Perhaps each of you needs to go back and reread it to refresh your memories."

She watched as they leafed through their Bibles to the page. She saw, on each of their faces, first consternation, then realization, then embarrassment as they read the verses about taming the tongue.

Karen gave a nervous little laugh.

"I don't think I've ever been reprimanded in quite that fashion," she said. "Thank you, Greta."

The other four nodded in agreement, and Peggy began the Bible study.

Wednesday turned out to be a rather difficult day at work for Greta. During the morning it seemed like everything that could go wrong, did. The safe didn't want to open to allow them access to the money for the cash drawer. Vanessa, her co-worker, had pinched her finger in the front door of the store as she came in. And an order that Greta had expected first thing in the morning didn't arrive. When Greta checked into it she discovered it had somehow never been filed properly to be filled.

On top of all that, the girl who normally came in after school didn't show up, and Greta found herself working at the counter during the last two hours instead of finishing her own work. Bill Gordon came looking for some paperwork from her, and she had to say that it wasn't done. He walked away disgruntled.

With all that, Greta was glad to finally leave the drugstore and head home. She sank gratefully into the driver's seat of her car and slid a tape of Christian music into the tape player to help her unwind on the way home.

But, within two blocks of the store, the car sputtered and died.

She used a payphone to call Dan at his garage. He was quick to come and check out the car, and, when he couldn't discover the problem immediately, he gave Greta a lift home, telling her that he'd tow the car to his place.

When she walked into the house, Greta could hear music playing in the living room. She hung up her jacket and headed in that direction.

Galen was sitting on the couch with a pad of paper on his lap. He looked up when she walked in.

"Hi, Mom. You're a little late."

"Car broke down," she said in a tired voice as she sank onto the couch. "Mr. Edwards brought me home. He's going to take care of the car."

Galen put his pad and pen on the coffee table.

"Mr. Lancaster called a few minutes ago."

"To cancel tonight?" Greta asked hopefully.

Galen shook his head.

"To say he'd forgotten to tell you that his meeting is at six."

"Six?" she groaned, glancing at her watch.

It was ten minutes before six.

At that moment the doorbell rang. Greta groaned, burying her head in her hands for a moment.

"I'll let them in," Galen said, getting up to head for the door.

Greta heard the door open, then Ash's voice.

"Your mother isn't here yet?"

"She's here," Greta heard Galen tell him. "Her car broke down on her way home."

Greta stood up just as Ash appeared in the doorway.

"How did you get home?" he asked, concern written all over his face.

"Dan," she replied, smiling at his reaction. "He's taking care of my car. Hopefully it's nothing major and he can get it back to me quickly."

Ash frowned slightly, coming further into the living room.

"Have you had dinner?"

Greta shook her head as she said, "No. I just came in myself."

He ran his hand through his hair, rumpling the neatness that had been there.

"Maybe Chase should come with me," he told her. "He can do his work there."

"He can work on his report while I get something for Galen and I to eat," Greta assured him. "We'll probably just have a sandwich here in the living room."

"Are you sure you don't mind?" he asked, giving her a serious look.

"Go to your meeting, Ash," she encouraged him gently. "We'll be fine."

He looked at her for another moment, then nodded and turned back toward the hallway. Greta saw Chase grin at Galen as his father passed them.

At the living room doorway, Ash stopped and looked back at Greta for a moment.

"You have to be the world's most stubborn woman, Greta Jorgenson."

Greta smiled as he disappeared. She heard the front door close behind him and she sank back down onto the couch. Chase came over to the couch and sat down also, while Galen grabbed his paper and pen from the coffee table and moved to a chair.

"I'm glad you let me stay," Chase admitted. "I don't really like sitting around waiting for Dad to get done with his meeting."

Greta smiled at him.

"How far have you gotten on your report?" she asked.

"I'm almost done copying it," he replied eagerly. "I didn't tell Dad cause I was afraid he'd make me go with him instead of coming here."

"I see," Greta said thoughtfully, then stood up. "Well, you can sit here and finish your copying. Galen is busy writing something also. I'll go make sandwiches, and be back shortly. Are you hungry at all?"

Chase shook his head.

"Dad made us chicken and vegetables tonight. I'm stuffed."

Greta nodded, then she headed for the kitchen.

While she made the sandwiches for herself and Galen she thought about Ash's concern for her, and her reaction to it. She realized that she had become accustomed to taking care of everything for herself and Galen since Bob's death. In a way, having a man concerned about her was nice, but part of her almost resented his attitude. It seemed as if he saw her as being a helpless female.

Greta pushed the idea away, knowing it to be untrue.

"I know Ash respects me," she said out loud, but softly. "He even said he admires me for the way I've handled things."

No, his concern was just simply concern caused by the situation at hand.

Greta whispered a quiet prayer of thankfulness and took the sandwiches out to the living room.

It was seven-thirty before Ash came back. Greta had

begun to be concerned, because usually his meetings went for one hour. Galen and Chase had disappeared upstairs, and Greta had decided to relax on the couch with some music while she waited. She wasn't entirely relaxed though, and the later it got, the more un-relaxed she became.

When the doorbell rang, she jumped up to answer it. Ash stood on the porch, his hands tucked into his jacket pockets.

"I see your car is back," he said.

"Is it?" She looked out to the driveway, frowning slightly as she said, "I wonder why Dan didn't come to the door and let me know."

"Maybe you were in the kitchen when he came."

Greta shook her head.

"I've been relaxing in the living room. Chase finished his report and went upstairs with Galen."

"I like your music," he commented.

Greta suddenly realized she hadn't asked him to come in. A cold wind blew and she shivered involuntarily.

"Come on in," she said as she moved aside. "You must be cold. I'll get Chase."

Ash stepped into the house and closed the door.

"He won't mind waiting a couple more minutes," Ash said as she started up the stairs. "Unless you really don't want to talk to me."

Greta turned around.

"I always want to talk to you. But your meeting ran late, and..."

Ash laughed gently. Greta remained where she was on the bottom step as he came towards her. When he stopped in front of her, she realized that he was still a bit taller than she was. Ash looked at her for a moment, then said, "The first time I saw you, I thought your eyes reminded me of Tucson's, very soft."

Greta felt herself tremble a little.

"Later I considered you a very feisty little creature." She smiled slightly and he continued.

"Tonight I called you stubborn."

"Yes, you did," she agreed with a nod.

Ash smiled, leaning forward to kiss her lightly. Greta trembled even more.

"Are you going to invite me into your living room to sit and talk?"

"Are you going to let me off this step?"

Ash stepped aside, chuckling softly. Greta felt a bit weak as she went into the living room ahead of him. When she sat in a chair, she saw Ash smile.

"Not going to take any chances?" he asked jokingly.

"What do you mean?"

He looked pointedly at the couch as he sat down in the other chair. Greta blushed as she laughed.

"I see you aren't either."

"I know better than to put myself in questionable situations," he replied, shaking his head.

They were both silent for a moment. Greta thought he looked rather tired, and she spotted a smudge of something on his chin.

"Were you and Bob unable to have any more children?" he suddenly asked, surprising her. "Or were you content with just Galen?"

"Are you going to answer the same question for me?" she countered, not sure she was ready to share her story.

Ash laughed.

"I could sit here and say, 'I asked you first', but I won't," he said. "Margaret had a hard time giving birth to

Chase. She didn't want another child. She went and had her tubes tied without ever talking to me about it."

Greta saw his pain, but it disappeared quickly as he said, "Your turn." She closed her eyes for a moment, her own pain making her wish that this job was already over and done with.

"Bob and I were in a car accident when Galen was a little over two," she said, opening her eyes to look at him again. "Fortunately he was not in the car with us. I had to have emergency surgery once they got me out of the car. When I woke up the doctor informed me that I could never bear any more children. I was four months pregnant at the time, but the child didn't survive the accident."

Ash bowed his head for a moment. When he looked at her again, Greta saw a muscle in his cheek twitch slightly.

"I'm sorry. I shouldn't have asked."

"The only way you learn things is by asking." she replied. "I could have changed the subject if I didn't want you to know."

"Yes, you could have." He studied her for a moment, then said, "So, you grew up on a horse ranch, and you married a man in the service. Anything else I should know about you?"

"Are you asking if I have any secrets?" she said with a smile.

"Yes."

"If they're secrets, I shouldn't tell them to you."

Ash laughed.

"Ok, I can live with that," he said, glancing towards the stereo system in the corner as her tape clicked off. "Do you always listen to Christian music?"

"Most of the time," she said, getting up to slide in

another tape. "As long as we're playing twenty questions, I have one for you."

"Go for it."

She turned the new tape on and sat down again before asking, "Was it just for Chase that you came to our church?"

"It's an Assembly of God church," he replied. "If I was going to go anywhere, I was going to stick with my grandfather's beliefs. He was a vibrant speaker, and knew the Bible inside and out. He could recite a lot of it by memory, and said there was an answer for every question in it." He paused, then added, "But, no. It wasn't just for Chase. I stayed up for hours the night before wrestling with a few of my demons. I knew I had to go back to the church. Make my peace with God and start doing what I know to be right."

Greta nodded silently, glad that he could be so open about his thoughts and feelings.

They talked for a few more minutes, then she called the boys downstairs so Ash and Chase could get home. Not that she really wanted them to go, but she could see how tired Ash was.

On the way home, Chase expressed a wish to have Greta and Galen visit them again. Ash suggested have Peggy and Jimmy come as well, but Chase didn't seem to care for that idea and Ash had the feeling the boy was trying to find a way to leave him alone with Greta. That provoked a serious conversation that lasted the rest of the way home. As they drove up the farm lane, Chase told him that Jimmy liked one of the girls in his class and wanted to take her to the movies.

"Galen told him that he probably shouldn't do that,"

Chase went on. "He said his mom told him that he should think very carefully before choosing to date any girl. Is that what you're saying too?"

"Pretty much," Ash stated, nodding his head.

"Dad," Chase said rather hesitantly. "Mrs. Jorgenson said I shouldn't repeat personal information that I hear in conversations. Did I just do that?"

"Not entirely, Chase. If Jimmy had taken the girl out, and told you and Galen all about the date, then it would be gossip if you passed it along to me. In this case you were sharing someone's good opinion about a topic we were discussing."

"I'm glad I didn't do anything wrong. I like Mrs. Jorgenson and I wouldn't want her to be hurt by something I do."

"I feel the same way, Chase," Ash said as he parked the pickup. "Which is why I'm not entirely sure we should have her out to the farm without Mrs. Edwards, or someone else."

Once in the house, Chase had another question.

"Dad, you know an awful lot about the Bible, don't you?"

"When I was your age," Ash said, guiding Chase to the couch and taking a seat, "I had a very special grandfather, Chase. He was a pastor of a church in the town where I grew up. He taught me a lot about the Bible, and encouraged me to trust what it said. Through him I learned to trust and obey God too."

"Then how come we didn't go to church?"

"Because I was running away from God all during the time I was married to your mom. After your Uncle Grant was killed, and your grandmother died, I left home. I tried to shut God out. I never totally succeeded. That's why I was still reading my Bible."

"Have you quit running now?" Chase asked very seriously.

"Do you remember when I went up to the altar a couple weeks ago?"

"Yes," the boy answered slowly.

"I rededicated my life to Christ that morning," Ash told him. "I asked God to forgive me for running away, and for my anger. I told him that I wanted Him to be the Lord of my life again, and to show me how he wants me to live." He laid his hand on Chase's shoulder as he continued. "When I was a teenager, Chase, I decided to become a pastor, like my grandfather. I don't know if God still wants me to do that, but we need to be ready if he does."

Chase's eyes widened.

"Do pastors live on farms?"

"Pastors live wherever God puts them, Chase."

"Do pastors get married?"

Ash grinned.

"If God wants them to."

Chase looked thoughtful, and Ash wondered just what was going through his mind. He didn't have to wait long to find out.

"How old do you have to be to give your life to God?"

"However old you are at the moment you realize that you're a sinner and you need a Savior to redeem you, that's exactly the right age to do it."

"Would I have to go to the altar at church like you did?" Chase asked.

"Anywhere you are, God is. I went to the altar because I wanted to rededicate my life to God in a public way. I had already made my peace with him right here at home, the night before we first went to church."

"I want to give my life to God too, Dad. I think I really need him around."

Ash took the boy's small hands in his own large ones and closed his eyes as Chase began talking to God about his need.

Chapter 15

Her car was running perfectly when she drove to work Thursday morning. Greta called Dan at his shop from her office and thanked him for doing the work so quickly. He was silent for so long that she thought she might have lost the connection.

"Uh...gee, Greta, I...um...I didn't actually fix your car," he finally said.

"What do you mean? It works perfectly."

"Oh, it's fixed alright," he replied. "It just wasn't me that fixed it."

Greta was confused by his words. She knew that Dan didn't have anyone working for him, though he had thought seriously of hiring someone lately.

"I still don't understand," she said. "How did my car get fixed?"

"Well..." he said hesitantly, then she heard him sigh. "Ash fixed your car, Greta."

"Ash? But he was at a meeting!"

"Uh...He skipped his meeting, and I probably shouldn't have said anything since he obviously didn't."

"Well, I'm glad you did," Greta told him. "Do I owe you for parts or anything."

"Ash took care of that," Dan said reluctantly, then rushed on. "He went over your car with a fine-toothed comb too, and you shouldn't have any more problems for a long time."

Greta was glad she was sitting down. The immensity of what Ash had done amazed her.

Before they hung up, Dan told her that Ash was a jack-of-all-trades who could fix all sorts of machinery and do carpentry and work a farm like an expert. By the end of the call, she was laughing with him over the fact that Ash had sat in her house for close to half an hour without saying a word.

On the way to church Sunday morning, Ash decided that he was ready to take a step forward in his relationship with Greta Jorgenson. When Chase began to turn into the row of chairs behind her, Ash stopped him and pointed to the empty seat beside Greta. Chase eagerly entered her row and sat down beside Greta, launching into a conversation before she could even offer a good morning.

"Mrs. Moore collected our reports Friday," he told her. "She said she would tell us our marks tomorrow."

"I'll be waiting to hear what you got then," Greta replied.

"I learned a lot while working on it," Chase admitted. "I always thought horses were just horses."

"That's why Mrs. Moore has you write those reports," Greta told him. "It gives you a chance to learn new things."

"Lots of the kids don't like them. Tommy Nichols was a bit jealous cause I have you to help me. He says his parents make him do his reports all by himself."

"Do you think I should help him too?" she asked, a smile lighting up her face.

"He could sure use help!" Chase exclaimed, smiling up at her. "Now that he's not teasing me, we've gotten to be pretty good friends. He brought his model airplane to school to show it to me. He said he made a couple mistakes while putting it together, but it still looks real nice. Dad said maybe I could get a kit and put it together."

Greta looked over at Ash and he thought again of how soft her eyes seemed to him. He wanted to reach out to touch her face. Instead, he just smiled back at her.

The service started then, and Chase leaned against him. Ash slid his arm across the back of the boy's chair. He could feel the warmth from Greta on his hand. Carefully he turned his attention to the front of the church.

After the service ended, and the boys headed for the foyer, Greta turned to Ash as she said, "I need to thank you."

"For what?"

"My car," she stated firmly. "Dan said you were the one who actually fixed it. You shouldn't have skipped your meeting to do that."

"There will always be other meetings," he replied easily.

"You didn't have to do it though."

"No," he said, with a slight shake of his head, "but I

wanted to."

Greta nodded. She felt a little overwhelmed by his kindness, but also pleased.

"Chase is worried that we won't see much of you now that his report is done," Ash said, changing the subject. "He's hoping Mrs. Moore will assign another one right away."

Greta laughed. Then she told Ash that Chase was welcome to come just for the fun of it, especially on a Saturday.

"Or when you have another meeting," she added.

"I'll remember that," he replied, turning to look towards the back of the sanctuary.

Greta took the moment to drink in her fill of him, admiring his strong features and the dark, curly hair that brushed the collar of his shirt. She found herself wondering how it would feel under her fingers. Then Ash turned back and caught her watching him. Greta looked away quickly, but she was sure the color of her face was enough to give her thoughts away.

"I get the feeling that you have already made up your mind about me, Mrs. Jorgenson," Ash said quietly, his fingers touching her hair.

"What makes you think that?" she asked, looking at him again.

"I don't think you're the sort of woman who would initiate a kiss without having a commitment to back it up with," he replied. "I've been doing a lot of thinking this week about that kiss."

"And...?" she said, not daring to think that he was saying he wanted more from her.

"Sooner or later I'm going to ask you to marry me," he said. "I have no choice."

"No choice?" Greta exclaimed, her heart galloping. "That makes it sound like a hardship of some sort."

Ash chuckled, shaking his head.

"Not a hardship at all," he said. "But I think that I haven't had any choice in this since the day I walked into that drug store to check you out. Only God could have put you in my path and given me such a strong attraction."

Greta wanted to reach out and touch him, but she restrained herself. Although he had chosen to sit with her during church, and the fact that he had stated his future intentions, she had the feeling that he still had some thinking to do.

"I think I feel the same way," she admitted. "Shortly after I began tutoring Chase, Galen asked me if I ever thought about getting married. I told him that God would have to send down lightning or something to identify the man for me. The day you and I took that walk, it happened."

"I don't remember any lightning that day," he commented with a smile.

"No, but when you told me that you needed me to be part of your life, the ground under me moved."

Ash was silent. Greta picked up her Bible, shifting in her chair in readiness to stand up. Then she said, "I did my best to ignore God, telling myself that you were in no shape to take on a wife. The day we all came to the farm I could no longer ignore his nudging though. You were so nervous that day, and I had such a very strong feeling that I was supposed to kiss you that I couldn't stop myself."

Ash smiled, nodding his head. He stood up, holding out a hand to help her up.

"I still think you're one feisty little creature," he commented once she was standing beside him.

Greta's legs threatened to buckle under her at the caressing tone in his voice, but she forced herself to turn and make her way out of their row.

Monday morning the big bell began ringing while Ash was mucking Tucson's stall. When he answered the phone, Dan's voice filled his ear.

"What are you and Chase doing for Thanksgiving Thursday?"

Ash wiped the sweat off his forehead with his sleeve.

"Haven't thought about it," he admitted.

"Good. Peggy said to invite you over. We'll eat around one, but you're welcome to come whenever the chores get done."

"Don't think Peggy would really appreciate if I come straight from chores," Ash said with a chuckle. "Could we possibly wash up a bit first?"

Dan laughed.

"I think some of Greta's wit is rubbing off on you, Ash," he said. "And yes, we're inviting her and Galen as well. Sorry, old friend, but I can't exactly stop my wife's matchmaking efforts."

Ash chuckled.

"Don't think they're needed," he jested. "I wouldn't come if she wasn't."

Dan's laughter rang out and Ash felt pleased with himself for admitting that he wanted to spend Thanksgiving with Greta. He told Dan that he and Chase would aim for ten that morning, and they ended the call. Ash went back to his work, but as he tossed wet smelly straw into the wheelbarrow, he wondered if Greta was ready for his sort of life. Knowing that she had grown up on a horse ranch made him feel better about things, but she'd been away from smelly barns and hard physical labor for a long time. Margaret had never really gotten used to farm life. That was why he had always humored her when she wanted things like stone walkways and trips to the city. Margaret like the busy-ness of Boston, with its shops and museums. She had never complained though. That was one of the things he had loved about her.

Greta's face popped into his mind, and he rested his hands on the handle of the pitchfork for a moment. Without meaning to, he thought about the day he had kissed her.

She had been so insistent on knowing why he had asked for another tutor. She had said she wasn't going to leave without an explanation. Ash had suddenly wanted to shake her composure, to expose her to some of what he was feeling. Before he knew it, he had pulled her against him and was kissing her. Rather violently kissing her.

Ash tried to stop his thoughts, but his entire body fought against him. He could feel her slight form against him, and smell the scent of her perfume. He wanted to laugh, knowing he was standing in a smelly barn, ankle deep in straw that had been under Tucson's feet all night.

Suddenly, Ash knew the momentary response in her. The tiny shift in her posture that brought her closer to him. And with that realization came the knowledge that that was what had made him thrust her away. And he had done it so quickly that Greta nearly fell. He'd had to steady her. All he wanted to do was to get away from her, yet he took the time to steady her so she wouldn't fall.

With a groan, Ash carefully leaned the pitchfork

against the side of the stall and walked out of the barn.
He strode across the yard and entered the house through
the mudroom, yanking off his smelly boots as he went.
He took the stairs two at a time and walked into his
bedroom, the room he had shared with Margaret. He
pulled the box of pictures out from under the bed and
opened it, quickly finding his favorite picture of her.
Then he dropped to his knees and began praying,
earnestly seeking God's touch, God's wisdom, and God's
peace.

"Ok., ladies," Peggy said, pulling them all from their
conversations, "Tonight we get to talk about rich people."
She grinned as she added, "And just because none of us
are rich, it doesn't mean that James 5:1-6 isn't speaking to
us also."

"It isn't just that these people are rich," said Ann, who
was sitting next to Greta on the couch. "It's that they're
selfishly rich. Look at verse four where it says they have
cheated their workers."

Vetta and Karen nodded their heads.

"Verse five talks about how they had been satisfying
their every whim," Karen said. "I think we can be rich
and use our riches for God instead of ourselves."

"Right," Alexi said. "There's that verse elsewhere that
people sort of mix up at times. They say that money is
the root of all evil. What the Bible actually says is that
the *love* of money is the root of all evil."

"My parents were pretty well off," Greta said quietly,
"but they never flaunted it. I don't know how much they
gave to the church, but I do know they always tithed.
And their workers were well taken care of. I can
remember how all the workers came to the main house for

Thanksgiving and Christmas dinner."

Vetta was staring at her.

"I never knew you came from that sort of background, Greta," she said in amazement. "You are definitely not like the rich kids I used to know."

Greta smiled.

"Believe me, I've known some of the other type," she told them. "Some of the girls I went to school with didn't care too much for some my friends. I never limited myself where friendship was concerned the way they did."

"You still don't, Greta Jorgenson," Karen said with a laugh.

Ann and Alexi both giggled slightly. Greta looked around the room, wondering what was going on. Peggy grimaced.

"I didn't say anything, Greta," she promised, causing Greta to be prepared for what came next.

"You are a sly one, Greta," Ann said, reaching over to pat her hand, "but it's getting sort of obvious that Ash Lancaster has an interest in you."

"You could have knocked me over with a feather when he actually sat with you in church Sunday!" exclaimed Alexi.

Greta blushed.

"I tutor his son, Chase," she said hastily. "We've become friends."

"Are you telling us that's as far as it goes?" asked Karen.

Greta sighed, glancing at Peggy. Then she said, "Ash has had a very hard time with his wife's death. I don't mind if you all want to tease me about this, but I'd appreciate it if you keep it to that. I really wouldn't want our lives to become a part of town gossip. I will admit to all of you that there is an attraction between us, and that we're having Thanksgiving dinner here with Peggy's family. But that's all."

"And what does God say about it?" Peggy asked curiously.

Greta grinned at her.

"James 4:10," she said, making them flip through their Bibles to that page.

Ann began laughing.

"You always bring everything back into perspective, Greta," she said, getting up to give Greta a quick hug. "Always pointing to God."

Chapter 16

Greta let the dishwater drain out of the sink, then dried her hands and reached for the photograph on the windowsill. She ran a finger over Bob's face, whispering, "Life changes so quickly here where I am, Bob. Ash is a good man. I wouldn't consider any other sort, of course. He'll be good for Galen too, I'm sure."

She moved to the table and sat down, pressed the photograph to her chest and closed her eyes.

"Lord, I commit my life to you," she said. "I will follow where you lead. I will accept what you want for me."

She stayed where she was for several minutes, allowing the silence to surround her. Then she replaced the photograph on the windowsill and turned to leave the room. Galen was standing in the doorway.

"Is everything ok, Mom?" he asked, looking a bit worried.

Greta smiled.

"Everything is ok, Galen."

"You always look at Dad's picture when you're worried, or sad, or you feel like life is crashing around your ears. Are you sure things are fine?"

Greta laughed, crossing the room to give him a quick hug. As she did, she realized that in the last two months he had gained another inch in height.

"Let's go sit in the living room together," she said as she turned him around. "We can talk about tomorrow."

"It's going to be different having Thanksgiving dinner at Jimmy's," he said as they went to sit on the couch. "Real turkey, and lots of people."

"Real turkey?" she repeated curiously. "We've always had real turkey."

"Not a whole turkey, Mom. Last year we had frozen turkey dinners. The year before we had deli turkey."

Greta sighed, knowing just how right he was. She hadn't really felt like cooking a Thanksgiving meal, nor like going out to a restaurant.

"So how come you were looking at Dad's picture?" Galen asked.

"I was just...well...just trying to catch up with myself, I guess," she mused. "Things seem to be changing so fast around here. You're growing up, and..."

"And Mr. Lancaster is getting closer?" Galen said, finishing her thought.

Greta smiled, reaching to give his knee a pat.

"I could live at the farm," Galen said, "if that's what you're sort of trying to ask. I'd miss being so close to Jimmy, of course, but he likes going out there already."

"And who says we're moving to the farm?" she asked, trying hard to keep from laughing.

Galen grinned as he said, "Mr. Lancaster sat with you

in church, Mom. Everybody knows that means it's getting serious."

She laughed, relieved that he was so accepting of what was happening.

"Ok," she said, nodding her head. "He hasn't officially asked, but he has spoken of marriage. In some ways I feel like things are happening too fast, but I feel that God is behind it all. God brought us together, and he's working it out on his own timetable."

"And you want to marry him?" Galen asked.

"I do," she replied. "It feels right."

"So how come...?" he said, waving a hand in the direction of the kitchen.

"Your father and I shared a lot of years together," she explained. "A lot of joys, a lot of tears. But those memories can't come between Ash and I. Can you understand that?"

"You were sort of saying goodbye?"

"You scare me sometimes," Greta said, her eyes widening. "Too wise for your age."

"You're the one who helped me be this way," he replied with a grin. "You and Dad both. If God wanted us to move to China as missionaries, I'd be ready, I think."

Greta slid across the space between them to give him a hug, telling him that she was very thankful that he was so grown up.

"You do realize that not all families do so well after a death, right?"

"Like Chase and his dad? Yeah, I know, Mom."

She patted his leg again, then stood up.

"I have to get up early to make sweet potatoes and an apple pie," she said. "Want to help?"

"Yeah!" he exclaimed. "Your apple pie is the best."

"I'll wake you then. And right now, I'm going to listen to some music, I think. I need to unwind before bed. Sure am glad I do not have to work tomorrow."

She was headed for the stereo when Galen said, "Hey, maybe you won't have to work once you're married. I'd like that. I miss having you here when I get home from school."

Greta turned to look at him, wondering why she hadn't even considered that side of things.

Ash smiled as he looked across the table at Chase. The boy was still half asleep, but he'd been so eager for the day to begin that he'd set his own alarm clock to go off shortly after Ash's. Ash had come in from his early chores to find the boy sleeping at the kitchen table, which Chase had set for breakfast.

As Chase emptied his bowl, Ash leaned back in his chair.

"Do you remember telling me to keep Mrs. Jorgenson in mind when I was ready to remarry?" he asked.

Chase looked up with a grin, suddenly waking up a bit more.

"You're ready?"

"Thought I'd ask her today."

Chase leaped out of his chair so quickly that it fell over backwards. The boy was too excited to pick it up, and he threw himself on Ash.

"That's great, Dad! That's the best news ever! That's even better than the B+ on my report!"

Ash chuckled.

"I guess that means you approve."

Chase leaned back a little to look him in the face.

"You knew I would, Dad," he said, trying to act as if he were frowning. "I like Mrs. Jorgenson. And it'll be neat having Galen for a brother." He paused, then asked, rather thoughtfully, "Would I still have to call her Mrs. Jorgenson? I mean she wouldn't be Mrs. Jorgenson anymore. She'd be Mrs. Lancaster."

"I think maybe you could call her Greta, unless you want to call her Mom."

Chase shook his head, getting up to go back and pick up his chair.

"I don't think I could do that," he replied seriously as he set the chair upright. "Greta will be fine."

"Not until I've asked her to marry me though," Ash reminded him quickly. "You're going to have to keep this a secret until I've had a chance to ask her."

"How will I know when you've asked her?"

"I hope to have a moment alone with her before dinner," Ash admitted, making a face at the thought of how many people would be around. "If I manage that, perhaps we could announce it during the meal."

"Galen and I will help. We've already left you two alone lots."

"So I noticed," Ash said with a slight laugh.

Chase grinned at him, but then a slight frown creased his forehead.

"What if she says no?"

Ash smiled at the boy's worried expression.

"I already know she won't say no," he said in a confidential whisper, then winked at Chase before adding, "We discussed it Sunday."

"Why didn't you just ask her then?" Chase wanted to know.

"I'm afraid I wasn't quite ready then to ask her," Ash

admitted honestly.

"But you are now?"

Ash nodded.

"I have one last thing to do, though, with your help."

"What's that?"

"After breakfast, would you get your book? I need to read the story in it about Uncle Grant and I. Perhaps you could read it with me?"

Chase's face lit up.

"Yeah!" he exclaimed, then suddenly looked very thoughtful. "Dad, do you still smell things around here? You know, like bread and chocolate chip cookies?"

Ash shook his head.

"Not since I rededicated my life to God, Chase."

"Do you still think it was God? That he was trying to get our attention?"

Ash nodded.

"Are you ever going to tell Mrs...I...I mean Greta, about them?"

"Now that's a good question," Ash said. "Maybe I will...someday. Go get your book. I'll meet you in the living room."

Chase left the room and Ash glanced around it, suddenly grateful that it was different now. This would be Greta's kitchen, not Margaret's. He certainly didn't want Greta to be uncomfortable in it, which made him decide to not tell her about the smells and sounds issuing from it for the past year.

He heard Chase's footsteps coming back down the stairway. Though his heart quaked at the thought of reading that book, he headed for the living room, eager to do what he had not dared to do before.

Greta didn't see Ash's pickup when she parked her Chevy in front of Peggy's house. It was a little after ten, which was the time Peggy had said Ash was aiming for, so Greta figured he'd arrive at any time.

Peggy opened her door before they even had time to knock, and she took the pie out of Galen's hands as she told him that Jimmy was in his room. Galen headed up the stairs.

"This pie smells delicious," she said as she led Greta to the kitchen. "And I bet you did the sweet potatoes with marshmallows? I love it that way."

"So does Galen," Greta said, setting her burden onto the counter. "They're going to need to be warmed up a bit before we eat."

"I'll slip them into the oven after the turkey comes out," Peggy told her.

They went back out to the living room and Peggy supplied the information that Dan was outside trying to clean up the last of the leaves in the backyard.

"Jimmy and I did most of it yesterday," she said. "Dan decided to get some exercise by finishing the job."

Greta slipped off her jacket and sat down in a chair, laying the jacket across her knees. She forced herself to listen to Peggy, to even respond, but every inch of her being was waiting for Ash to arrive.

"This will be a very different Thanksgiving for us," Peggy explained. "We used to go to Dan's childhood home every year and have Thanksgiving with his parents and two brothers. Their families too, of course. Last year we stayed home. Dan was sick, and Margaret had her accident at the end of September. I think Dan would have stayed home even if he'd been well, just to support Ash. Not that Ash was open to support."

"And this year?" Greta asked. "Dan didn't want to go home?"

"His mother wasn't up to doing a big family thing this year," Peggy said. "She hasn't been too well this year. Dan went out to see her in August. They live in the western part of the state. Small town, like this one."

Greta heard the pickup outside and relaxed, earning herself a laugh from Peggy.

"I take it Ash just arrived?" she asked.

Greta blushed, nodding her head.

"Am I that obvious?"

"Well, you've been all nerves since you walked in," Peggy said, getting up to go let Ash and Chase in.

Greta groaned as she got to her feet also. She didn't want to seem so eager to see Ash. He hadn't called her all week and Greta wasn't sure how today was going to go. All she did know was that she longed to see him.

Chase came in first, glancing quickly at her, then looking around.

"The boys are upstairs, Chase," Peggy said. "You can go ahead up."

He raced up the stairs and disappeared, and Greta finally turned to look at Ash. He was busy taking off his jacket and saying hello to Peggy, and Greta took a moment to study him. She had the impression that he was very relaxed, more relaxed than she'd ever seen him before.

"Chase has been very eager for today to arrive," he was saying to Peggy. "We didn't actually have Thanksgiving last year, so being with everyone this year is extra special."

He turned to Greta, gave her a warm smile, then reached out to take her jacket. As he hung it up beside his he kidded Peggy about the number of hooks she had, reminding her of what she'd done the last time they were both there. Peggy had the grace to blush.

"Dan is out back," Peggy told him. "You're welcome to join him, if..."

"Hey, Mom!" Jimmy shouted as he and the other two boys came bounding down the stairway. "You gotta see this! Come on!"

He grabbed her arm, turning her toward the living room as Galen and Chase followed. Greta would have gone too, but Ash held her back.

"I wondered how they'd manage it," he said with a chuckle, "but the resourcefulness of our boys is well known."

Greta looked at him quizzically and he pulled her closer to him.

"Not sure how long I'm going to have here, so I'm going to make it quick," he said, gathering her into his arms.

When she realized his intention, Greta slid her arms up over his shoulders and buried her fingers in his dark hair. His kiss sent little spikes of electricity through her, but it didn't last at all long enough. She had no more than started to respond when he set her away from him, grinning at her unsteadiness.

"You responded to me that other time too," he said, keeping his hands on her shoulders. "That was why I shoved you away. I had expected a slap across the face, not an invitation."

Greta nodded slowly. She wasn't sure what to say, but Ash didn't give her any time for a reply anyway.

"How soon can we get married?" he asked, smiling down at her.

"Are you asking me to marry you?" she said, tipping her head to one side. "Or are you telling me that I'm going to?"

"Both," he said immediately.

Greta pretended to consider her options, stretching the moment out. Ash's smile grew.

"Maybe if I could have one more kiss it would help with my decision," she finally said, rather mischievously.

"You're a tease," he told her, but he pulled her against him again.

Greta felt the world spin around as he kissed her, this time a bit longer. When he finally set her away from him she was breathless.

"I think I'd better marry you quickly," she said a bit shakily. "Those kisses are a bit too heady for me. I'll be in big trouble if we wait very long."

Ash laughed, pulling her close once more, but this time he didn't kiss her. Instead he just wrapped his arms around her and held her.

"I read the article in Chase's book this morning," he said, his voice drifting down to her from above her head. "And yesterday I took a trip to the cemetery. Took flowers to Margaret's grave and said goodbye."

"I said goodbye to Bob last night," Greta confessed. "Galen caught me at it."

"So maybe he wasn't too surprised when Chase wanted his help in providing me with some uninterrupted moments with you this morning? That was the only concern in our plan. I was afraid you might not have said anything to him."

"You mean that was at your instigation?" she asked, leaning back to look up at him.

Ash grinned as he nodded.

"I told Chase he could announce our plans at dinner," he said. "I hope that's ok with you."

"I think that would be fine," she replied with a smile, anticipating Peggy's reaction to the news.

They heard the back door bang and Ash stepped away from her. By the time Peggy came into the living room, they were there also.

"I don't know about those boys," she said as she tugged off her jacket. "They were all excited over some weird bird in our backyard. When we got out there, nothing. Course, how could there be with Dan still working out there?" She went to the hallway and hung up her jacket, then came back to them. "You could have made yourselves comfortable," she commented. "Grab a chair. I'm going to check on our turkey. It smells heavenly."

When it came time to eat, they were packed in like sardines around the kitchen table, with no room between them. Ash found himself pressed close to Greta, with Chase on his other side. Greta giggled as she slid her napkin onto her lap.

"I sure hope no one is left handed or we aren't going to be able to eat like this," she said. "This is snug!"

Peggy laughed.

"It's cozy this way, I think," she said as she glanced around at them all. Then, looking at Dan, she asked, "Shall we stick to our tradition?"

"I think so," Dan said, glancing around also as he explained. "Before our meal each year, my family goes around the table and we all say what we're thankful for. I'll start by telling you that I'm thankful for old friendships renewed and new friendships formed."

"I'm thankful for God's presence in our lives," said Peggy who was next to him.

Chase was next. Ash saw him think for a moment, then the boy looked up at him with a question in his eyes. Ash nodded, and a slow smile spread across Chase's face. He leaned forward to look at Greta, then he looked around the whole table.

"I'm thankful that Greta and my dad are going to get married," he said proudly.

Galen and Jimmy both gave a glad shout and slapped hands with each other in a high five. Peggy squealed in delight, jumping up to run around the table to hug them both. Dan sat there staring at Ash for a moment, then said, "All right!" As Peggy went back to her seat, Ash slid his arm around Greta.

"Sorry about your wild goose chase this morning, Peggy," he said. "I'm afraid it was my fault."

"What do you mean?" she asked, jiggling her chair to get it back into place.

"Well, the boys have been so good at thinking up ways to get Greta and I alone, I figured they could come up with something to keep you and Dan out of the house long enough for me to ask the question."

"You mean...?" She looked around at the three boys, then laughed. "There was no weird bird! I should have suspected something when the two of you didn't come out. I never even thought about it."

Dan gave her a hug, then he told Ash it was his turn to share what he was thankful for. Ash looked at Greta beside him, a warm tender feeling welling up inside him.

"I'm thankful for feisty little creatures that won't go away," he said softly.

"And I'm thankful for sidewalks that move, and for an

awesome God who always knows what's best for us," Greta said, smiling at him.

"Sidewalks that move?" Peggy asked curiously.

"Guess he didn't use lightning," Galen joked. "He probably figured that might fry her anyway."

Ash grinned as Peggy look hopelessly from Greta to Galen. He knew that she would grill his bride-to-be about it later. He smiled at Greta, then looked beyond her at Galen.

"Your turn," he said.

"I'm thankful for Chase needing tutoring," Galen told them, "and for my gift of words, and for strong men to be my role models." He looked at Ash as he added, "Do I have to call you Mr. Lancaster still? I noticed Chase called my mom Greta."

Ash smiled at him.

"Either Ash or Dad would be fine. Whichever you feel the most comfortable with."

Galen nodded, then reached out his hand toward Ash. Ash took it, giving Galen a firm handshake as the boy said "I'd like to call you Ash for now, sir."

Ash nodded in agreement, then glanced at Jimmy.

"You're last, I believe."

"I'm thankful for both my mom and dad, of course," Jimmy said. "But I'm really thankful to have Galen and Chase for my best friends. Even though Chase is younger than me, he's a role model for me too."

Both Peggy and Greta were obviously moved by his words. Ash gave Greta a slight squeeze of encouragement. Then he bowed his head as Dan spoke a blessing over their meal.

After dinner they played kickball in the back yard.

Greta was a little unsure of what to expect from Ash, but he joined into the game with gusto, kicking the ball with a good bit of precision, and cheering Chase on around the bases even though he was on the other team.

The game ended when Peggy and Greta pleaded exhaustion, falling onto the ground in the middle of the playing field. Ash came over and dropped down beside her as Greta sat there catching her breath. He stretched himself out full length in the grass and heaved a sigh of relief.

"Don't know when I last did something like that," he said, closing his eyes. "I think I'm too old for it too."

Greta looked down at him, suddenly realizing that she had no idea just how old he actually was.

"How old are you?" she asked, the question escaping before she could stop it.

"I thought we adults weren't supposed to divulge our age," Ash said without opening his eyes.

"That's only for women," Peggy chimed in.

Chase dropped onto the grass beside his father.

"What does 'divulge' mean?"

"Means 'tell', son," said Ash with a smile. He opened his eyes to look at Chase. "Women don't like people to know how old they are after they reach a certain point in their life."

Chase looked over at Greta.

"Have you reached that point?"

Greta laughed, reaching across Ash to give Chase a playful punch on the shoulder.

"I couldn't care less if the whole world knows I'm thirty-seven, Chase," she told him. "I'm proud of my age, though I have to admit that I used to consider anything over thirty ancient."

"Funny how that works," said Peggy. "When I turned thirty I thought I was over the hill, because everyone said that. But at thirty-eight I don't feel I could possibly be headed down the other side yet."

Ash looked towards Dan, sitting next to Peggy.

"How about you, Dan? Do you feel like an old man yet?"

"Don't think so. I'm the same age as Peggy, so if she's not heading down the other side, then neither am I."

Ash grunted.

"You're just a bunch of spring chickens," he said quietly, closing his eyes again.

"What's a 'spring chicken'?" asked Jimmy.

Galen laughed.

"Means he must be the oldest one here."

Greta giggled as Ash sat up to give Galen a meaningful look.

"I got a nice barn for you to sleep in," he said threateningly. "Bit smelly, but the straw is clean."

Chase roared with laughter, rolling on the ground. Galen smiled.

"I guess that means you sort of like me. I don't think you would have teased me like that a month ago."

Ash laughed.

"A month ago I probably would have knocked your head off for a remark like that," he admitted. "Though usually my anger goes into some stupid project."

Everyone laughed at that one and Greta was thrilled by the sound of it. It was very obvious by his casual jesting that Ash had completely come to terms with the past, and with Margaret's death. She silently thanked God for the healing that had occured in him.

Dan got to his feet, reaching out a hand to help Peggy

up also.

"I don't know about the rest of you," he commented, "but I'm ready for some dessert."

Ash started to stand up, but Greta reached out a hand to stop him.

"Not so fast there, Mr. Lancaster," she said. "Thought you were going to get away with it, didn't you?"

"With what?" he asked, a puzzled look on his face.

"You're the only one who hasn't yet divulged their age," Greta told him, determined to find out now just how much older he was. "If the rest of us can do it, I think you should be able to also."

Ash grinned at her as the others laughed.

"Four times Chase," he said, then quickly moved out of her reach and stood up.

Greta smiled thoughtfully as she got to her feet.

"Forty is good," she said, nodded her head. "Nice and mature, without being too old." She paused, still nodding. "Yes, I think I like forty."

Ash looked at her rather suspiciously.

"What is this?" he said. "You aren't going to tease me about it?"

"Oh, no," she said, shaking her head and looking quite serious. "I want another one of those kisses before I go home today."

Peggy collapsed on the ground again, laughing. Dan slapped a hand over his mouth to smother his laughter, while all three boys stared at Ash, waiting to see what he would do.

The look in Ash's eyes made Greta melt inside. He stood very still in front of her, and she saw the muscle twitch in his cheek.

"I would gladly oblige right now," he said quietly, "but

I have more of an audience than I would like. So I think I'll use a bit of self-control, and go into the house for some dessert. I think I earned it after all the hard work I just got done doing."

He turned around and put one arm over Galen's shoulder. Catching Chase's hand with his free one, he headed for the house, motioning with his head for Jimmy to go too.

"Don't ever let a woman have the upper hand, you three," he said, loud enough for her to hear. "It's going to be difficult, but you always have to stay one step ahead of them."

The three boys were laughing as they disappeared into the house. Greta shook her head wordlessly as she watched them go.

After dessert, the boys went upstairs to Jimmy's room. The four adults sat around the living room talking. Ash deliberately took a chair, not trusting himself to sit on the couch with Greta. He smiled slightly as he saw Greta do the same, leaving the couch for Dan and Peggy.

Gradually the talk turned to church. After a brief conversation about the pastor's sermon the previous Sunday, Dan asked Ash if he had given any thought to his place in ministry. Ash considered the question for a moment, then he said, "To tell you the truth, Dan, I regret living with Margaret for twelve years and never once talking to her about Christ. I never once asked her to read the Bible with me, or to pray with me. I totally shut her out of that part of my life. That's going to take a while to digest."

"God has already forgiven you," Dan said quickly.

"I know that," Ash replied, nodding his head. "But

that doesn't help me to not remember my failure. I promised God when I was seventeen that I would live my life for Him, and spread His word to the best of my ability. In the end, I couldn't even spread it to my own wife." He leaned forward and rested his arms on his knees, giving Dan a very serious look. "I want to begin again to honor God with my life, Dan. I realize that I've started just by going up to the altar, but for me, it isn't enough. I had a passion for Him once that overshadowed all my other desires. Even flying didn't fulfill me as much as my love for God did. Flying was fun, but I always knew I was going to quit and go into the ministry because I was drawn to it. Everything in me went haywire as I watched Grant's plane spiral silently down out of the sky and my mother collapse. Now, because of Greta and Chase and Galen, I want that passion back. I don't know if God will call me into ministry this time around."

He stopped, turning to look at Greta. Her eyes glistened with unshed tears, but she smiled at him slightly. Ash was very sure that she understood exactly what he was talking about.

Greta slid into bed later with a deep sigh. It had been a very full day, and everything in her felt tired. Muscles that hadn't been used in a while ached a bit, and she almost regretted the kickball game after their Thanksgiving dinner.

As she lay there allowing her muscles to relax, Ash's words lingered in her mind.

"I had a passion for him once that overshadowed all my other desires."

"He would have been an excellent pastor, I think," she

said out loud.

She tried to imagine herself as a pastor's wife, but couldn't. Imagining that she was a farmer's wife was much easier, and she smiled as she pictured herself mucking out Tucson's stall and weeding in the vegetable garden.

But when she tried to imagine herself in Ash's house, a small thread of doubt wormed it's way into her thoughts. She laid there looking around her cozy room, the room she had shared with Bob, and wondered what Ash's bedroom was like.

'Does it face the dawn or the sunset? And how am I going to feel about sleeping in the bed he shared with Margaret.'

"I know he redecorated that room, but it was still their bedroom," she said quietly.

She was to see the entire house on Saturday. Ash and Chase were expecting her and Galen to arrive at lunchtime. Greta smiled as she thought of Chase's reaction to the plan. He had looked up at his father and said, "Without Mrs. Edwards or anyone else?" Ash had crouched down beside the boy and smiled at him. "Greta and I are to be married, Chase. That sort of changes what's acceptable behavior. It doesn't mean I can let down my guard about all those emotions yet, but it does mean that her honor will not be messed up by being in my house alone with us." Chase had nodded in understanding, as though the two of them had discussed the topic before.

"In the world as it is today, Ash is pretty amazing," Greta told herself as she lay there in her bed. "In fact, knowing his past, it's hard to believe he still thinks the way he does. God certainly protected him from all sorts of disastrous choices."

She pushed away her doubts about their sleeping arrangements, reaching for her Bible.

Chapter 17

Friday dragged by. Greta spent her time at the drug store fighting to stay focused on her work. She was glad that Peggy had invited Galen to spend the day with Jimmy. At least she didn't have to worry about him at home by himself all day. Galen's remark about her not having to work once she and Ash got married sounded better and better to her. Not that Ash had mentioned it yet. It was possible that he would need her to continue working. Adding two people to the household would add more expenses as well.

When they drove up the farm lane on Saturday, Greta was surprised to see Ash come out onto the front porch of the house.

"So they do use the front door at times," Galen said beside her, echoing her own thought.

The truck was parked across the lane ahead of her, so Greta slowed to a stop. Galen rolled his window down as Ash came over to the car.

"You can leave the car right here," he said, leaning down to smile at them through the window. "Today you use the front door."

Greta wondered why, but she didn't say anything as she turned the car off and opened her door to get out. Ash waited for her to walk around the car, then he took her hand and led her over to the front porch. After climbing the steps, he stopped in front of the open door.

"All set, Chase?" he called.

"Yeah. You can let them in."

His voice was rather faint, and Greta looked at Galen.

"Do you know what's going on?" she asked suspiciously.

"No," he said slowly. "I do know they're acting a little weird though."

Ash stepped aside and waved them in.

The front door opened into the living room. Greta had been in the room just once, but she thought it looked the same as it had then. Chase was nowhere to be seen.

"We decided you should see the upstairs first, Greta," Ash said. "You've already seen most of the downstairs anyway. This, of course, is the living room. It's the biggest room in the house, and hasn't been used all that much this past year. I expect you'll want some of your own furniture, so feel free to make whatever changes you want."

He led the way across the room to a door she hadn't noticed before. When he opened it, she found herself looking at a flight of stairs going up.

"The door is so the upper parts of the house can be closed off during the winter," Ash explained as she and Galen joined him. "Conserves heat. There is a bathroom upstairs, but we close the door to that in the winter time too. The bedrooms don't need to be as warm as the bathroom."

"Are they heated at all?" she inquired.

Ash nodded, then motioned for her to go up the stairs.

"Where is Chase?" she asked curiously, not really sure she wanted to go upstairs.

"Around," he said with a grin. "Are you going up?"

Greta reluctantly went up the stairs, with Galen following. Ash came last. At the top of the stairs was a hallway. From behind, Ash told her to go in the door to the right. As soon as she stepped in, Greta knew that this was Ash's bedroom, the room he had shared with Margaret. There was a double bed, with a nightstand on each side of it, and two dressers. The door to the closet stood open, and she saw his clothes hanging neatly inside. A small table stood in one corner. On it was a picture of Ash and Chase, with a woman standing beside them. All three were smiling into the camera.

Ash was directly behind her and Greta closed her eyes for a moment.

'This is not going to work,' she thought. 'I cannot sleep in the same bed he shared with Margaret. I just can't do it.'

Ash touched her arm.

"The room across the hall will be Galen's," he said.

She moved with them to the room across the hall, feeling somewhat trapped, but willing herself to not show any of the emotions that were within her. Ash tapped on a closed door and said it led up to the attic, then motioned them in through an open door beside it. This room was smaller than the master bedroom, and had bunk beds in it.

"Hey, neat," said Galen. "Maybe Jimmy can stay overnight sometimes. I'm going to miss not being able to go over there after school."

Greta groaned inwardly. Again, Ash touched her arm.

"The next room is Chase's," he said as he led them down the hallway.

This room was similar to Galen's and also had bunk beds in it.

"The bunk beds can be taken apart and used separately. When I built them I figured that Chase wouldn't always want bunks."

"You built both sets at the same time?" she asked without looking at him.

"At the time I thought we would have more kids," he said quietly. "I didn't know then what Margaret had done."

Greta silently made the decision to never tell him how she felt about sleeping in that other room. She was not going to hurt him by revealing her selfish feelings.

"One more room up here, plus the bathroom," he said.

They went back out into the hallway and Ash pointed to the closed door at the end, telling them that it was the bathroom.

"When we moved in all the fixtures were very old, and we had a lot of trouble with it. I finally just tore the whole thing out and had new pipes put in, and all new fixtures. You can peek in there in a minute."

He reached for the doorknob of the last room and opened it. Greta stepped into the room, stopping abruptly just across the threshold. Her hand flew to her mouth as she took in the double bed with Chase on top of it, holding a large sign that said, "This is your wedding gift. Love, Ash." She gasped in delight as she realized the spread, which was a mixture of browns and greens, had appaloosa horses running across it. Then, as it sunk in that this was their bedroom, tears began cascading from her eyes and she turned to bury her face in Ash's chest. His arms closed around her. Greta tried to stem the flow of tears, but it was like some big faucet had been turned on and got stuck. She felt movement around her and tried to step away, but Ash simply pulled her closer to himself.

Greta had no idea how long she cried. And when there were no tears left, she continued to stand there clutching his shirt and pressing her face into his chest.

"Not exactly the reaction I expected," he finally said above her, his voice rumbling in his chest as well. "I sent the boys downstairs."

"I'm sorry," she murmured.

He stepped back, forcing her to stand on her own, though he did keep his hands on her shoulders. Greta bowed her head and mumbled, "I must look a mess."

"A beautiful mess," he replied, lifting her chin with one hand and surveying her face. After a moment he reached behind him and produced a large hanky. "It's a clean one," he said, offering it to her. "I put it in my pocket an hour ago."

Greta smiled as she took it. She turned away from him and began wiping her face, glancing around the room as she did so. The bed had a nightstand on each side, and there were two dressers, one with a mirror. A small desk and chair sat in one corner. The room looked as if it was newly decorated and she was sure that Ash had done it before asking her to marry him.

"Morning sun comes in here," Ash commented behind her as she went to stand in front of the window. "Not that I'm still in bed when it comes up. I'm an early riser."

"Why did you do this?" she asked, turning to look at him.

Ash ran a hand through his hair, glanced at the bed, then looked at her again.

"I knew I would be uncomfortable sleeping in the bed that you shared with Bob," he explained. "I'm already asking you to live in the house that I shared with Margaret. How could I possibly ask you to sleep in the bed that I shared with her too? This room is ours, with no history to it."

Greta nodded.

"I was miserable when I stood in that other room," she admitted. "I'm sorry."

"Don't be," he said, moving to take her into his arms again. "Don't be sorry. I didn't dare look at you while we were in there for fear of what I'd see in your face. I wanted to only remember what I'd see in here."

"And I drenched your shirt," she said, picking at the wet place on the front of his shirt, laughing slightly.

"I have plenty of shirts. I have only one Greta."

She hugged him tightly.

"So...do you like it?" he whispered above her.

"I love it," she replied. "It's very special to me."

She felt his muscles relax at her words, and she smiled, her face pressed against the dampness that her tears had left behind.

When she and Ash walked into the kitchen a few minutes later, they found that the boys had been busy getting lunch onto the table. Greta went over to Chase and gave him a hug, then glanced at the shelf in front of the picture window. Four appaloosa horses stood there, all made of china and in different poses. One was obviously a stallion, one a mare, and two were foals.

"Now I know why you asked about my favorite

breed," she said, looking at Chase. She moved to where Galen was standing and gave him a hug also. He surveyed her face in exactly the same way Ash had upstairs.

"I haven't seen you cry like that since Dad died," he said quietly. "Are you ok?"

"I'm fine, Galen," Greta replied, giving him a second hug. "I think I've been so busy being strong for you that I haven't had time to cry. When I saw that room, it was just so...so special. Once started, I...I couldn't stop."

She felt Chase's arms go around her waist, then Ash slid his arms around both her and Galen. Greta felt very warm and loved as the four of them stood there together.

"Will he carry more than one person?" Galen asked, looking at the big horse in front of them. "Could my mom get on him with me?"

"I don't think Tucson would mind doing that," Ash said, smiling at Galen.

He gave Galen a hand up, then Greta. As he watched her settle onto Tucson's back, he was amazed again at how comfortable she looked there. He stepped away, listening as she repeated the instructions he had given the last time. She nudged Tucson forward, and they walked around the corral once, with her guiding the big horse. Her voice was soft as she continued talking to Galen about their ride. When she stopped in front of Ash again, she smiled down at him.

"He's definitely the gentlest creature I've ever ridden," she said.

Ash grinned.

"Can I try making him go now?" Galen asked.

"Want me to stay on? Or do you want to do it alone?"

"Stay on, please. I haven't gotten the hang of this yet."

They went around the corral again. Ash stood with Chase, his arm across the boy's shoulders. Chase looked up at him.

"She rides good."

"Yes, she does."

"How come Mom never rode Tucson?"

"Your mom wasn't a horse person, Chase," Ash told him, glancing down as he added, "Truth is, your mom wasn't all that keen on the farm. She lived here because we lived here."

"I guess I sort of knew that," the boy said, looking down at the dirt around their feet. "She never came out here much. She always stayed close to the house."

Ash didn't respond to his words. He returned his gaze to Greta and Galen, keeping his arm on Chase's shoulders as they stood there silently watching Galen finish the circle.

Ash felt a peacefulness inside as he watched Greta. He knew now that she would be a perfect farmer's wife. She didn't mind getting dirty, and she obviously liked Tucson. He was pretty sure she wasn't going to mind the cows, or working in the vegetable garden, or any of the other jobs required of her.

After several more rides, the boys asked if they could take Tucson out to the field to ride. Ash looked at Greta.

"It's your call."

She looked at Galen as she said, "You feel you're ready for that?"

"Tucson is real gentle," he said eagerly, nodding his head. "I'm not nervous anymore. Chase can help me if he needs to."

Greta nodded her head. Both boys got up onto the big horse and Ash opened the gate. Chase guided Tucson out.

"Leave him in the field when you're done, Chase," he called after them. "We'll let him graze out there for a while."

He grabbed Greta's hand and led her out of the corral.

"Worried?" he asked as they walked to the fence that enclosed the field where the boys were now riding.

"Not really," she said, wiping some hair out of her face. "Galen wouldn't have gone if he didn't feel ready for it."

Ash nodded. He leaned on the fence, turning slightly so he could watch Greta. She had her arms on the top rail of the fence and was watching the two boys, and Ash thought she looked very peaceful. He was looking forward to having her around all the time.

"The boards," she said suddenly, startling him. "That's what you were cutting the boards for. That's when you remodeled the kitchen window."

Ash chuckled, sliding his arm around her.

"I've been wondering if that question would ever come up again," he said.

"You did the window because of me, didn't you? Because you were upset."

"If I ever decide to tear something apart," he mused, "you might better make me sit down and talk to you. I have this tendency to do extra hard work when I need to plow through some difficult thoughts. That window got me into trouble too. I ended up having to set my pride aside and hire someone to help me get it into place."

"Dan couldn't help?" Greta asked.

Ash shook his head.

"Didn't want to ask," he admitted ruefully. "That

would have peaked Peggy's interest."

Greta laughed, nodding her head. Ash released her, but he continued to look at her. Finally he reached out to touch her hair. Greta turned to smile at him.

"If the time comes that God wants me in the ministry, are you prepared to do that?" he asked quietly.

Greta's smile grew slightly, and a twinkle came into her eyes.

"Where you go, I will go," she said. "Where you stay, I will stay. Your people will be my people. Your God will be my God. May the Lord deal with me, be it ever so severely, if anything but death separates you and me."

Ash smiled as he recognized the quote from the book of Ruth.

"You'd make a good pastor's wife," he told her.

"And you?" she asked, turning slightly. "Are you ready to give up your jeans and flannel shirts for a three piece suit if God wants you to?"

Ash looked down at himself and grinned.

"I used to own one suit. It's buried out there in the woods, about six feet deep. I swore I'd never wear one again after Margaret's funeral."

"Does that mean you're going to get married dressed like that?" she asked, turning to look him up and down.

Ash frowned, running a hand through his hair as he realized the impossibility of such an action. He doubted that even Greta would allow him to do that.

"Guess I have some shopping to do," he said.

She was silent for a moment, then she said, "How long do you have to shop?"

Ash looked at her quizzically, wondering if he'd ever understand how her mind worked.

"How long?" he asked, totally confused by her

question.

"When are you getting married?"

Ash laughed, reaching to pull her into his arms for a quick hug. He released her almost immediately, looked around the farm, then said, "I'm getting married just before Christmas. I want to wake up Christmas morning beside my bride so we can celebrate the birth of our Lord together." He paused, looked at her, and added, "So I have less than a month to shop."

Greta smiled and he slid his arms around her.

"Is that enough time for you?" he asked.

"More than enough," she replied. "I was afraid that the man I'm marrying was in such a hurry that he might want to marry me next week."

"He does," Ash admitted with a chuckle. "But I think I can convince him to wait."

Greta reached up to touch his cheek, and Ash felt an instant urge to kiss her. He stood very still, feeling the warmth flood through him as she traced the line of his jaw with her finger. He felt like he wanted to stand there with her all day, and the urge to kiss her grew stronger. Then he heard the boys' laughter and he tore his eyes away from her, dropping his arms and turning to lean against the fence again.

"I must have been crazy to agree to a month," he muttered.

Greta laughed, turning to lean against the fence also.

Another comfortable silence spread over them. Ash found himself thinking of his grandfather, and he remembered Greta's question about leaving God behind. He continued watching the boys as he began to tell her his story.

"When I was packing my things to leave home after

Grant's death, my grandfather came to see me. He was my mother's father, so he had just lost his daughter. He knew my pain. I was closing my suitcase when he handed me my Bible. I pushed it away. I had no plans to take it with me. My grandfather made me look him straight in the eye, and he said, 'Ashland, I know something of what you're feeling right now, but you can't leave this Bible behind. God has his hand on you, and he's not about to take it off.' He put the Bible into my suitcase, and closed the lid."

"Did you ever see him again?" she asked.

Ash nodded.

"He kept track of me until he died," he told her. "That's how I knew when my father died. No matter how many times I moved, my grandfather would always find me. He'd come to see me, to show me that I couldn't get away from him. I finally began writing letters to him, letting him know what was going on in my life, about Margaret, and about Chase's birth. It was just after Chase was born that he passed away. A close friend of his, someone he had confided in, sent me the article about his death, as well as his journals and a few other personal possessions, as Gramps had asked him to do. I hid them in the attic where Margaret wouldn't find them. I've read his journals. He always wrote down his prayers about our family. It was a habit in him that I liked. His journals showed me that he had continued to pray for me all those years. I guess sometime I should dig them out for Chase. A good legacy to pass on."

"And your Bible?" she asked.

"It didn't take me long to begin reading it again," Ash confessed, smiling at the memory. "It comforted some of the pain, but, until Chase asked me to, I've never set foot in a church. Margaret couldn't understand why I read my Bible when I didn't even go to church. What she didn't know was that my grandfather gave me that Bible the day I decided to go into the ministry. It's still my Bible of choice, though I know there's plenty of other versions around." He sighed, glancing at her for a moment. "I really regret that Margaret died without ever really knowing who I was, Greta. I regret even more that I never told her about Jesus. I do not want that to ever happen again."

He turned back to watch Galen and Chase as they took turns riding Tucson around the field. Greta stood near him without speaking, and he felt a peacefulness surround him. He knew without a doubt that he would marry this woman. She carried with her all his secrets, his doubts and fears, even his desires. And he knew that she was God's gift to him in his time of greatest need. He reached out and slid his arm around her, pulling her close to him, and they stood there together, watching the boys.

Epilogue

Greta smiled as she looked at the small, three shelf bookcase that was almost hidden in the corner of the living room near the kitchen door. It was made of sturdy oak and had a set of wheels to make it easier to move around, and it was home to a number of craft and cookbooks as well as a few novels.

'It's the one place in this house that Ash never did anything about,' she thought to herself as she ran her finger through the dust on top of one of the books.

When they were first married she had marveled at how clean he had kept everything. Even the bookshelves in the study had been dusted. At first she hadn't noticed this one, but when she did, she had kidded Ash about the dust on it. He had stared at it for a moment, a frown marring his features, then he had told her that it had been Margaret's. The books on it had been some of her favorites, and it had originally sat in the kitchen. He'd moved it when he had remodeled the kitchen after her death.

After explaining that, Ash had rubbed his forehead as if to erase his frown, then he'd muttered that they could put it in Chase's room. But nothing had ever been done with it. Greta had left it alone, though occasionally she had dusted the top and the edges of each shelf.

Now something seemed to be compelling her to tear it apart and really clean it.

Greta pulled the books out of the top shelf, dusting each one carefully and setting it aside. Several times she sneezed as the dust drifted around her. As she worked, she thought about all the changes that had come about in the last six months since their wedding.

Galen was now very comfortable on Tucson, riding with the same confidence that Chase did. He had grown another two inches, and had formed new muscles as he worked alongside Ash and Chase around the farm. His writing was maturing right along with the rest of him, and his teacher had helped him get two more of his reports accepted by a magazine. Greta was very proud of his acheivements.

Chase was now reading confidently, and he was quickly becoming a leader among his school friends. His knowledge of the Bible was growing by leaps and bounds, and he used what he knew to help the other boys to change some of their actions. Mrs. Moore had had high praise for him when the school year had ended the week before.

Ash had bought a second horse in February, after Tucson had stumbled while dragging a log. The new horse was black, with white markings on his legs. Tucson now spent his days in the pasture, enjoying the sunshine and a never-ending supply of grass. The boys continued to ride him, and Greta was glad that the old horse was still their favorite.

On her own birthday in May, Ash had brought home another horse, a beautiful appaloosa, complete with saddle and bridle. Galen and Chase had pooled their money to buy a horse blanket for her. She'd cried when she saw everything, then scolded Ash for giving such an extravagant gift. He had just grinned, much to the boys' amusement.

Ash had expressed a wish to have her at home, so Greta was no longer working at Gordon's Drug Store. She had gladly quit right after Christmas, and now she poured all her energy into the house, the two boys, and Ash. He'd been rather pleased when she showed up in the barn to help him muck out the stalls, and he had quickly gotten used to her appearing to help wherever he happened to be working.

For Greta, the changes in Ash had been the most fascinating of all. He had begun pouring himself into the work of the church, taking on several small jobs that no one else wanted, including cleaning the building once each month. And every Saturday, he and the boys headed for the church to work around the property, mowing the grass, trimming bushes, and making sure no trash littered the area. He had also begun meeting with the pastor on a regular basis to pray with him about church concerns.

Greta finished cleaning the top shelf and replaced all the books onto it. Then she began pulling the books off the second one. One had slipped behind the others and she picked it up to add to her pile. Then she realized it was a Bible. Puzzled, Greta turned it over in her hands several times before opening it.

Someone had written in the margins of various pages. She flipped through the pages and saw the same neat handwriting again and again, as if someone had read the book on a regular basis. Finally she opened the front cover to see if there was a name on the flyleaf. A folded piece of paper dropped out. Greta ignored it however, as she saw Margaret's name staring out at her from the flyleaf of the Bible.

"Margaret had a Bible?" she said softly.

After staring for a moment at the name, which was written in the same neat handwriting as the notes inside the Bible, Greta picked up the piece of paper from the floor and carefully opened it.

'Oh Lord, how I wish I could talk to Ash about you,' the note said. 'That part of his life is so shut off.'

Greta gasped, and stopped reading. Tossing her dust cloth away, she scrambled up from the floor and ran through the kitchen to the back door.

Ash was out in the field working. She could see him and the boys, and she ducked through the rails of the fence to go to them, clutching the Bible to her chest.

"Ash!" she called loudly. "Ash!"

All three of them looked up, and Ash started toward her. As he got closer, Greta saw concern written on his face. She stopped, brushing away her tears and gasping for breath.

"What's wrong?" Ash said as he stopped in front of her.

Greta shook her head, silently holding the Bible out to him. He dusted his hands off and took it from her, with a question in his eyes.

"It's Margaret's," she whispered.

Ash stared at her for a moment, then he opened the

Bible.

"In the front cover, Ash," she said quickly. "There's a note."

He opened the front cover and took out the note just as Galen and Chase came up behind him. Ash ran his hand over the neat handwriting, then he began to read the note out loud.

'Oh Lord, how I wish I could talk to Ash about you. That part of his life is so shut off. He reads his Bible, and it's obvious that it means something to him, but he refuses to talk about it at all.

'I think now that I was wrong to not tell him that I'm a born-again Christian. When we got married I kept thinking I would wait for the right moment, sure that he would soften on the subject. But the right moment never came, and he didn't soften. I'm so sorry, Lord, for my failure in this. I kept thinking that since he reads the Bible, he would come on the truth himself.

'I put them both in your hands, Lord. I pray that you will find a way to reach Ash. I know that if you reach Ash, you will also reach Chase. I'm so very glad that Ash reads the Bible to our son.

'Thank you, Lord, for honoring me with your presence in my life. I trust you to work your will in our lives in whatever way you need to.'

Ash sank to his knees, clutching the note and the Bible. Greta knelt beside him in the warm earth.

"She knew, Greta," he said softly. "She knew about Jesus." He shook his head, a sad look crossing his face as he murmured, "All those years. We lived together for all those years without ever knowing the truth about each other."

Greta reached out and laid her hand on his shoulder.

Ash looked her, the sad expression softening into an expression of awe and wonder.

"Gramps was right!" he exclaimed. "God never did take his hand off me!"

Greta looked up and saw that Galen was standing with his arm around Chase, who had buried his face in Galen's sweat-stained shirt. She moved closer to Ash, sliding her arm around him, and she motioned Galen to bring Chase over. As the two boys knelt in front of them, Ash slid an arm around Chase and Greta put hers around Galen.

"The Lord worked his will in our lives," Ash said quietly as the four of them knelt there together. "Just as Margaret asked him to do. And he wanted us to know the truth." He closed his eyes as he went on. "I thank you so much, Lord, for showing Greta where to find this Bible. And I thank you, again, for making the four of us a family."

Greta closed her eyes, nodding in agreement as tears of joy ran down her face.

Brenda Stacy Mastromonaco

Made in the USA
Middletown, DE
05 March 2020

85870605R00159